FATE OF THE UNION

Approve

ENTER Comment for me
Ruth Ann

Cannibalizing

For Ruth Ann, It was Fate!

FATE OF THE UNION

MAX ALLAN COLLINS
WITH MATTHEW V. CLEMENS

Matthew V. Clemens

THOMAS & MERCER

Published by Thomas & Mercer, Seattle

www.apub.com

Amazon, the Amazon logo, and Thomas & Mercer are trademarks of Amazon.com, Inc., or its affiliates.

ISBN-13: 9781503947405
ISBN-10: 1503947408

Cover design by Ray Lundgren

Printed in the United States of America

In memory of Rob Cimmarusti,
who joined us on this journey

"The cause of America is, in a great measure, the cause of all mankind."

Thomas Paine (Common Sense, *1776*), *American political activist at the time of the Revolutionary War.*

ONE

Chris Bryson knew he was in over his head.

And not just out of his depth—more like going down for the third time, still conscious but holding his breath, waiting for the darkness to come.

Of course he was not in the water at all, and in fact he was already sitting in the near dark—a former Secret Service agent and Congressional Medal of Honor winner holed up like a bank robber in a seedy two-story motel/hotel in Chantilly, Virginia, where he could hear the overhead rumble and whine of the metal beasts of Washington Dulles International Airport. On the one hand, they promised escape, on the other threatened to consume him.

He grunted a laugh through the slit in his face that wasn't quite a smile. Such melodramatic thoughts were part and parcel, he supposed, of hiding out in a place called the Skyway Farer. Not that he couldn't take care of himself, normally. But sometimes even the strongest, most confident man could use a little goddamn help.

And right now the only person he could think of, who might be up to helping him out of this deep a hole, was Joe Reeder. He only hoped, with everything that had happened to Joe in the last year or so, that help from him wasn't out of the question.

Five feet nine and in damn good shape for his midfifties, Bryson kept his sandy-colored hair military short, the gray barely showing, all of which conspired with his boyish features to make him look forty-something. At work he wore contacts, glasses at home.

Now, though, in this low-rent motel room, in the dim light of a bedside lamp, his eyes burned from too many contact-lens hours, and he'd left his glasses on his desk at his office. He wished he could take the damned things out, but that just wasn't going to happen—he had to stay alert and—small detail—he had to be able to see.

There was something else he wished he didn't have to wear. Even as he sat on the bed, legs stretched out, a pillow propped against the wobbly headboard, he was ever aware of the shoulder rig with loaded Glock, a round in the chamber. His suit pants were getting wrinkled, the fabric as loose as a used parachute, but looking sharp was not exactly a priority. The sleeves of his white shirt were rolled up, his tie loose as a noose before the executioner snugged it.

The room was decorated in Early Twenty-First Century Urban Blight with its Wi-Fi hook-up, small flat-screen TV, and high curved shower rod so that fat-ass businessmen could fit inside. His suit coat hung on the back of the office-type chair at a meager table of a workstation where his laptop sat, open, screen saver on. Random light trails blundered to the edges of the screen, then bounced and dissipated, a sad reminder of what might become of him if Reeder couldn't help. Right now he would kill for a drink, but the only cocktail available was the mingled odor of sweat and fear.

In a room silent but for the muffled drone of televisions in the rooms on either side of him, Bryson pricked his ears, searching for the slightest sound from the hallway. Fear was nothing new to him. Sometimes it was like a friend whose advice was irritating but worth listening to. This nagging friend had aided him in combat, and when he stood post on the presidential detail.

But this time—was it his age?—the fear was not a friend, but some out of control stranger blurting false alarms.

Only not quite a stranger.

He'd met this kind of fear before. Like the day his fellow agent Reeder had taken a bullet for President Gregory Bennett. Yet never before *this* bad—he hadn't been this fucking scared when he and a gaggle of other agents had jumped on that would-be presidential assassin and disarmed him.

No, this was different.

This was fear bordering on panic, and not just for himself—he could handle that, and maybe that was why this felt so different. This time the stranger had come to shout warnings about Beth.

His wife, Beth, who he hadn't even dared call yet. Who he knew might come under that terrible designation of collateral damage, generating in him a fear for her safety that dwarfed anything he might feel for himself.

And what of his son, Christopher? A man by the calendar, but still just a boy compared to his father's years. That this might touch his son was so terrible a thought, it refused to fully form.

That's why he needed Reeder.

Working as a one-man security operation, Bryson didn't have anyone in his current life who could handle this level of shitstorm. And he was so far out of the national security loop, he didn't know who to call that could be trusted.

Except Joe Reeder.

If it came to a shoot-out, Reeder would be on top of it, and the man had the kind of unique standing that meant Bryson could come in from the cold. With Reeder at his side, anyway.

In the motel room's near darkness, Bryson shook his head. *How the hell had he gotten himself into so much trouble so fast?*

It had begun as just another routine gig, just some normal digging—a simple background check for Christ's sake! And now, somehow, he was running for his life—if holing up in a sleazy shithole, with his loaded gun on and his burning contacts in, qualified as "running."

More like running in place. Waiting for help that might not come, help he hadn't been able to even ask for yet. Of course, if he didn't get hold of Reeder soon, his fears, his worries, would soon be over . . .

Last night, as part of his security work, Bryson had committed the first real crime of his career—not the middling corner-cutting anybody in his line might pull, no. But outright breaking and entering—into somewhere he should not have been, where he'd seen something he wasn't supposed to see.

He'd known the instant he found the thing that it was bigger than he could handle himself. He hadn't even expected to find it, had been hoping this was just a wild goose chase, a wild hair up his ass. It was neither. Although he had barely *touched* the damn thing, taking just one photo with his digital camera, he knew instantly he was looking at major-league trouble.

And ran.

Even though his discovery had been an almost random action, he was aware that they were onto him, that his knowledge of what they'd figuratively buried could literally bury him.

He pulled out the burner phone he'd bought from Reeder's guy, DeMarcus. No way to trace it, no way for his pursuers to know he would go to Reeder. And no sign of them, either, now that he'd gone to ground.

Should be safe to make the call. Right? *Right?* Still, he went through every possibility again before telling himself, *No, it's fine, the call will be safe.* He punched in Reeder's number and waited while it rang. And rang.

And rang.

Where the hell was he?

It wasn't like Joe Reeder had a social life. *Why wasn't he answering?* Bryson's blood pressure rose in tandem with his growing panic.

Did he dare leave a voice mail?

Fuck it, too much at stake not to. When the beep came, he said in a rush, "Joe, Chris Bryson. Call this number when you get this. Life and death, brother—don't let me down."

He hit END CALL and stared at the phone in his palm as if Reeder might immediately ring back. When that didn't happen, he kept staring, willing the thing to ring. When it refused to, he slipped it into his pants pocket. Watched pot never boils, watched cell never rings.

If he stayed in this room much longer, he would start bouncing off the walls. His blood sugar was dipping, his mind racing. No one knew he was here in this anonymous area—just another business traveler, right? No harm in going out for a late steak and a drink.

It'll be fine, he told himself. *No worries.*

Rising, he smoothed his pants and if wrinkles could laugh, they would have. He snugged the tie a little, but not completely, the hangman image lingering. Looking like a businessman who'd had a hell of a day was in character, wasn't it? Would help him blend in, explain the red eyes, sweat-stained collar, and five o'clock shadow that had long since lapped itself. The last he'd shaved had been yesterday morning, thinking it was just another Monday.

Now it was Tuesday evening, a day later . . . or was that a week, or a month? Two days had blended into a waking nightmare with some intermittent sleep last night but nothing more than a catnap since. He dare not risk more than that, at least not until he'd convinced Reeder to step up.

He went into the bathroom, ran some cold water, rinsed his face, then dried it. The face in the mirror was his, but he had never seen it look so . . . so *stricken* before. So old, so desperate, so frazzled. Didn't look forty-something now; more like sixty. He had to do something about that.

He considered his options—color his hair? Different color contacts? These days you could get contacts at a strip-mall optician's in under an hour. Blue-collar apparel maybe? That was easy enough. He tried smiling at himself but the bastard in the mirror wouldn't have any.

The bastard in the mirror knew that none of that cosmetic crap mattered, that those coming after him would have access to facial recognition software and to the CCTV cameras that were fucking everywhere. With his security training, Bryson felt fairly confident that he'd done a decent enough job of avoiding them so far; but the odds—and time—were against him.

Though he knew his way around hotels, airports, and banks, and was careful at unfamiliar corners, constantly assessing his surroundings, sooner or later a camera would catch him, if it hadn't already. He was old enough to remember when London-style CCTV surveillance wasn't the norm in this country; that now seemed the distant past, and an all too real present carried an inevitability he could only put off for so long.

He pulled his suit coat off the chair, shrugged into it, patted the phone in his pocket, accepting the idea that Reeder wasn't going to be calling back immediately. He'd risk that steak and that drink—just one drink, though. Couldn't stand to lose whatever edge he had left after these endless two days.

At the door, he stopped, listened hard, heard nothing, then opened it as slowly as if it were the lid on a box of snakes. He looked both ways, stepped out into the corridor. Turned toward the elevator, then heard the door across the hall open.

He spun, but it was too late.

Two men were coming toward him; his hand swept toward the shoulder-holstered Glock. But behind him, on his side of the hall, another door opened, only with those two men bearing down, he'd have to take his chances that this was some other guest who'd happened to open that door just then, about to blunder innocently into something bad going down, stalling Bryson's attackers just long enough . . . and Bryson's hand was on the gun butt when he felt a bee sting his neck.

He reached up, as if to swat that bee, and his fingers felt the dart there, and plucked it out.

Already his legs were rubber and the floor came up and took him. He fumbled with his pistol, but his hand was weighed down with leaden fingers, his arm even heavier, yet somehow it merely drifted to his side.

He could not move. He waited to black out but that kept not happening. Sprawled on the cheap carpeting, his breathing shallow, his eyes wide open, he could manage only to stare up at the four men looming, huddling, over him. They all wore small smiles that had some sneer; none had bothered wearing a mask.

His body was paralyzed, but his brain wasn't. It kept computing. The lack of masks meant two things: this quartet wasn't worried about the security camera at the other end of the hall, and didn't care if he saw their faces because they felt sure he would never describe them to anybody. Though they were dressed business casual, fitting in well at the Skyway Farer, they had the hard hooded-eyed look of the mercenary.

Just above him, a muscular blond man, with flecks of scars

scattered around his handsome face like ugly confetti, said, "Get his key card—haul his ass back into his room before someone sees."

Bryson tried to yell, but his vocal cords were nonfunctional. Within seconds, they had dragged him back into his room, locking the door behind them. Helpless down on a carpet smelling of stale food and dust, he found he couldn't even work up a sneeze.

The trip out of and then back into his room had taken less than a minute. He doubted anyone had heard anything, let alone seen anything, and the camera was surely broken or blocked.

Why hadn't they just killed him in the corridor?

That would have been easy enough, had that been their aim. Instead, they had taken him down with a dart, like a beast in the jungle. Was it possible that they didn't intend to kill him? How could that be, since he could identify them all? Or did they mean to . . . to torture him?

The blond leaned down. "Succinylcholine, sux. You know what that is, right? What it does?"

Bryson did know the drug—a neuromuscular paralytic used in presurgery anesthesia to relax the trachea, making it easier to intubate a patient. Also a part of the chemical mixture used in lethal injection, which explained why he was having so much trouble breathing. Wouldn't be long now, he knew, before his breathing stopped altogether. Without benefit of the sedative combined during both of the drug's normal uses, dying would be unbearably painful, too. The logical part of his brain reported these facts as the emotional layer screamed.

Silently screamed.

The blond grinned at the fear he saw in Bryson's eyes. "Don't worry, Mr. Bryson, we didn't administer enough to kill you—just to make you compliant." The grin became a wide smile, scar flecks on both upper and lower lips. "We're not here to murder you."

No use fighting it. He still could not move, and wondered if he'd ever move again. Maybe if he cooperated. Maybe he could save himself. *But at what cost?*

Businesslike, the blond asked, "Can you blink?"

Not trying to, he blinked.

"Good. One blink for yes, two blinks for no. Now. Did you tell anyone what you found?"

He didn't blink at all, thinking, *How many blinks for fuck you, asshole!*

The blond smiled pleasantly, or as close to pleasantly as he was capable. "Maybe you told that pretty wife of yours. How about it?"

He blinked twice. He saw himself overcoming the drug, reaching up and strangling the son of a bitch. In reality, he remained motionless, the ability to blink the only thing left to him. But that meant the sux was starting to wear off. He needed this bastard to keep talking just a little longer and maybe he would have a chance.

The blond knew about Bryson, anyway enough so to ask him if he'd entrusted anything to half a dozen friends, from business associates to a pal down the block. Each time Bryson blinked three or four or five times—never giving the blond the satisfaction of a single or double blink—and felt himself start the hint of a smile. He'd figured out how to blink, "Fuck you," after all!

Finally, the blond sighed and said, "I said we weren't here to murder you. What's the point in killing a man who's about to commit suicide?"

Two of the others stepped forward and one held him while the other got his belt off him. The blond and another guy grabbed him and carried him to the bathroom, trailed by the pair with the belt, which they worked around the shower rod, inches from the ceiling, while the blond and his helper propped Bryson up. The blond wound the belt around Bryson's neck, not making eye contact. It was as if the man already considered him dead.

That was the terrible part, not the pain, not the certainty that death was coming, but knowing that after a little time had passed, they would call on Beth, to see what he had or hadn't told her.

As they held him up, Bryson tried to kick, but his legs remained slack and the belt cut more deeply into his neck, shutting off even more of the meager oxygen he was managing to suck in.

The blond let go of him and Bryson's feet slipped down the outside of the tub until the belt was taut, and he was barely off the floor, the shower rod holding.

Maybe it would give—maybe it would break before anything inside his neck did!

Alone in the bathroom now, he could feel his eyes bulge and his chest burn, as he fought to draw in even a molecule of air without success.

He heard the outer door close. They weren't even going to stay around to make sure he died! He had to think of something, had to do something. He tried to bend his feet, to touch the floor, but they barely moved. He tried to lift his hands but they were useless things, floating yet heavy.

The burning in his throat grew hotter. Sweat poured out of him like the shower was on, and he struggled to draw a breath of any kind.

Stars exploded in ghastly Fourth of July bursts as his vision darkened. He thought of Beth and begged her forgiveness, as if she could hear a pain-racked apology that would never leave his head. He hadn't meant for any of this to happen, it was just a job, no, not even that, just him looking into something he had overheard. Something he had overheard that had gotten him killed and probably her, too, without Reeder's help. Shit! Shit!

He loved her, always had. Now, all he wanted was to hold her one last time.

Beth, I love you, I'm sorry. Christopher, son—always said you were the man . . . now you are *the man . . .*

In the darkness, he felt sensation begin to flow through his limbs, his body, most of it pain, but goddamn, sensation.

The last sensation he felt was the burner phone in his pocket, vibrating.

"If it happens, it happens . . . we can't stop living."

Walter Reed, US Army physician who postulated and proved that yellow fever is transmitted by mosquitos. Section 3, Lot 1864, Grid T/U-16.5, Arlington National Cemetery.

TWO

Joe Reeder hated being called a hero.

The idea that he, or anybody for that matter, realistically fit that designation seemed to him absurd. Heroic actions, yes—Audie Murphy in combat—but a hero? Maybe the kind Murphy played in those ancient cowboy movies. But not in life. In life America's most decorated soldier of World War II had been a troubled alcoholic, possibly psychotic in his worst moments.

Yet according to the media, and most everybody else he ran into these days, Joe Reeder was a genuine American hero twice over, larger than life and then some. This dated back to his Secret Service days, when he had taken a bullet for President Gregory Bennett, a man whose politics he deplored. Even now—especially in the dead of winter like this—his left shoulder reminded him of that bullet and his actions, nudging his mind to recall the reactions. Deskbound afterward, he'd been unable to stomach the politics and particularly the underhanded tactics of President Bennett and his cronies, and had let his feelings slip.

Mistake.

The Secret Service was necessarily apolitical—though finding a left-of-center agent in those ranks could be a trick—and Reeder had become a pariah in government circles for his indiscretion. That had driven him from the Service and he had, out of necessity, begun his security business, which proved rewarding in several senses. The private sector only knew him as the "hero" who saved President Bennett, and ABC Security—the ABC standing for nothing more than good placement in alphabetical listings—had flourished from day one.

That success multiplied many times over when he was designated a hero a second time.

On that occasion, he'd saved the Chief Justice of the Supreme Court from a potential assassin. The rewards had been great, for his security business at least, but the price for that newfound wealth had been the life of his best friend, FBI agent Gabriel Sloan.

Joseph Reeder, twice a national hero. Twice suffering the ignominy of media fame.

Hero? You can have it.

Reeder was six one and pushing fifty, with regular features that the years had lent some craggy character. His eyes were brown, his hair white and cropped near-military short, his eyebrows white as well. During his years as an agent, he'd had to conceal that premature distinctiveness with hair dye.

Back in his Secret Service life, he'd been nicknamed "Peep" by Gabe and others, a joking acknowledgment of his ability to read people. An expert at kinesics, the study of body language, Reeder had spotted President Bennett's would-be assassin in the crowd a split second before the shooter fired.

Walking through Arlington National Cemetery before the tourists were let in at 8:00 a.m., Reeder enjoyed the feel and sound of snow crunching under his Rocky-brand oxfords, and didn't mind the cold on his face or that the weather made his eyes water.

This was the place on earth where he felt the most at home, where peace enveloped him. Right now he was in Section Three, unofficially known as the "hospital section," where he stopped at the grave of Dr. Walter Reed.

Pulling his ABC Security parka a little tighter, he gazed down at the dark granite headstone, set atop a white granite base displaying the doctor's last name. A bronze plaque provided information about Reed and concluded with the quote: "He gave to man control over that dreadful scourge—yellow fever."

He thought about all the stupid media acclaim he'd gotten for being a "hero," while here rested a man who just might be worthy of the word. Of all those who knew the name Reeder today, how many remembered a doctor named Reed? Yes, there was a hospital in Bethesda, Maryland, that bore the man's name, but now—the late 2020s—how many knew why the building had been named after a physician dead since 1902?

Dr. Walter Reed. Who had never taken a life, and had in fact saved many. During the building of the Panama Canal, Reed's team had proven that yellow fever was not passed by way of bedding, towels, and other materials from the stricken, rather the result of a simple mosquito bite. From this rose the fields of epidemiology and biomedicine.

That was heroic work, far outweighing catching a bullet or killing a couple of potential political assassins.

Though he'd been up only a few hours, he found himself yawning. Ever since the night of that suburban shoot-out, he'd gotten only fitful sleep. Getting through the day was no problem. Always something to do—a desk filled with work, staff meetings, client luncheons, even occasional interviews with the more trustworthy members of the media, since being a goddamn hero was keeping his business flush.

But at home, darkness out the windows, with nothing to keep him company but TV and books and a beer or two, Reeder found the nights endless. Today he'd change that. He would go home this afternoon instead of tonight. Maybe take some mild over-the-counter sleep aid. Get to bed early, snare that elusive good night's sleep. The kind of sleep where dreams don't come and peaceful rest does.

The dreams he so hoped to avoid were not nightmares, more recollections, some pleasant, even very pleasant, *his daughter Amy with her friend Kathy . . . sharing beers with Gabe at a ball game . . .* then not so pleasant, *Amy at Kathy's funeral . . . Kathy's father Gabe crying into his shoulder . . . and then sudden violence, bullets flying, the dark of night all around . . .*

Wake up bathed in sweat. Plump the pillow, drop back down, start the whole cycle again.

That had been his nights for almost a year.

Last night, though, had been different. Usually he got right to sleep before the fitfulness crept in, to wake him every hour or two with the fresh taste of recurrent dreams lining his brain. Last night? Worry was nagging him, and a guilty feeling that he should be doing something about that call he'd received, just before he crawled in the sack.

Well, not that he'd *received*—he'd missed the call. These days Reeder ignored his phone, where media types frequently bothered him and left him messages that had no chance of return. But he did check periodically, and before he went to bed he had.

He didn't recognize the number, and there'd been no caller ID. He damn near ignored it, but his gut told him not to, and he'd learned not to blow off his inner warning system.

The call had been from an old friend, one he rarely saw, a fellow retired Secret Service agent who had a security outfit of his own now . . . okay, really just a PI office with some twenty-first-century trappings. Chris Bryson was one of those friends with whom he felt guilty about not keeping in closer touch, as the years crawled and raced by, in their contradictory way.

The message had been simple enough: "*Call this number when you get this. Life and death, brother—don't let me down.*"

A lot of people used that phrase—to some, getting to FedEx on time could be a matter of life and death. Not to ex-agents like Bryson and himself. Reeder had returned the call but it went to voice mail.

"Chris, get back to me," Reeder told his cell. "I'm waiting, buddy. Just tell me what you need, where to come. No matter the time."

He tried Bryson's other number and it went right to voice mail, too, and he left a similar message. He didn't have Beth Bryson's number. Bryson's wife and his ex-wife Melanie were good friends.

Which meant the next logical step would've been to call Melanie, but somehow he couldn't force himself across that small social barrier. The call might be answered by the husband who'd replaced him, Donald Graham, and hearing the lobbyist's buttery voice always gave Reeder a pain.

So he told himself Chris was a pro who could handle himself. Put the phone on ringer, turned the ringer up, and deposited it on his nightstand, waited for it to ring.

Which it never did.

Behind him, he felt more than heard someone coming, but he didn't turn. Judging by the person's boots crunching lightly on brittle snow, this someone was not very heavy.

Did Dr. Reed have descendants who regularly came to pay their respects? More likely someone knew to find Reeder here, but that was a short list. He didn't have a lot of friends, and Amy—Christmas break over—would be in class or at her new job. So would her boyfriend Bobby Landon, who was growing on him.

Patti Rogers maybe? The FBI agent had been Gabe Sloan's partner till last year when she teamed up briefly with Reeder, who was consulting on the Supreme Court task force. He and Patti remained tight, and those light footfalls could be hers.

The caretakers of the cemetery had little to do in the winter and, anyway, gave him a wide berth. If the media had tracked Reeder here, keeping his temper would be a challenge. A tiny part of him thought it might be a threat, and he was unarmed, so—despite not wanting to invite conversation with a reporter or intrude upon someone's privacy in a cemetery—he finally turned.

And saw his ex-wife trudging up the slope toward him in the snow.

"Jesus, Joe," she said, half-kidding, "give a girl a hand, why don't you?"

He stepped toward her, held out a leather-gloved hand. She held out a cotton-gloved one. Tall, her slender form plumped as if for an Arctic expedition in navy and black and touches of red and Ugg boots, she gave him a small smile so white, the snow might have envied it. Her long brown hair was tucked under a fashionable red-and-black stocking cap, her brown eyes impossibly large with long natural lashes, her model-sharp cheeks pinked with cold.

The divorce had been the right thing for the marriage, he knew that, but he would never stop loving her. Though they spoke on the phone regularly, he hadn't seen her in many months. His heart raced a little, as it had when they had first met, so many years ago.

She positioned herself beside him, leaving her gloved hand in his, as they both looked down at the headstone. Magie Noire, her favorite perfume, found its way through the chill to warm his nostrils.

She said, "It's fuh-fuh-fuh-*freezing* out here."

"You trudged all this way with that news flash?" He meant to tease but it didn't quite come out that way.

She pursed her lips, a precursor to a familiar frown.

"Just making conversation. And hello to you, too, Joe."

"Sorry. Trying to be funny."

A tiny smirk. "You suck at 'funny.'"

Last year's tragedy had brought Reeder and his ex-wife closer than they'd been in years. Daughter Amy had seemed happier now that her parents were getting along again.

But last summer, Reeder had gone over for a family cookout that included Amy and boyfriend Bobby. Hubby #2, Donald, was grilling in the backyard, taking on a role that had been Hubby #1's. Though a registered Democrat, Reeder found the combination of the liberal lobbyist's cynicism and Bobby's idealistic socialism hard to stomach. It was a wonder he hadn't slapped them both around with a greasy spatula. He thought he'd hidden his feelings pretty well.

But privately Melanie scolded him for his "unrelenting sarcasm," and invites to family dinners were not repeated.

Reeder did still meet Amy and Bobby for dinner once every week or so, but hadn't seen Mel since the ill-fated barbecue.

Suddenly here she was at his side, in his Fortress of Solitude. But Arlington was a big place, and even though she knew the five or six graves that were among his regular stops, she had gone to considerable trouble in frigid weather to track him down.

Whatever had brought her here was in-person important. Why wasn't she getting to it?

Concern spiked in him. "Is Amy all right?"

"Yes, yes," she said, waving a gloved hand. "Amy is fine. Bobby, too. This isn't that."

"What *is* it?"

Her voice sounded small against the wind. "Beth Bryson called this morning."

"Oh. About Chris?"

Her eyes tensed. "Yes . . . but . . ."

"Dead?"

The face under the stocking cap goggled at him. "You *knew?*"

"No. Seeing you here . . . just meant . . ." He gulped air and breathed it out like cold cigarette smoke, then told her about the missed call from his friend.

"I let him *down*, goddamnit."

"Joe . . . you couldn't know this would happen."

"What did happen? Killed on a job?"

"No. Nothing like that. Joe . . . I'm sorry . . . but Chris took his own life last night."

"Shit," he said.

They both knew the suicide rate among Secret Service agents, both active and retired, was not exactly low.

"At home? Hell, did Beth *find* him . . . ?"

Melanie shook her head. "No, she says he was in a hotel or motel somewhere near Dulles. Evidently, he . . . hanged himself."

"Doesn't sound like the guy."

"Joe, we never know what's really going on inside other people's lives . . . do we?"

"No. And Chris had been out of mine for too long. But damnit, he *turned* to me and I didn't come."

"How could you? Don't beat yourself up over something you couldn't control."

They stared at the headstone.

His kinesics expertise had been an issue in their marriage, Melanie constantly accusing him of reading her. Like she expected him to turn it off, somehow. Even now, as she shoved her hands into the pockets of her coat and hunched her shoulders, he took in the classic defensive postures. Or, hell—maybe she was just cold. It was an inexact science.

The longer they silently stood there, the more he knew she wasn't done with him yet—this was more than just delivering some bad news about an old friend. She could have phoned him, right? And he and Chris had been friends, but never Gabe Sloan tight.

Or was she worried about how losing another friend, any friend, would hit him?

Finally, she let out a long steamy breath. "Beth asked me to get ahold of you."

"Oh? To deliver the bad news?"

"To ask you to come talk to her."

"Do I look like a priest?"

She turned toward him, eyes flashing. "Your dead friend's wife wants to talk to you. Should I have asked for a reason? To see if it's important enough to interrupt your busy schedule walking around a graveyard?"

"That came out harsher than I meant it to."

"Me, too." She shuddered, some of it the cold. "Really bad morning."

"Sorry."

"Joe . . . how long have we been snipping at each other, anyway?"

"Too long."

"Cease-fire, then?"

"Cease-fire. Mel . . . did Beth have any explanation for why Chris would do this?"

She shook her head. "Says they were happy, never better, actually. Doesn't believe Chris killed himself. That's why—"

"Why she wants me to look into it."

"Yes."

"You do know she should be talking to the police, not your ex-husband."

Her expression bordered on pleading. "*Talk* to her, Joe. She thinks someone who knew Chris might get a handle on this where the

21

police wouldn't. And you could look into it . . . discreetly. Anyway, she seems to think you can do anything."

"Right," he said. "I'm a hero."

Her head tilted, her smile taking its own sideways tilt. "That's how some people see you."

"How about you, honey?"

The automatic expression of affection embarrassed her, and she looked away. "I don't think I believe in heroes, anymore."

"We have that in common."

A gloved hand came from a pocket and rested on his sleeve. "But I believe in *you*, Joe. Always have, always will."

He grinned at her. "If you're going to play my heartstrings, maybe I should unzip the parka."

She laughed a little. Maybe he didn't entirely suck at "funny" after all.

He said, "Of course I'll go see Beth. Of course I'll talk to her. But how will she feel when she hears that Chris called me, and I failed him?"

Melanie waved that off. "You didn't fail him. She'll know that."

She kissed him on the cheek.

Even in the chill, he felt the old heat.

"Do you have Beth's number?" she asked.

He shook his head.

"Give me your phone and I'll put it in."

He did and she did.

Then she was turning and walking away, footsteps crisp in the snow. He caught up and walked her to her car. They didn't speak until he was holding the door open for her.

"I'll call you with a report," he said.

That small white smile again. "I'm not a client, Joe. But I would appreciate that."

She drove away, giving him a tiny wave, and he watched until she was out of sight. Then he climbed behind the wheel of his Prius and got the motor and heat going. He withdrew his cell from a parka pocket.

First he tried Beth Bryson and got voice mail. He left a fairly lengthy message, hoping she was screening calls, but she never picked up. Since she wanted to talk to him, that meant she was off dealing with matters related to her husband's demise—cops, funeral home, obit.

So he called Carl Bishop, the veteran DC Homicide detective who had also worked on the Supreme Court task force last year, and who'd been a friend well before that. The beefy bald cop would likely be in the know on the Bryson investigation.

One homicide bureau covered the entire DC area now. Over the years, two facts had emerged: criminals didn't care about jurisdictional lines, and budgets grew ever tighter.

Bishop was ahead of him. "Callin' about Chris, aren't you?" This was in lieu of a greeting.

"You got it," Reeder said. "What do we know so far?"

"Is that the editorial 'we,' or the what-do-I-know-so-I-can-tell-*you* 'we.'"

"Dealer's choice."

There was a shrug in Bishop's voice. "Not my case, Peep, but from what I'm hearing? Looks like a pretty straight-up suicide."

"His wife doesn't think he would kill himself."

"No wife wants to think she missed the signs."

"Bish . . . she wants me to look into it."

"You like wasting your time, son? Go for it."

"Maybe I will. I could start with Chris leaving me a message on my cell the night he died."

Reeder could almost hear the switch click as Bishop turned total cop.

"Jesus, Peep, what did Chris say?"

"That it was a matter of life and death. And he strongly implied he could use my help, and right now. Which obviously I didn't provide."

Reeder told him of his attempt to call back.

Bishop said, "You're saying he was murdered."

"How the hell do I know? I haven't talked to the guy in over a year. I can tell you that he didn't sound suicidal."

"How *did* he sound?"

"Uneasy. The kind of uneasy that coming from a seasoned pro like Chris means scared shitless."

Silence.

Then: "So, then, Peep . . . you plan to make this an ABC Security issue?"

"I'm going to talk that over with Beth Bryson, after I hear why *she* believes Chris was murdered. Whose case is it, Bish?"

"Graveyard-shift detective named Pete Woods. You know him?"

"No."

"He's a pup, barely paper-trained," Bishop said. "But he has the makings of a good detective. If this *isn't* a suicide, he'll listen to you if you find something. I mean, hell, who wouldn't be impressed when the great Joe Reeder expresses an interest?"

"Screw you, buddy . . . and thanks for the info. You wouldn't have any idea where Beth Bryson is about now?"

"Woods went out to pick her up. He was taking her to the morgue for the official ID. Been gone about an hour. My guess, if you hustle, you can catch them there."

Great, track down the widow at the morgue. Still, it might be better than meeting her at home, surrounded by memories.

The morgue and the Office of the Chief Medical Examiner were located in what had once been a cutting-edge facility, the Consolidated Forensics Building on E Street SW. Now, nearly twenty years after its opening, the glass, concrete, and steel shell of its once-modern self had a worn, dirty look.

Inside, the building had held up better, though its along-the-wall lobby seats were worn, with cushions flattened by countless behinds. Antiseptic scent hung in the air in this hospital whose refrigerated patients were on trays and in drawers downstairs.

But Reeder didn't make a trip to the basement, nor did he check for Beth at the medical examiner's office. Instead, he treated his ass to one of those flat-cushioned lobby chairs. He had barely settled in when Beth emerged from the elevator, with Chris Jr. supporting her as she made it slowly across the lobby. No sign of their cop escort.

The son had his father's sandy hair, blue eyes, and solid build on a shortish frame. Thirty or so, an insurance salesman by profession, he wore a gray suit with a light-blue shirt and a striped tie.

Short, blonde Beth wore black slacks and a black jacket over a black silk blouse—not necessarily in mourning, as she preferred black and navy shades, perhaps because she was just slightly on the heavy side. Her face was heart-shaped with a pug nose and Kewpie-doll lips overwhelmed by big light-blue eyes. Her chin rose as she saw Reeder approaching, then she stepped forward and fell into his arms.

As they hugged, he said, "I'm sorry, Beth. So very sorry."

"Thank you, Peep," she said, stepping back.

He shook hands with Christopher, who gave him a solemn nod. Reeder said to Beth, "Where's Detective Woods?"

"Still with the coroner. Nice enough young man. He'll be driving us home. We just wanted to . . . get out of there."

"I understand. While you wait, could we talk for a moment?"

"Please," she said, some eagerness in it.

He ushered her to the terrible chairs and he sat on one side of her with her son on the other. Christopher sat forward, keeping an eye on his mother.

Looking from one to the other, Reeder said, "When I say I'm sorry, that's not just condolences."

And he told them about the call he'd received from Chris, and apologized for not following it up better.

"No apology necessary," she said, eyes bright but shimmering. "What you say confirms my suspicions. It really does."

"If you want my help," Reeder said, "you have it."

She swallowed and reached out to clutch his hand. "You *knew* Chris, Peep. He didn't kill himself. He would never kill himself."

"Right now the cops seem to think he did. But I'll talk to them. The phone message should change things."

"It *has* to. Peep, we had such a good marriage. Never even a speed bump. He treated me like I was still the slim little girl he met in college. Just a week ago or so, we booked a second-honeymoon trip to Europe. Why would Chris do such a thing, if he was in the kind of bad place where he might not be *alive* in three months to take it?"

Reeder knew that people could crash faster than that, but he didn't think that was the case here, and kept it to himself.

"Chris said it was a matter of life and death," Reeder said. "What was he mixed up in, Beth?"

"I don't know, Peep." She looked to her son, who shook his head, then back to Reeder. "Chris didn't talk much about work—I don't have to tell *you* about the security business."

He gave her a smile. "Confidentiality on one hand, boredom on the other. Missed meals and late nights."

She managed a small smile in return, then shrugged. "Everything seemed fine until a few days ago."

"What happened then?"

Those big blue eyes were really quite lovely. "Nothing specific. Chris just seemed . . . preoccupied. I'd ask him something and he didn't seem to hear me until I repeated it. Just very . . . distracted.

FATE OF THE UNION

Worried, but not in a depressed way, *that's* not it! Anyway, on Sunday, I asked him what was wrong, pressed him a little, and he said something odd."

"What?"

"That he shouldn't have looked into that . . . sink.'"

"Sink? Like a bathroom sink? Are we talking plumbing here?"

"No sink problems at home or at the office either, Peep." She frowned in thought. "Could it be . . . a name?"

"Maybe."

Her chin crinkled. "Now I'm so *mad* at myself."

"Why would you be?"

"I mean, why didn't I *ask* him? Why didn't I ask what he was talking about? But I just . . . wanted to respect his space. His privacy. Now I wonder if he was trying to protect me."

"When did you see him last?"

"Monday. He said he had to do something out of town Monday night, and should be back by yesterday."

"*Where* out of town?"

"No idea."

"Did you hear from him?"

She shook her head. "Not once. Which is kind of unusual. He almost always called, nightly, from his hotel room, but . . . I wasn't alarmed or anything. I wish I had been. You don't think I missed something, Peep, do you? That maybe he *was* depressed?"

"I don't. But if I dig into this for you, you have to be prepared—you might not like what I find."

She looked to her son and they exchanged brave smiles. Then to Reeder she said, "We'll just have to take that chance, won't we? But I'm confident it won't be a reason for suicide. That just wasn't Chris."

"I agree."

He didn't share with her a major reason why he felt that way—a cop uses his gun to kill himself. And for Chris to hang himself like that, to choose to die in such an excruciating, non-immediate, self-punishing way? No damn chance.

But telling Beth that would be less than comforting.

"So you'll do it?" she asked, eyes wide, the eagerness shimmering in their teary setting, glancing from Reeder to her son and back again.

The dead man's son spoke for the first time. "Then you will look into it, Mr. Reeder?"

"I already am," he told them.

He gave Beth a kiss on the cheek, shook hands with Christopher again, and slipped out. He wasn't ready to talk to the detective on the case just yet.

"Integrity is the lifeblood of democracy. Deceit is a poison in its veins."

Edward "Ted" Kennedy, fourth-longest-serving United States Senator, Commonwealth of Massachusetts, 1962–2009.
Section S, Site 45-B, Arlington National Cemetery.

THREE

FBI Special Agent Patti Rogers hadn't been in the Verdict Chophouse since task force days. Not that she'd spent nearly a year consciously avoiding the place—it was well out of her normal civil-servant price range—but this was where Joe Reeder suggested they meet tonight.

He had even gone so far as to say, "My turn to pick up the check," which it wasn't, but she knew he wanted her to feel comfortable.

Now, sitting at a table in the bar, not far from where Associate Justice Venter had died, she felt woefully underdressed in her navy business suit, white silk blouse, and sensible shoes. She felt like a Goodwill shopper who had wandered into a Brooks Brothers world, especially compared to the living wax museum around her of heavy hitters from political and financial arenas.

Though Joe had ultimately taken the lead in the Supreme Court investigation, he had gone out of his way to give her equal credit at its successful conclusion. That meant a nice promotion for her to head up the new Special Situations Task Force. Now if the hottest young investigator in the Bureau could just locate that MIA personal life of hers . . .

"I'm Joe," said a resonant male voice above her. "I'll be your server this evening."

She looked up into Reeder's unreadable brown eyes and that slight smile in which she'd finally learned to locate warmth.

"Won the age discrimination lawsuit," she asked with a smirk, "did you, Joe?"

And to her it was always "Joe"—she'd learned that the "Peep" nickname was one colleagues had foisted on Reeder, and that he'd never really liked it.

"It was this," he said, "or greeter at Walmart."

He sat down across from her. His suit was well tailored and his tie probably two hundred bucks. But she knew he was a sweatshirt and jeans guy at heart.

"A past murder scene," she said, "is your idea of memories, memories? There are cheaper ways to reminisce."

His smile broadened. "I'm not a government worker anymore, remember? I'm a high-priced consultant. Let me show you how much an average citizen like me appreciates you hardworking G-gals and guys."

"I smell an ulterior motive," she said.

"Well, you've got a cop's nose. Or maybe it's my Clive Christian Number One."

"Is *that* what you're wearing?"

"Hell no. Aqua Velva. Don't laugh. It's a step up from Old Spice. Listen, Patti. Thanks for this."

She toasted him with her empty martini glass. "Thank *you*. It's overdue. Been almost a month."

A real waiter arrived and raised an eyebrow at Reeder by way of a question.

"Arnold Palmer for me," Reeder said, "and . . . another martini for the lady?"

She nodded, thinking how twentieth century her former partner always sounded, and the waiter left.

"Rough day at the office?" he asked, knowing she rarely had a first cocktail, let alone a second.

She shrugged. "Uneasy the head that wears the crown."

"Fuckin' A," he said.

These dinner meetings, not really dates, occurred every couple of weeks. The two had an easy chemistry developed in a case that had finally gone somewhere very dark. At first, they had met to talk about that, their shared trauma so to speak, and their dinner chats had evolved into a casual frankness. Joe Reeder seemed to her much less the mystery man now and more a good friend.

"But you're okay?" he asked, with understated but genuine concern.

In the low-key lighting of the bar, the planes of his rugged face had an undeniable attractiveness, emphasized by the whiteness of his hair, including those eyebrows, against a tanned complexion left over from a Florida trip.

The fresh martini came, she sipped it, the waiter disappeared, and she said to Reeder, "I'm going to ask you an embarrassing question."

"Do my best not to wet myself."

"Joe—in all this time . . . I'm just wondering . . . why is it you've never, you know . . ."

"Hit on you?"

She nodded.

He chuckled and a wave of embarrassment washed over her.

"You can ask that with a straight face?" he said. "I'm something like fifteen years older than you, easy."

"Like that has ever stopped any man from hitting on a woman! Particularly with your kind of sugar daddy potential."

A grin flashed. "I like that. Sugar daddy potential. But what's the use, kid? I mean, after all, you're gay."

Red rushed to her cheeks. "What do you mean? I . . . I've had boyfriends."

"Okay, then. Let's say you're bi. An old goat like me has *two* sexes to compete with? No thank you. Even if you are cute as lace pants."

She laughed. "Maybe that should offend me."

"No it shouldn't. Potential sugar daddies get to say politically inexcusable things to nice-looking women in bars. Anyway, you should be flattered—I was quoting Raymond Chandler."

"No you weren't."

He sipped his Arnold Palmer. "I certainly was."

"You were quoting Philip Marlowe, and that's a completely different thing."

The white eyebrows went up. "I stand corrected. And impressed by your investigator's eye for accuracy."

The waiter returned and took their order.

"Okay," she said. "So much for repartee. Why are we here? I mean, we've established we're not going to be an item."

His face turned serious—not grave, not somber. But decidedly serious. He tilted his head as if he were looking over the tops of glasses he wasn't wearing. "I need to ask a favor."

"The steak that's on its way to me," she said, with a touch of lightness, "will buy you a pretty good favor. Not to invoke unpleasant memories, Joe—but shoot."

"Not so fast, kid. Even for filet béarnaise, this might not be worth the risk."

She leaned forward and almost whispered. "You saved my life, Joe. Gay, straight, bisexual, it's a life I don't mind living. What do you need?"

His shrug was barely perceptible. "I'm looking into a suicide."

She arched a brow. "The president of ABC Security is looking into—"

"*Supposed* suicide of a friend," he said. "Retired Secret Service agent. Worked with him back in the day."

"'Supposed suicide' says you think it's murder."

"I do. And his wife thinks the same. I'd like to say the man saved my life . . ."

As he had saved hers.

". . . but that's not the case. He wasn't best man at my wedding. He was no Gabe Sloan. Just a guy I occasionally worked with. But, Patti—he was one of us. He deserves better."

She set her martini to one side. "Spell it out."

He did.

Then she said, "And the cops are *buying* this? They think a guy with a Glock in a shoulder holster chose to *hang* himself? Ridiculous."

"My read exactly. Of course, they formed their theory before I let Carl Bishop know I'd received that phone message from Chris. Bish thinks I can get the detective in charge to listen, but I'd like to have something more to show the guy."

She flicked him a smile. "Sounds like this is where the favor comes in."

"Almost certainly Bryson called me from a burner phone. But the police are not about to let me get into his records."

She shrugged. "Play the hero card. You're Joe frickin' Reeder, for Pete's sake."

"Is that your third martini? Fourth maybe? In what world do cops adore ex-feds who get a lot of play in the media?"

She nodded; he was right again. "And you want to know if he called anybody else on that phone?"

"Could be a good jumping-off point—see if the police are missing anything."

Nodding again, she said, "Give me both numbers, normal cell and burner one. It wasn't a blocked number, was it?"

"No. I have that for you. Both of them."

"Good. I'm in. Hey, I'm the boss of a task force, remember?"

"It's good to be king," Reeder said, and handed her a slip of paper with both numbers.

She held it up by thumb and middle finger, like evidence she didn't want to spoil. "You *knew* I'd say yes."

"No. High probability. Particularly after I said you were nice looking."

She grunted a laugh. "Sugar daddy."

They went silent as their food arrived. When the waiter left, they ate slowly, enjoying their steaks, which was a skill cops like Rogers and Reeder had to develop, in a life filled with so many on-the-fly meals.

When they had finished, and a busboy had cleared the table, she noticed him staring at her.

"What, broccoli in my teeth?"

He glanced around them, then said quietly, "If this really *was* a suicide, and I suppose it could be, well . . . it's no big thing. Just another guy the job caught up with. But if it's *murder* . . . ?"

"Yeah?"

He leaned in. "Patti, Chris Bryson was good, really good. He made presidential detail in the Service. He was successful as a one-man operation in this corporate world."

"Okay . . ."

He gave her the over-the-invisible-glasses look again. "If somebody took him out, and managed to get the better of him? So *much* the better of him that they could make his murder look like it was his idea . . . ?"

"Then they're good, too," she said. "Really goddamn good."

"Yeah. You know how people say 'Take care' instead of good-bye?"

"Sure."

"Well, Patti—*take care.*"

The next morning, in her office at the J. Edgar Hoover Building, Patti Rogers sat sipping coffee at her desk, looking at the slip of paper with two phone numbers written in Reeder's concise hand. Nothing to it, feeding them into the computer to call up the records.

Even though President Devlin Harrison had replaced the two assassinated Supreme Court justices with jurists closer to his own Democratic politics, the legacy of a gutted Fourth Amendment and expanded Patriot Act remained. Rogers, who did not wear her slightly right-of-center politics on her sleeve, approved. That Reeder was an old-school JFK-style liberal made for ironic amusement here, since those conservative-bred changes allowed her to do his dirty work—specifically, Rogers had the right to look into the phone records of any citizen.

The new court had also overturned *Roe v. Wade*, after President Harrison selected one liberal judge and one conservative to fill the two vacancies. Arguably the court was more balanced than before, but it still leaned clearly right.

The President's stated intention had been to exercise bipartisan fairness to bring the country together. Instead, the assassinations of two justices and their replacement appointments had only pushed the two sides further apart. The only unity between right and left today was a shared anger at Harrison.

Even with the new Supreme Court's blessing, however, running Bryson's phone numbers wouldn't be enough.

With Reeder's advice to "take care" foremost in her mind, Rogers went to see Miguel Altuve, her colleague and friend from the Supreme Court task force. A computer expert who could coax the most obscure information out of the net, Miggie played his keyboard with the skill and artistry of a great jazz musician.

In an office of his own now—roomy enough to include a small conference table with chairs—Miggie looked up from a trio of fanned-out monitors to answer Rogers's knock at the frame of his open door.

"Patti Rogers," he said with an instant smile, rising to welcome her. "Let me lie to myself that this is a social call before you tell me what you want."

"Well, you *are* looking sharp, Miggie."

Now that he was heading up a unit hunting cyberterrorists, a slimmed-down Altuve evidenced undergoing a considerable makeover— center-parted black hair exchanged for swept-back razor-cut, wireframe glasses supplanted by contacts, red-and-black power tie in place of his former-trademark clip-on bow tie.

And that charcoal suit had clearly set him back.

They shook hands and shared the awkward smiles of two former coworkers with mutual affection but little to say to each other. When your respective jobs were shrouded in secrecy, small talk was a problem.

"Got a second?" she asked, her smile starting to feel frozen.

"A second? I might even scrounge up a minute."

He gestured to the small conference table and she took a seat there while he came over and sat across from her. He folded his hands in a saying-grace fashion and leaned forward, eyes bright with curiosity.

"So what can I do for you, Patti?"

"Not for me exactly. Actually . . . for Joe Reeder."

Miggie's eyebrows rose; frankly the contacts gave him something of a glazed look. Nerds die hard. "He working for the Bureau again?"

"No. That's what makes this a little sticky. Let's say I'm keeping an eye on something he's looking into."

There was nothing negative in Miggie's frown. "Are we on the down-low here?"

Slowly, Rogers nodded. "Yes. So far it's nothing even vaguely work-related. Law enforcement–related, but not Bureau."

"You haven't scared me off yet. Keep going."

"It concerns a friend of Joe's from his Secret Service days. Another retired agent . . . who committed suicide under what Joe considers suspicious circumstances."

"Who am I to argue with Reeder's instincts? Few computers can compete with that mind. Lay it all out."

She did.

Then she said, "If this *wasn't* suicide, the killer or more likely killers took out a very capable agent. Retired but hardly over the hill. I guess we know better than most that if an agent from any government law enforcement agency dies, under even vaguely suspicious circumstances, something bad may have happened. And that could mean somebody in government covering up."

"I'll stop you when you get to something I don't know."

She nodded. "Good. On the same page, then?"

"Same page."

She clapped once. "So . . . take precautions, cover your newly slender ass, and don't get cocky."

"You're talking to somebody who can look at three monitors and over his shoulder, all at the same time."

She smiled a little. "Then you're just the guy." Handing him Reeder's slip of paper, she said, "Let know what you find."

He glanced at the two numbers and said, "Be on the safe side—give me a couple hours."

She left him to it and returned to her office. The Special Situations Task Force was investigating a string of four homicides in the DC area that might or might not be related. Of the 109 murders in the

District over the course of this year, these four stuck out as something different. The team was getting together for a briefing this morning.

The bullpen housed a cozy half a dozen desks with Rogers's office in back. She stood looking out at her busy crew—four agents and a behaviorist that made up the task force.

Behavioral expert Trevor Ivanek was a skeletal six-footer with a talking-skull head home to a fuzzy cap of hair, broad forehead, and dark deep-set eyes. The latter were bright and inquisitive, and he smiled readily, for a man who spent so much time inside the heads of monsters.

The other four agents were divided into two teams. The more senior duo, Jerry Bohannon and Reggie Wade, had over thirty years experience between them.

Handsome Bohannon—whose hair had become mysteriously darker since his divorce, even as his wardrobe got sharper—had become something of a mentor to Rogers. When the unit was assembled, she had expected some pushback from the more veteran agents. The most senior of these, Bohannon, had set a respectful example.

Wade—six four, African American, trimly bearded, a former college basketball player—always managed to just skirt Bureau's apparel regs with his *GQ* wardrobe. Rogers suspected Wade was serving as his recently unmarried partner's sartorial adviser. Wade, too, had shown her nothing but support, despite having logged more years.

Lucas Hardesy, lead agent of the other pair, was less than impressed with Rogers, though never outright insubordinate. Head shaved, clothes immaculate, shoes spit-shined, he was gung-ho ex-military and clearly resented taking orders from someone with less time in.

Rogers sensed no sexism in Hardesy's attitude—his trust and respect for his partner, Anne Nichols, making that unlikely.

Younger than Rogers, African American Nichols managed to balance badass with beauty. Patti's own default setting was to underplay her appearance, even going for an asexual vibe with her short hair and neutral wardrobe. She could only admire Nichols for pulling off the tough but feminine gambit. That blue suit with suede navy collar and cuffs, and the simple touch of lace at Anne's throat, were beyond Rogers's confidence and imagination.

Even if Reeder *had* said she was cute as lace pants . . .

"So," Rogers said, putting enough into it to raise everyone's eyes from their reports, monitors, and coffee to her direct gaze. "Anybody come up with anything new this morning?"

Ivanek said, "This still doesn't feel like a serial killer to me. Victimology doesn't match—three men, one an African American, and one Latina female. Serial killers don't usually break racial lines. Plus, these are impersonal kills. They could be hits, with nothing to tie the victims together. Beyond that, boss—I just don't know."

At his desk nearby, Hardesy was nodding. "Seems to me we're treading water here. Feels like the Sharpshooter Fallacy."

The Sharpshooter Fallacy was the psychologist's example of a cowboy shooting random holes on the side of a barn and then painting a bull's-eye target around the biggest cluster.

"It does," Ivanek said, just faintly cranky, "if by that you mean superimposing your target over my words."

A frowning Anne Nichols held up four fingers. "Four victims, different walks of life, all seemingly killed for no reason. No robbery, no enemies."

"Coincidence," Hardesy said.

Wade said, "Luke—did I just hear a law enforcement professional use the word 'coincidence,' as if there were such a thing?"

Shrugging, the ex-Army sergeant said, "Shit does happen."

Rogers said, "Let's key off Anne's view here. The murders were clean, no mess. Professional."

Bohannon said, "Double-taps don't really sound like serial killer ritual."

All the victims had died by twin bullets to the back of the head.

"Jerry," Ivanek said, straining for patience, "there's no template for serial killer ritual."

"Could be he's just one smart son of a bitch," Wade offered. "Nobody's looking into these murders as possibly related, except the people in this room." He grinned. "Experts *all*, of course."

"Experts," Nichols said, "who can't find a single damn thread that connects these victims."

"Doesn't have to be one," Rogers said. "The killer may see some vague connection that seems significant to him or her. Look at eye color, hair color, age, hobbies, shared job aspects. What do we have? An accountant, a librarian, a congressional aide, and a factory supervisor—"

"Go into a bar," Hardesy interrupted.

There were a couple of chuckles. And Rogers hid her irritation under a mild smile.

"Okay," Rogers said. "So it sounds like a bad joke . . . but *Deputy Director Fisk* and I think that, somehow, these killings may well be connected. So . . . let's keep digging. We'll meet up at the end of the day and see if we're anywhere closer."

But when they met in the afternoon, they'd made zero progress tying in the four victims, finding a motive for the murders, or even identifying a possible killer from security footage from around the victims' lives.

Rogers sat at her desk, a headache trying to win her attention and starting to succeed. She ran a hand over her face, lied to herself that the headache had gone away, then sat straight up and said "Shit," remembering she hadn't checked back with Miggie Altuve all day.

Quickly she found two e-mails, two text messages, and a voice mail, all from Miggie, all saying they needed to talk.

Finding him (no surprise) transfixed before his trio of monitors, she was about to knock at his open door when—without looking at her—Miggie said, "Should I have tried semaphores?"

"Sorry," she said with a chagrined grin, still poised in the doorway. "Busy day . . . So, you found something?"

He turned to her and raised eyebrows that had been trimmed into submission, then took a sip of his latest cup of coffee. Free-trade Sumatran, most likely—that was how Miggie rolled these days.

"Quite a lot," he said. "Also, nothing."

She frowned. "Why don't you connect those two dots for me."

"Okay, I'll give it a shot."

They returned to the small conference table and sat.

The computer expert said, "Start with the burner phone. Once upon a time it was stolen from a brick-and-mortar. Day he died, Bryson probably bought it black market."

"Any way to know who he bought it from?"

He shook his head. "On the street or from some dealer in such items. Maybe Bryson had somebody regular he used. No partner or coworker or even secretary to check with. Still, maybe there's someone out there who might know who his contacts were. That would be a nice break."

"Did he call anyone besides Reeder?"

"No. My guess? He bought it *to* call Reeder."

"We got nothing from that phone?"

Miggie smiled, just a little. "Not exactly. That's why I said a lot and nothing. Someone was tracking it."

Rogers sat forward. "Who?"

"No idea, but they're good. Someone remotely turned on that burner's GPS without Bryson knowing. Tracking him the whole time he had it."

She stared at her own clenched fists. "So *they* know who he bought it from. Or maybe who he bought it from turned the GPS on . . . ?"

"Maybe. Or they could have been following him and saw him buy the burner and turned it on remotely."

"How would they do that?"

He just looked at her.

She smirked. "Okay, so you smart computer guys can do anything."

"Not *anything*, but . . . I saw a couple of footprints they left behind. They were careful, but few of us are ever careful enough."

"Does that mean you have an idea of who they are, or might be?"

Another head shake. "No, but I can tell you this—they're as good as I am . . . maybe better, hard as that might be to believe. Whoever this is has had extensive training in concealing themselves."

"Training from where? By whom?"

He shrugged. "Maybe us, maybe Homeland, or NSA . . . could be anyone really. Wouldn't have to be American, foreign government even . . . but this is no ordinary hacker."

She waited for him to continue, and when he didn't, she said, "Is that it?"

"That's it for the burner phone. His personal phone, that's off-line. Bryson probably smashed it to bits in some trash can, after an attack of righteous paranoia. It went off-line late the night *before* Bryson died . . . and never came back on."

"Can you tell me anything about it?"

Miggie flipped a hand. "Normally, I could give you the cell's search history, websites visited, all kinds of information."

"But because it's off-line you can't?"

He gave her the sadly patronizing gaze of the computer geek. "No, Patti—it's because Bryson only used the device as a *phone*. Like a lot of older guys, he didn't use ten percent of the device's capabilities. You gotta understand—this guy grew up in *landline* days."

"Great—so there's nothing there?"

"Just the call log."

That was something at least. "Anything interesting?"

"Not really. Well . . . one item of possible interest—starting a couple of weeks before he died, Bryson got some calls from CSI."

"From *what* CSI? Local cops?"

This amused him. "No, and not the old TV show, either—Common Sense Investments. Actually, it's called CSII, if you add the 'Incorporated' on."

She frowned. "*Adam Benjamin's* investment company?"

"Right on the money. Literally."

Benjamin was her generation's Warren Buffett, just a regular guy who had parlayed his savings account into a billion-dollar investment firm by staying smart and keeping it simple. He had never fallen prey to the self-indulgences that usually come with wealth.

A childless widower for the last twenty-five of his nearly seventy years, all Benjamin did was make money, teach others how to make money, and donate money through several charities. Money, money, money. Yet he still lived in the same Defiance, Ohio, house that he and his late wife had bought almost fifty years ago.

What possible connection could there be between a dead small-time security consultant and the richest man in America?

She said, "Chris Bryson worked his whole life—he probably had something put away."

"Probably. Might have been moving money around. I didn't check his financials."

She raised an eyebrow.

Miggie shrugged. "Hey, I ran with what you asked me to. I *did* confirm a PI license. As a security consultant, Bryson could've been doing an investigation for CSI."

She noted that mentally. "Any other corporate calls?"

"A few, but nothing that added up to more than one or two."

She patted the table with both hands. "So, then—that's it?"

A crisp nod. "Afraid so. Can you get me Bryson's computer? If I had that, I could tell you anything you want to know about the guy."

"I'll have Reeder check with Mrs. Bryson."

"I'm not talking about his home computer so much, though I'd be happy to take a look. A guy who travels, in the security business? Get me his tablet or even laptop . . . dinosaur like Bryson, a laptop wouldn't surprise me. *That's* his safe—that's where we'll find all his secrets."

Reeder hadn't mentioned any computer of Bryson's. She wondered where the hell any computer of his might be, and more important . . .

. . . *was there something on it that got the man killed?*

"The World is my country,
all mankind are my brethren,
and to do good is my religion."

Thomas Paine

FOUR

Joe Reeder was a new man where his cell phone was concerned. Missing the call that could have saved Chris Bryson was obviously part of what inspired his new attitude. But Patti Rogers might check in with information, and so might Carl Bishop. For right now, anyway, Reeder was a field agent again—a private detective of sorts, with a client of one: himself.

And a field agent on the job lived and died by his phone. Just ask Bryson.

Seated on a bench one hundred yards east of (and down the hill from) the Tomb of the Unknowns, Reeder sent his eyes across the Potomac toward the Washington Monument, then to the National Mall and finally the Capitol, its dome currently encased in a cocoon of steel scaffolding. Last summer DC had suffered an earthquake in comparable magnitude to the 5.8 quake of '11 that had necessitated repairs to the Washington Monument. Now the Capitol, sporting cracks in its cast-iron dome, was undergoing restoration and reinforcement for the first time since 2014.

Reeder rarely visited Arlington during the cemetery's open-to-the-public hours; having saved a President's life, he had the unique perk of roaming the grounds whenever he chose. In those early morning hours, the place was his alone—his and the fallen around him, whose company he generally preferred to the living. Anyway, few tourists made a visit in this kind of cold and snow, and he needed his Fortress of Solitude to clear his head.

After all, it wasn't every morning he answered his cell before 6:00 a.m. Wasn't every night that he put that cell on his nightstand, either, leaving the ringer on. But it wasn't every day that he received a phone call from Adam Benjamin.

No day ever before, actually.

He'd bolted upright in the bed, like a buck private who found his commanding officer looming over his cot. Ready to blink the sleep out of his eyes and salute.

For a man who did not believe in heroes, Reeder made an exception for Adam Benjamin. The man had overcome adversity in the too-early death of his wife, and transformed himself by hard work and brains from a simple small-college economics prof into one of the richest men in the world. He'd done it all himself, and he'd done it honestly.

The billionaire investor had gradually become such a figure of American popularity that a groundswell movement based on his idea of common-sense centrism was gaining not just economic traction, but political momentum. Cable news outlets, right and left, spoke of a grassroots group that, if they could ever get themselves organized, would draft him to run independently for president.

There'd been no secretary or assistant on the line, saying, "Hold for Mr. Benjamin." Just that familiar, much-imitated voice from television interviews, distinctive in its warm Midwestern baritone, almost—but not quite—folksy.

So familiar and imitated was the voice that Reeder wondered if this might not be a prank, worked by somebody at the ABC Security office who knew how much he admired the guy.

"This is Adam Benjamin. Am I speaking to Joe Reeder?"

He had nearly clicked off, rolled over and gone back to sleep. "Hell it is."

"The hell it *is*," the voice said with a chuckle. "Mr. Reeder, I assure you that you enjoy the dubious honor of speaking to Adam Benjamin. Or do I really sound that much like those late-night comics would have it?"

A hearty laugh followed, indicating this wasn't the first time someone had not believed his caller.

Businesslike, Reeder said, "If this is Adam Benjamin, would you mind telling me how you got this number? And why you didn't call me at work? That number is listed."

"I apologize for the early hour. It's actually earlier here in Ohio, but still I understand that this is an imposition. As for getting your number, might I immodestly mention that I own some portion of every phone company in this country? And a few elsewhere. As for my reason for calling so early, that will become apparent, if you allow this conversation to continue."

Seemed to be Benjamin, all right. Strength, courtesy, and confidence.

"Okay, Mr. Benjamin. What's the reason for this wake-up call?"

"Call me 'Adam,' if you would."

"Not just yet. And I'm fine with 'Mr. Reeder' till I know what's going on. There remains at least some possibility I'm speaking to an imposter."

With a smile in his voice, the caller said, "But you're the 'people reader.'"

"Not over the phone I'm not. I need faces. Whole bodies when necessary."

"Understood. The reason for my call, Mr. Reeder, is to discuss some business that we might do."

"I don't do endorsements, and all my money is tied up in my own firm or already securely invested."

The tiniest hint of irritation came through. "Mr. Reeder, I have a reputation for being something of a 'good ol' boy,' but this is hardly phone solicitation. I have others to do that kind of thing for me."

Reeder smiled. "Well, I guess you would. That was just my way of suggesting you be more specific about what it is you want with me . . . or from me."

Silence.

Then: "Fair enough, but I don't want to talk about our potential business on *any* phone, nor do I wish to be seen walking into your corporate headquarters."

"Might be a little below your standards at that."

"We both know that it's not," the caller said. "In fact, your business has never been better."

"What do you have in mind, Mr. Benjamin?"

"Could we talk about that this evening? Over dinner?"

"All right. Where?"

"The Holiday Inn Express in Falls Church, Virginia."

Part of the greater DC metro area, but out of the way enough not to attract media attention. Made sense. But the Holiday Inn Express?

"Why that, uh, venue?"

"Well, it's where I'll be staying tonight."

"You're kidding, right? Anyway, you said dinner. The only meal they serve is breakfast, and I'm pretty sure we'll be past the cutoff."

The warm laugh again. "We'll come up with something to eat, Mr. Reeder. I'm not asking you to brown bag it. As for the . . . accommodations? I like my privacy, including coming and going as I please. Under the radar, so to speak."

"I think it's time for you to start calling me Joe."

"Not 'Peep,' as the media would have it?"

"No. I hate that nickname."

"You could have it worse. As a boy they called me 'Adam Ant.' So make it Adam."

"All right, Adam. But frankly, with your money, you could rent a floor at a five-star hotel and have plenty of privacy, and they'd probably get you in and out without anyone knowing."

"I could. But it's easier for me to rent an entire Holiday Inn Express in the suburbs, have them put 'Welcome Conventioneers' on their sign, and keep a truly low profile. Which would you choose?"

"If I had the dough," he admitted, "probably your way."

"It's only common sense," Benjamin said, invoking the catch-phrase that had been his calling card since he began his investment business.

"I do apologize for the early call," he went on, "but I have to allow for making my way to you, and there are arrangements to handle. Shall we say six? Just go to the front desk."

The rest of the day, Reeder wondered what kind of business Benjamin might have for him. Hiring ABC Security didn't require one CEO calling the other. Several years ago, Reeder had sold 49 percent of his firm to investors—he wondered if Benjamin had secretly been one of them.

Now that ABC was making more money than ever, was America's savviest investor coming after the rest of the company? If so, Benjamin approaching Reeder personally might have to do with a sort of celebrity-to-celebrity courtesy. Otherwise, in the greater scheme of things, ABC would seem small damn potatoes to a wheeler-dealer like that.

Benjamin's astounding phone call had brought Reeder to Arlington National Cemetery to think things through, to mull it over. Back up the hill, he heard the guard at the Tomb of the Unknowns click his heels together. Judging from a sound Reeder had heard many times, the guard was at the north end of the mat. So was Reeder. The guard would turn toward the tomb and face east, but wouldn't see Reeder. His bench at the bottom of the hill was behind a low wall. Of course, the guard might note the plume of Reeder's breath.

Silently, Reeder counted to twenty-one with the guard.

As Reeder's lips formed the last number, the guard's heels clicked and the count began again. In twenty-one seconds, the guard would take twenty-one paces south, click his heels, then turn east again. Reeder knew the ritual as well as any guard who ever walked the mat.

To him it meant peace and serenity, its symbolism and every click of the guard's heels giving him a little surge of patriotism, of purpose. He never spoke of this, had never shared it even with his late friend Sloan, and certainly not Melanie or Amy. Patti Rogers might get it, former Army MP that she was. He knew some, perhaps many, would consider him an aging cornball, mired in a red-white-and-blue past that never really existed. Their loss.

With a sigh, he rose. Ready for the meeting, whatever it might be.

Back in his Prius, just reaching to turn the key, he was interrupted by the trill of his cell. No more ignoring that! He checked the caller ID—PATTI ROGERS.

"Hey, Patti. Anything yet?"

Her hello was: "Do you have your friend's computer?"

"No, but I can get to any home computers through his wife. The cops would probably have any work machine."

"What would your friend Chris have had with him on a job? In his motel room? A tablet maybe?"

Reeder thought for a moment. "Seems like the last time I was at his office, he used a laptop. Cops should have that, too. I'll check. What about his two phones?"

"Nothing much on either. Miggie says Chris's computers are our best shot."

"Thanks, Patti. I'll talk to his wife, Beth, later tonight. Right now I've got a meeting with Adam Benjamin, of all people."

"Did you *already* talk to Miggie?"

"Huh?" How had she made a leap from a billionaire to a computer geek? "Why would you—"

Interrupting, she said, "Only thing Miggie found on your friend's cell were a couple calls from that Common Sense Investments group of Benjamin's."

"Huh. You think Chris may have had money with them?"

"Don't know," she said. "My bad for not running his financials."

"I'll ask Beth," Reeder said, mostly to himself.

"Should I have Miggie run those financials?"

"Please."

"Anything else?"

"No." He smiled at the phone. "But it's nice to know Uncle Sam's finest is at my beck and call."

"Anything for a taxpayer. But there's a quid pro quo here—I want to run something past you, next time we're together."

"Yeah?"

"Something my unit's getting nowhere with."

"Sure. Dinner tomorrow night?"

She said, "Right. I'll buy. I'll pick where."

Even with rush hour traffic, the drive to Falls Church wasn't bad, though it got dark quickly once he got going. At the Holiday Inn Express, Reeder saw at once that things looked off. Three black SUVs were parked at the curb in front of the entry doors. Though neighboring motels and restaurants were doing good business, the Holiday Inn Express lot was empty but for a half-dozen vehicles along one side of the building, employees probably. Those conventioneers welcomed by the hotel's marquee must have been out on the town . . .

So Reeder didn't have a whole lot of trouble finding a parking place. Inside, past the automatic doors, he saw a female desk clerk at left and four men scattered around the small lobby—sofa, easy chair, table by the breakfast area, one casually chatting up the young glazed-looking brunette. They wore black suits and various one-tone ties and guns tough to spot under their suit coats. Tough if you weren't an ex–Secret Service agent.

The sofa guy rose. At fifty-something, he was ten or more years older than the others, and might have been ex–Secret Service himself, earpiece, wrist mic. Dark hair clipped close, brown eyes wary.

Reeder skipped the desk clerk and her chaperone and went over to the man who'd risen upon his entry.

"Mr. Reeder?" he asked. Voice polite, eyes hard.

As if Reeder's mug and white hair hadn't been splashed all over cable news for the last year. "Right. Here to see Mr. Benjamin. But you know that."

He nodded. "If you'll follow me . . ."

While the two who were still seated stayed behind, the desk clerk's chaperone fell in behind Reeder and his escort, in a kind of hi-ho-hi-ho line. They walked down a corridor a short distance to a first-floor room.

The fiftyish bodyguard, Reeder just behind him, knocked at room 103.

A security man inside opened the door and allowed them in. Just another Holiday Inn Express room, not fancy but acceptable, if you were some midlevel or lower executive. Across the room, a man and a woman sat on opposite sides of a round table, sleek high-end laptops back to back. Both sexes wore business suits in shades of gray; midthirties, shortish dark hair, the female's a lighter shade of brown, tied up in a bun.

When Reeder entered, neither acknowledged him even with a glance, though both closed the lids of their computers. Sitting in a wing chair in one corner, a guy around Reeder's age did not take his attention from his smartphone at this new arrival; his suit coat lay folded on the back of the chair with a military care that went with his short brown hair. An inch-and-a-half scar along his right cheekbone started just under his eye.

They were all businesspeople, no doubt, although the scarred man's business might be security. The laptop pair were minions of the man who was not in the room: Adam Benjamin.

Reeder's fiftyish escort exited, closing the door behind him. The inside bodyguard took his post there, remaining silent. Everybody remained silent, including Reeder. If they didn't want to talk to him, he didn't want to talk to them. Then a flush, running water, and the bathroom door opened.

Adam Benjamin strode out, a smile splitting his face as he saw Reeder, coming right over to offer a hand.

Though dark-framed, large-lensed glasses provided a hint of the professor he'd once been, Adam Benjamin was clearly no weakling refugee from academia. According to Benjamin's most recent book, *Common Sense for the Uncommon Man*—which Reeder had read on a plane last year—the man worked out daily (he'd played football at Ohio State), ate well but sensibly (cheeseburgers an unguilty pleasure), and steered clear of tailored clothing, as evidenced by his navy blue, red-pinstriped cardigan with open-throat white dress shirt, navy slacks, and well-worn black loafers.

His silver hair still showing some dark brown, Benjamin was approaching seventy, but looked some years younger, his oval face handsome, in an avuncular way—strong Roman nose, wide thin-lipped mouth, kind dark eyes. In the flesh as on television, he personified the middle-class values that he extolled in the media.

"Joe," he said as they shook hands. "Adam Benjamin."

"Yeah. I recognized you."

That chuckle was even warmer in person. "And I you."

And still they shook, Benjamin's grip firm but no self-conscious knuckle crusher. Reeder met the pressure.

"I may not have sounded like it on the phone, Adam, but I am a fan."

"That's flattering. As am I of you, sir."

Reeder finally stopped the handshake. It had gone on too long and, anyway, this mutual appreciation society routine was getting a bit much.

The scarred guy in the wing chair had put the smartphone away. He was on his feet, climbing into his jacket.

"Joe," Benjamin said, gesturing, "this is my majordomo, Frank Elmore."

Reeder shook hands with the man, just a single firm shake. Elmore's eyes were on Benjamin. The guy knew which side the butter went on, and who wielded the butter knife.

He said, in an emotionless baritone, "Will there be anything else, sir?"

"Not now, Frank. Get yourself something to eat. I'll call."

The laptop pair tagged after Elmore, pausing just long enough for Benjamin to identify them: "My VP of Special Projects, Lynn Barr, and my chief accountant, Lawrence Schafer. I'm sure you recognize Joe Reeder."

With small meaningless smiles, the pair exchanged nods but not handshakes with Reeder, then followed Elmore out. But for the bodyguard just inside the door, this would seem to be a private meeting.

Big wide smile from Benjamin. "Joe, have a seat."

His host waved Reeder toward the round table—the laptops had gone along with the lapdogs. He'd barely sat before a knock came at the door. He glanced that way as the bodyguard opened the door, accepted two white paper bags, then closed it. He came over and gave the larger bag to the former professor, who had not yet joined Reeder at the table.

"Thanks, Len," Benjamin said. "That's all for now."

Len and the smaller bag went out, closing the door behind him. *Private meeting, all right.* Of course, Reeder figured the bodyguard would remain on duty in the corridor.

Alone now with the richest man in the United States, Reeder ignored the questions bubbling in his brain. He'd learned to keep quiet while standing presidential detail. And Benjamin somehow invoked that in him, that special respect that came with high office and, well, high finance.

Benjamin came over, grinning like a kid as he showed his guest the label on the bag—a hamburger chain long famous in the DC area.

"Five Guys," Reeder read, grinning back.

"Hope this is all right with you. It's not the Old Ebbitt Grill, but it's my second favorite."

"Five Guys was good enough for Obama and the press corps, and good enough for me."

"You were on presidential detail back then?"

Reeder shook his head. "I came on two years into President Mathis's term."

Benjamin's sigh was somber. "There's a real tragedy and a damn shame."

"Agreed," Reeder said.

Just over halfway through his first term, President Edward Mathis was diagnosed with leukemia. Serving out his term, he chose not to run for a second. Instead, his GOP-picked successor, neocon Gregory Bennett, had taken over.

Reeder had been no supporter of Mathis's right of center politics, but the late President had been a good man and an honest one, a small miracle considering what it took to get elected to the land's highest office. Mathis died less than a year after leaving the White House, with President Bennett already pursuing a much farther-right agenda.

Benjamin handed a foil-wrapped burger to Reeder, kept one for himself, and handed Reeder a pack of fries, too. His host jerked a thumb. "Pop and water in the fridge."

Reeder got up and went there, thinking, *"Pop" and "fridge," two good old-fashioned Midwestern words.*

Kneeling as he made his selection, he asked Benjamin, "Want something?"

"Just water—pop gives me the burps anymore."

Reeder came back and sat down with two bottles of water whose labels were those of an Ohio grocery chain. Benjamin had brought his own water rather than pay for the minibar. Reeder's kind of guy.

As they ate, Benjamin asked, maybe too casually, "How would you like to sell me your company, Joe?"

"Not on the market, sorry. Hope the meeting isn't over, 'cause I'm really enjoying the burger."

That patented chuckle again. "Figured as much, but you never know unless you ask. ABC has been successful in its own right, but now with your superstar status . . ."

"Adam, please. I'm eating." He shrugged. "ABC does okay. Has since the start."

"Right, and then one Joe Reeder kicked ass on the Supreme Court task force, and now your business has doubled."

"You do your homework."

"I do. I have help, of course. But mostly it's still me. Key to my success, if you were wondering."

"That and common sense."

Benjamin chewed some cheeseburger, savoring it, then swallowed and said, "We both know common sense has been in short supply in this country for some while."

Reeder popped a couple of fries, said nothing.

Benjamin went on: "Someone needs to help return this country to the sort of common sense that Thomas Paine first wrote about, back in 1776."

"I don't disagree," Reeder said.

Given recent media talk that Benjamin might be planning a run at the White House, this turn in the conversation didn't surprise Reeder.

Benjamin continued: "Paine said, 'From the errors of other nations, let us . . .'"

"'. . . learn wisdom,'" Reeder finished.

Benjamin's burger halted midair. "So you've read *Common Sense.*"

"Years ago. In high school, and again in college."

He sat forward. "But now, Joe, we need to follow Paine's lead, and learn wisdom from our own errors, coming together to fix what is broken in this country."

With a faint smile, Reeder said, "Campaign speech?"

"No . . . just personal opinion. As far as seeking a certain oval-shaped office, I'm not convinced I'm the right candidate."

False modesty? The man's micro-expressions gave nothing away. He had obviously been trained to make his face as blank a mask as Reeder's own, under that layer of geniality.

"Adam, was that the business you wanted to discuss? Buying me out?"

"In part. You definitely have the kind of name that could be successfully franchised nationally."

"You mean, you like the ring of ABC Security?"

Now his host's smile turned wry. "No. I think you know what I mean . . . but I won't press. This is an idea you'll either come to or not. You might think on it and get back to me—who knows? In the meantime, I have another modest proposal."

"I hope it's not cannibalism."

"You know your Swift as well! A man of action and of the mind. I like that." His cheeseburger, like Thomas Paine, was history. He used his napkin. "Joe, I want you as head of my security team."

Reeder, also finished eating, raised a palm as if taking an oath. "I'm flattered, but no. I like being my own man. But I can offer you one of my best people . . . particularly if the assignment is temporary."

"It would be temporary, which is why I think you might want to take it on yourself. Given your track record, I would prefer you."

"Not a field agent anymore. Sorry."

Benjamin folded his hands, leaned forward just slightly. "Joe, I like you. My two offers could easily become one offer—sell me your company, then come to work for me . . . for just one year. At the end of that year, if you like, you can go back to running the DC office of ABC."

"That's a lot of letters, Adam."

"It'll be a lot of numbers, Joe, on the check I write. Amy will never have a financial worry in her entire life."

Reeder let out some air. "You really *do* do your homework—but no . . . though my offer of sending you my best man stands. Besides, you already have a head of security, don't you?"

"A former colleague of yours—Jay Akers," Benjamin said, nodding. "Jay has his strengths, but he's . . . how was it Ian Fleming described James Bond? A blunt instrument."

"Adam, if you have James Bond on your staff, who needs Joe Reeder?"

A warm chuckle grew into a full-throated laugh. "Look, Joe . . . for what I have planned, I need someone who can relate better within my corporate family. Who has a sense of subtlety and . . . discretion."

"What's your complaint with Jay? He's a good man."

"Perhaps, and I like having ex–Secret Service on my team . . . but Akers is rubbing my second-in-command, Frank Elmore, the wrong way. Claims Frank has me surrounded by mercenaries, for the most part. Not that there isn't some truth in it. Sometimes it's like I'm traveling with a band of thugs."

"Worked for Capone."

"But not for presidential candidates."

"Is that what you are, Adam?"

He ducked the question. "Having your respected presence on the scene, directing my security team—even the ones who do look like thugs—would frankly allow me to bask in your highly recognizable, heroic presence."

Hero again. He managed to keep the burger down.

Reeder said, "You'd like your personal detail to be more presidential. And I'm probably the most famous ex–Secret Service agent around. I get that. If you don't mind my asking, what exactly are your plans?"

Benjamin considered that. "I believe it's time I tested the presidential waters. See what the people think. See how a speaking tour might impact the polls. Then I can make a decision that makes sense."

"Yeah, common sense, I know."

Benjamin held Reeder's gaze. "Joe, you've been around the political circus a long time, and you know as well as I do that our country is in trouble. The right and the left continue to move farther apart, to a point where our two major parties are essentially radical fringe groups with unearned power."

"Been that way a while now," Reeder granted.

"The center, where most people live, has become disenfranchised as the extremes on both sides scream at the top of their lungs, drowning out any, yes, common sense. And so nothing gets done. Congress is paralyzed. It's time for the center to take back what is rightfully theirs. It's time for the majority to rule the country again. Time for common *sense* to prevail in this country once more."

Reeder had heard enough campaign speeches in his time to recognize one a mile away. "You aren't just testing the waters, Adam. You're going to do this thing, aren't you?"

"Probably," he admitted with a twinkle and a smile. "Almost certainly. But don't quote me."

"Big step," Reeder said.

"Yes it is—and we're kicking this off with what I'm calling 'A Citizen's State of the Union' speech next Tuesday, at Constitution Hall. It would be my pleasure, even if you're reluctant to come officially on staff, to have you join me at the rally. You and a guest, if you like. What say?"

Reeder gestured to the Five Guys bag, in which wadded-up wrappers and napkins now resided.

"After a feast like this," he said, "it would be ungracious of me to decline."

Benjamin leaned forward and clutched Reeder's forearm. "Joe, we're going to do great things together. Help me lead the country we love back to where there's some real harmony, and make these damn political parties work together, not against each other."

"We'll just start," Reeder said, "with me saying yes to your invite."

The billionaire's smile was an embarrassed one. "Got carried away a little, didn't I? Sorry. Thanks for coming, Joe. And I look forward to seeing you at the rally. I'll put the arrangements in motion."

Benjamin rose.

So did Reeder. "Uh, before I go . . . can I ask you something? Kind of out of left field?"

"Certainly."

"A friend of mine died the other night."

"Oh, I'm sorry to hear that."

"Thank you. The police call it suicide, but I know better. His name was Chris Bryson. In the weeks before his death, he received a few calls from your company."

"Which company?"

"CSI. He may have been an investor, or somebody of yours may have wanted him to look into something. He was a security consultant. Name doesn't mean anything to you, does it? Chris Bryson?"

"No, I'm sorry to say it doesn't. But you have my sympathies, and I'll check with my people and see what those calls were about."

"I'd appreciate that. Sorry to bother the CEO with such trivialities."

"The death of one good man is a loss to us all."

"Thomas Paine?"

He shook his head, smiled a little. "Adam Benjamin. And that you can quote."

Heading out to his car, Reeder admitted to himself that everything Benjamin said did make sense, common or otherwise. But a guy who stood up in public saying such things, particularly if that guy got some traction . . . ?

Might not get carried away as much as carted out.

On his back.

"The liberal left can be as rigid and destructive as any force in American life."

Daniel Patrick Moynihan, United States Senator from New York, 1977–2001, Ambassador to India and the United Nations.
Section 36, Lot 2261,
Arlington National Cemetery.

FIVE

Sometimes Amy Reeder longed for her father's gift at reading people—spotting and interpreting the tiny behavioral tells of their moods, their inner thoughts, their outright lies. Right now, for instance, she had no fricking idea what her boyfriend, Bobby Landon, might be thinking.

Well, one thing she *could* read: he was pissed.

Not that *that* was anything unusual lately.

Sitting on the couch in her Georgetown apartment, still in the gray suit she'd worn to her part-time job as a senatorial intern, Amy inconspicuously brushed away the beginnings of a tear.

She would not dignify Bobby's belligerence with a single drop.

Slender legs tucked under her, the twenty-one-year-old knew she was wrinkling her slacks, buying herself time with an iron or expense at a dry cleaners, but at this point didn't really give a damn. Her long brown hair, tucked up in a bun, stayed perfectly in place as she shook her head.

How many times had they had this same damn argument? Once a week? Maybe, for a while. Of late, more like daily.

Bobby tromped back in from the kitchen, brown eyes flaring, fists balled, ponytail swinging. The contrast between him in his ancient Che Guevara T-shirt, ragged jeans, and worn sneakers and her professional attire from Ann Taylor made her feel at once invaded and a stranger in her own apartment.

"I told you the Common Sense douche bags," he said, not quite yelling, "are holding a big-ass rally on Tuesday. You *knew* that."

"And *you* know," she said, working to keep her anger in check, "that I cannot go to events like that anymore. We had this talk before I accepted the internship."

"Which I was in favor of!"

"That's right, you were. And you were *fine* with it when I said working for a senator, participating in protests was out for me."

He stopped pacing. Breathed in and out, slowly, like a man fighting a panic attack. Finally he let out a long period-at-the-end-of-a-sentence sigh.

"You're right," he said, holding up surrender hands. "You're right, you're right. I'm sorry."

". . . What?"

He came over and sat next to her. "I'm way out of line. I encouraged you to take the damn job."

"You did," she said.

"Figured you were in a position to do some good from within. From inside the belly of the beast."

"But not in a subversive way, Bobby. I'm not a spy. I'm trying to see how the system operates, and see if I can have some small impact . . . and make that work in favor of what we believe in."

"I get that," he said, utterly calm now.

She arched an eyebrow at him. "This *is* still you, right? You aren't an alien or anything, and I'm going to find a pod in the kitchen?"

He smiled, embarrassed. "No. It's me. Hotheaded, frustrated me. I'm starting to feel like I'm on the inside looking out. You know what guys my age who go to protests alone are usually trying to do, don't you?"

"Get laid?" she asked with a half smile.

"I was trying to think of a more graceful way to say it. But you're not wrong. We've been a team, baby, and it's hard sitting on the bench. These are important times. We're on the brink here."

She patted his leg. "Every generation feels that way. And I trust you not to pick up some latter-day hippie chick at the rally."

He gave her a kiss. Small, sweet kiss.

"I get carried away sometimes," he said. "I'll be better."

She studied him. "I am a little surprised that you got worked up about these Common Sensers. What's so bad about standing in the middle of the road? Other than both sides trying to run you over."

He shrugged. "They're not as bad as the Spirit jagoffs, I'll give you that. But the Sensers sure as hell will slow any small progress we might make in this country."

"The Spirit" was more officially the Spirit of '76 Movement, a splinter off the old Tea Party that had sprouted into a tree.

Bobby was saying, "And Wilson Blount and his old-school right-wing cronies? You're right, they are *so* obviously *worse*. I mean, those assholes are *always* up to some damn self-interested thing."

"Goes without saying," she said, hoping to cut off what appeared to be a building rant.

No such luck: his eyes were flaring again.

"Did you know that old man Blount got that asshole Cunningham from Montana to sneak a line item into the highway construction bill? Lowering the age for becoming president from thirty-five to *thirty?*"

"I did know," she said calmly. "It got some media play. But Blount claims he's only trying to encourage the youth of America. To show younger people, young voters, that he respects them."

"That's blather for the idiots. Blount has his eyes on the presidency for that puke-face kid of his, Nicky."

"I haven't heard anything like that," she said, eyes narrowing. "Where did you get that?"

He raised and shook a "right on" fist. "Inhabit America website. Right now, they're at the top of a short list of anybody spreading the truth."

Inhabit America was viewed, at least by the left, as the next logical step after the old Occupy Movement. They espoused sweeping change to nearly every aspect of the country that was still touched by the neocon legacy of President Bennett. Inhabit America was Bobby's latest hobbyhorse.

Of course, Amy followed Inhabit America online, too; but her experience from her new job had already made her more skeptical of sites like Inhabit and their self-proclaimed "truth."

"So we have Blount and his bunch going after the White House," Bobby was saying, getting himself going again, "while these white-bread Common Sensers are preaching their 'Meet Us in the Middle' nonsense. They just *love* to go on talk radio and cable news and present their old-time Americana bull, boasting that they aren't on *either* side. Come on! Who isn't more on one side than the other? They need to get off the goddamn fence!"

When she had first met and started dating Bobby, his save-the-world progressive notions had seemed to her noble, and she had joined in willingly. But the more time she spent on the Hill, the more she realized that Bobby's simple answers were not reality-based. Governments had budgets, with thousands of programs, each begging for its share from the national coffers, each with defenders on the right or left.

People like Bobby never worried about the economics of a problem—just doing what they thought was right, damn the cost, practicality be damned.

"People like Bobby"—*my God, was* that *how she was thinking now, about the man she wanted to spend her life with?*

Whenever she tried to explain her revised, insider's views to him, he only called her naive. Now the roles had reversed—*he* seemed the naive one.

"What's so bad about a centrist movement?" she asked. "It's where most people in this country really stand. The people in the middle just get shouted down by the extremes. And maybe the Common Sense Movement *is* 'white-bread,' but their demographics go across ethnic and even religious divides."

He gave her that condescending smile she knew too well. "You're cute when you mimic your dad. Such a good little girl."

"Cute" was his code word for naive. And he had just crossed the line with this "good little girl." Not a pod in the kitchen at all, just a condescending prick lying momentarily low.

She flew to her feet and glared down at him. "Go screw yourself, Bobby, because trust me—that's your only option tonight!"

"Honey . . . sweetie . . ."

"Don't honey/sweetie me, you smug bastard. First you talk me into that intern position, then you treat me like shit for *taking* it! Who is it again that ought to get off the goddamn fence?"

He shrugged with open hands, and made his case—lamely: "I just thought you could do some good on the inside, and that we'd have the ear of a US senator."

"And by *we*," she said, still towering over him, "you mean *you* . . . pulling my strings?"

"No . . . that's not it. Not at all . . ."

Amy folded her arms, her anger shifting from hot to cold. "Senator Hackbarth isn't progressive enough for you, I suppose."

"She's a good person, sure, means well but—"

"What *would* satisfy you, Bobby? An anarchist maybe? Somebody who'd toss a bomb in the Senate and run away cackling?"

Senator Diane T. Hackbarth, Democrat from Wisconsin, was rated by the *National Journal* as among the most left-leaning members of Congress. That was about all Amy had known when she'd been assigned to the senator, but she'd quickly done her homework to get up to speed.

Since Day One as an intern in Hackbarth's office, the hours had been longer, the work harder, and the rewards greater than anything the young woman had ever done. All this was on top of her college workload.

Bobby had quickly gone from being her support system to a genuine pain in the ass. Like tonight—riding her about a protest at a political rally, which he knew damn well she couldn't attend; it was finally just too much.

He showed her the surrender hands again. "You're right, baby. I've been a real dick."

"Finally," she said, voice dripping venom, "we agree."

Bobby looked up at her like she'd slapped him. He just sat there, eyes wide and welling, mouth hanging slackly open.

She'd seen that look on her father's face when she watched secretly from the stairs that time, back when she was in junior high, when her mother had said much the same thing to him. *Was she channeling her mother now?* The woman she'd resented for being so tough on Daddy?

She sat next to Bobby. "See what happens," she said gently, "when worlds collide?" Then jokingly, "Card-carrying pod person like you should know that."

He said nothing, wearing the hurt like a drink she'd tossed in his face, dripping there.

"Baby," she said, "that came out really nasty. I'm sorry."

She kissed his cheek. At least he didn't pull away.

Then he said, "No apologies, sweetheart. Got what I deserved. I started in on you and it was unfair and I was a prick."

"Like I said," she said, no venom in her voice at all now, quite the opposite, "finally we agree . . ."

She kissed him on the mouth and it was sweet and then some urgency came in. Then they were in each other's arms, making out like the overage immature kids that they were, the blowup over as quickly as it began.

Bobby's hands starting roving, then tugging at her clothes, and her cell phone vibrated on the nearby coffee table, hopping around for attention like a child in its crib, wondering what strangeness its parents were up to.

"Shit," she said.

He was unbuttoning her blouse. "Ignore it."

"Could be work," she said, already pulling away.

"They'll leave a message," he tried. "It can wait a few minutes . . ."

She said, not sharply, "Is that all the time you figure you need?"

He smiled, laughed a little, took the pressure off and she reached for the phone, getting it just before voice mail kicked in.

"Senator Hackbarth," she said, having seen the caller ID. "What can I do for you, ma'am?"

The familiar businesslike alto: "Meet me tomorrow, breakfast. Seven a.m., Capitol restaurant."

"I, uh, thought the restaurant didn't open till eight thirty."

"It doesn't."

That was all the explanation Amy's boss gave—after all, rank has its privileges, and so does being a senator.

Hackbarth was saying, "Have you read the background material on the college-loan reform bill?"

"Yes," Amy said, not adding, *Some of it.* So not technically a lie.

The senator continued: "And since this law could affect you and a good number of your friends, I'll be eager to hear your opinion."

"Yes, ma'am. Thank you, Senator."

"*Informed* opinion, Ms. Reeder."

"Absolutely, yes, ma'am."

The line clicked dead in her ear.

She turned slowly toward Bobby. He was already sitting up, and when he saw her face, he rose.

"I'm sorry," she said.

"No more sorries tonight," he said pleasantly, but there was just the faintest strain in it. "I'm gonna catch some TV. Check in when you get a chance."

He went off toward the bedroom.

Allowing herself a plight-of-the-working-class sigh, she trudged to the dining room table, grabbed her new briefcase—a gift from Dad—and shambled back to the couch. In the bed where Bobby waited, it was doubtful the two would be able to get to their make-up sex, just as the notion of her getting any sleep at all was similarly unlikely.

Chances were, she'd be reading till dawn. Withdrawing the fat folder of material on the bill the senator wanted to be briefed on, Amy settled back into the couch.

Already it felt like a long night.

"I prefer peace.
But if trouble must come,
let it come in my time,
so that my children can live in peace."

Thomas Paine

SIX

Pulling out of the Holiday Inn Express in Falls Church, Joe Reeder turned his Prius toward another Virginia bedroom community, Fairfax Station, and the Bryson home. On the way, he hands-free phoned homicide detective Carl Bishop's cell and got him in two rings.

"What have I done," Bish said, over bullpen chatter, "to deserve a phone call from a celebrity?"

"Maybe it's that lucky day you've heard so much about. Listen, do you guys have Bryson's laptop? Or a home computer of his?"

"Not my case, Peep."

"Yeah, I remember. I just thought maybe a sharp guy like you might pick something up around the shop."

"Listen, I'm on my way out the door after a long damn day. Why don't you skip the middleman and talk to the kid in charge?"

"Why not?"

Reeder heard Bishop calling out: "Woods! My famous friend wants to talk to you. Try not to get all tongue-tied."

Soon a crisp tenor said, "Detective Woods, Mr. Reeder. What can I do for you?"

"Sounds like you don't get any more respect out of Bish than I do."

A light laugh. "I take it as a compliment. I assume you're calling about that suicide. Bish mentioned you and Bryson were friends."

"Yes—did he also tell you about the message Chris left me, that evening?"

"Yep. Wrote it down for me when you called it in, so I figured I didn't need to bother you. Pretty straightforward—coroner isn't requiring an inquest. Sorry for your loss—he was former Secret Service, too, I understand."

"Yes. You mind a question or two, Detective?"

"No. But like I said—"

"Straightforward, right. Mind humoring me?"

Just the slightest pause. "What would you like to know?"

"Did you take a computer into evidence? Something you might have found in the motel room—a laptop, maybe? That's what Chris used at work."

"No. Really, a laptop? Who uses those anymore?"

"Dinosaurs like Chris Bryson."

And me, Reeder thought.

"No laptop, Mr. Reeder. Or tablet, either."

"Strike you as suspicious?"

"Not really. A man who checks into a motel room to kill himself doesn't need a computer."

"And it wasn't in his car, either?"

"No. His wife and son picked up his stuff today, and didn't ask where his laptop was, if he did have one. We did find a Nikon, but nothing on it. And we didn't bring in the home computer, either, if that's your next question."

"Why not?"

"Mr. Reeder, this was a suicide, plain and simple."

"Did it occur to you, Detective, that hanging yourself with a belt is not a 'plain and simple' way out when you're a law enforcement professional with a weapon handy?"

"Suicides take all kinds of ways out."

"No suicide note?"

"No. But you *know* that's not unusual, either. I understand losing a friend can be tough—"

"Do I sound grief-stricken?"

"No, Mr. Reeder, you sound like a good friend in the same line of work who would rather not think that your friend might be capable of such a desperate act. This is nothing we haven't seen before."

"If you mean murder," Reeder said, "I agree . . . Thanks for your time, Detective. We'll talk again."

And clicked off before the detective could respond.

Reeder had been to the Bryson home on Fairview Woods Avenue in Fairfax Station more than once, and drove there easily, no GPS required. He pulled into the empty driveway of the wide, two-story brick-fronted home with attached garage. The first-floor lights were on, Beth expecting him—he'd called ahead.

Taking his time going up the shoveled walk, Reeder moved through the sloping snow-covered lawn, past white-flocked bushes and curtained windows, then up three steps to the front stoop. Rang the doorbell, the sound of which had barely died away when the windowless steel door swung open. Christopher Bryson, suit coat off, sleeves rolled up, tie loosened, stood there looking enough like his father to make Reeder think, *My God, have I gone back in time?*

"Mom's expecting you, Mr. Reeder," Christopher said, in a mid-range voice that also summoned memories of his dad. "Come in, come on in . . ."

"Make it 'Joe,'" Reeder said, taking off his gloves.

But the response was, "Yes sir," as the younger man stepped aside, taking Reeder's lined Burberry and hanging it in a closet of the wide foyer.

An expansive living room was on the left, kitchen straight ahead down a hall toward the back, while to the right a staircase curved to the second floor, with the den/home office at right. The house was immaculate, just as he remembered it, though he hadn't been there in years, a feeling underscored by well-maintained furniture that hadn't changed in decades. That time machine feeling again . . .

Beth, again in the black silk blouse and black slacks but absent the jacket, appeared at the living room's arched entrance, a tumbler of amber liquid in hand. Her eyes were red-rimmed, but she smiled upon seeing him.

"Thanks for coming, Joe," she said, as her son looked on with concern.

Beth seemed sober enough—he'd never known her to be a heavy drinker—but there was something as liquid about her walk as the Scotch in her glass. She waved with a tissue-stuffed hand for him to follow her into the living room.

The south wall, to his left, was almost entirely a window onto the front yard. Sheer curtains were drawn, but heavy drapes remained open, the world out there hazy. He faced the west wall, dominated by a fireplace above which was mounted a flat-screen TV with some mini snowmen sitting on cotton on the mantle; a pair of matching sofas were perpendicular to the hearth, a black enameled coffee table between them, a lidless cardboard box of plastic police evidence bags sitting somewhat awkwardly on top of an oversize art book.

His pleasantly plump blonde hostess sat at one end of one sofa, her son settling in next to her, Reeder sitting opposite.

"Have you spoken to the police?" she asked, too casually, between sips of Scotch.

"Just on the phone," Reeder said. "Had a conversation with Woods, the detective in charge, on the way over here."

"The whelp still thinks Chris killed himself," Beth said, and had another sip, as if to wash away the bitterness. "You agree with that assessment?"

"That Woods is a whelp? That might be premature. Wait till I've been face-to-face with the man and ask me again. Did Chris take his life? Highly doubtful . . . but I need to find something to convince Woods to take this investigation seriously."

Christopher said, "What investigation? It's already a closed file."

Beth ignored that, setting her tumbler on the coffee table. "What do you hope to find?"

Reeder answered the question with another. "Was Chris still using a laptop?"

Christopher grunted a laugh. "You kidding? He never switched to a tablet, just kept lugging that antique everywhere."

"Is it here? In the den maybe?"

Beth gestured to the cardboard box. "Isn't it in here?"

Christopher quickly said, "We haven't gone through those things of Dad's. Couldn't quite . . . you know, face it yet."

Reeder said, "I asked Detective Woods and he said there was no laptop on the inventory of effects found in the motel room."

Frowning, Christopher asked, "Where *is* it, then?"

"Could be a clerical glitch," Reeder said, then nodded toward the box. "Go ahead and check, would you, son?"

Christopher rose and did so, hunkering over the box, then looked up and shook his head. "Not here . . . I'll check the den."

And he went off to do that.

Beth was lost in thought.

Reeder said, "Something?"

She nodded. "I'm positive Chris had the laptop with him, when he left for work, that last day. Might be at his office."

"All right with you if I go have a look?"

"I'd be grateful if you did," Beth said, and gestured to the cardboard box. "His office keys should be in there."

"Did he ever use the home computer?"

"No. That's strictly mine, in my sewing room upstairs."

Christopher returned, reporting no luck in the den.

Beth said, "Joe, why don't you take the whole box with you. If it would be of any help." She met her son's eyes. "Is that all right with you, dear?"

"Take it, Joe," Christopher said. "Maybe *you'll* find something worthwhile in there. The police didn't even try."

Reeder thanked him, then went to the box and began riffling through the evidence bags. Right away, something jumped out at him—a cell phone. Not Chris's smartphone, rather a cheap flip phone, obviously the burner Chris had called him on.

A question popped into Reeder's head, one that should have occurred to him sooner—back in field-agent days, it would have. And the police should have asked the same question: *What did a man who was about to commit suicide need with a burner phone?*

Reeder sat back down and asked them both: "Can you think of any reason why Chris would have needed a burner?"

Beth said, "A what?"

Christopher answered: "A prepaid cell phone. Something you use once or twice and throw away . . . right, Mr. Reeder?"

"Right. Was that something Chris might've used on the job?"

Shaking his head, Christopher said, "The kind of investigation Dad normally got involved with wouldn't require anything like that. Last few years, he mostly did small-business and industry analyses, recommending security systems and procedures."

Reeder asked Beth, "You last saw him on Monday?"

"Yes, when he left for work."

"Did you hear from him after that at all?"

She shook her head. "The next thing was the call from the police the next day."

What the hell had gone wrong enough from Monday morning to Tuesday night to make Chris trash his own phone, pick up a burner, and call Reeder on a "life and death" matter? The answer clearly wasn't suicide.

Chris Bryson had been on the run.

On the run from what or whom, Reeder couldn't say. Yet.

Then another thought struck him, also one that might have come sooner back in his field-agent days. *Maybe Chris had called Reeder out of concern for his* family's *safety as much as his own.*

He looked from mother to son and back again. "Beth, is there somewhere you can go for a few days? Somewhere no one could track you?"

Her eyes widened. "Why?"

"If Chris was murdered—and it was made to look like a suicide—the likely reason is he'd found something out . . . possibly something about this person, place, or thing called 'Sink.'"

Alarmed, she asked, "How would *I* know anything?"

Christopher said, "Dad might have told you."

"Darling, he never shared anything about work with me."

"Mom—how could his murderer or murderers *know* that?"

"You're right, Christopher," Reeder said. "Short of a family friend, they couldn't. And, Beth, he *did* mention that word to you—'Sink'—if not what it meant. I would feel better if both of you weren't easily accessible for a while."

"I agree," Christopher said. "Mom? What do you say?"

Beth just sat there looking from her son to Reeder and back, a woman still dealing with her husband's death only to have this unexpected contingency sprung on her.

"But . . . where would we *go?*"

Christopher somehow summoned a small smile. "How about Key West? I've never been there, and neither have you."

"Why Key West?" Beth asked, clearly reeling.

He put a hand on his mother's shoulder. "*Because* we've never been there . . . and if we're going into hiding, why not at least be warm? Plenty of tourists to blend in with, too."

Reeder was nodding. "Look for a mom-and-pop motel—there still are some of those down there. Somewhere that still takes cash and won't demand a credit card. Someplace off the grid and away from security cameras. This is a strictly cash trip—no credit cards, no cell phones either."

"Understood," Christopher said.

Still reeling, Beth asked, "But how will we know when it's safe to come back?"

Reeder thought for a moment. "Get adjoining rooms and check in as Joan and Broderick Crawford."

Christopher frowned. "Who?"

"Two actors from a century ago or so, whose names won't mean anything to whoever might be looking for you—except me. Those names and Key West will be enough for me to track you."

Beth asked, "What if we need to talk to you?"

Should he take time to buy them burner phones from his guy, DeMarcus? No reputable prepaid cell could be used without leaving a trail. He reached into the evidence box, withdrew the bagged burner, and handed it to Christopher.

"If you need me, call the last number your dad dialed—it's mine.

Don't use it from where you're staying. You can only use it once, then you have to get as far away from it as you can."

"Got it."

Beth asked, "Can't that phone be traced?"

Reeder said, "Assuming Chris was murdered, the ones who did this left that cell behind. It means nothing to them now—they have no reason to trace it. A one-time use should be safe."

"All . . . all right," she said.

Reeder went over and sat next to her and took her hand. "You need to pack a few things, nothing fancy, everyday stuff that goes with a warm climate. Now scoot."

She rose and went upstairs without argument, leaving her Scotch behind.

With Beth gone, Reeder turned to her son. "If we're right, and your father was murdered, these people are obviously dangerous, and almost certainly professionals. Professional enough to fool DC Homicide. You've got to stay on top of things."

"I will, Joe."

"Now one more thing—do you own a gun?"

He frowned. "No."

"Do you know how to use one? A handgun, I mean."

"Yes. Dad used to take me to the firing range. It was a hobby when I was a kid that I lost interest in."

"Well, you know what they say about riding a bike. I'm going to assume your dad has a handgun somewhere in the house, and that you know where it is."

"I do. It's in a locked desk drawer in the den . . . but I know where the key is."

"Good. Let's have a look at the thing."

Reeder followed the younger man into the den, where a key hidden in the middle drawer opened a left-hand lower one. The gun, like Chris and for that matter Reeder, was not new to this world—a vintage Smith & Wesson Model 52, a .38 with a box of shells to go with it.

"Don't tell your mother," Reeder said.

"Don't worry."

After Beth came down with a single suitcase and a cosmetics case, she presented Reeder with her late husband's key ring, singling out the office one; the electronic flip-key to Chris's BMW was hooked on as well.

"Beth," Reeder asked, "where is Chris's car?"

"In the garage. The police turned it over to us with the box of evidence."

"Anything missing that you noticed?"

Christopher chimed in: "No—all the usual stuff was there, glove compartment, trunk. And, no—no laptop."

Reeder got out his small notebook and wrote down a phone number, tore out the page.

"Call this," he said. "A friend of mine will open up his used car lot after hours, just for you. I'll call ahead and tell him you're special clients of mine."

Christopher blinked. "Is that what we are?"

"That's what you are. Tell him you want something solid, old, and with papers. Leave your own car with him."

"How much will all that cost?"

"Nothing. My treat."

"Mr. Reeder . . ."

"It's Joe, remember? And I'll tell my pal to disconnect the GPS. You can find Florida, can't you? Now you and your mom go have a fun vacation. Just don't go out much—too much sun can be bad for you."

Fifteen minutes later, mother and son were pulling out of the driveway in the BMW, Christopher behind the wheel—they would stop by his apartment to gather some clothes and other things of his. After that, Joan Crawford and her son Broderick would leave the apartment and begin a long road trip.

Soon the box of Bryson's effects was tucked safely in Reeder's trunk, and so was their home computer, though he wasn't sure what he was going to do with the stuff now. Surely, hitting up Patti Rogers to run everything through the FBI lab was iffy, since the chain of custody had been broken. Even if Reeder demonstrated Chris had been murdered, nothing found on his late friend's clothes would be admissible now. Maybe Miggie could pry a clue or two from that home computer.

This time of night, the drive to Chris Bryson's office took less than fifteen minutes. Fairfax Corner South was a warren of stores, offices, and restaurants on Monument Corner Drive—evergreens lining the sidewalks, storefronts dark, streetlights providing the only illumination. Bryson Security occupied a corner space of a complex with an old-time downtown motif and limited parking.

A pale blue Nissan Altima—the only car here besides his own, showing no signs of the afternoon snow—was parked three store-fronts past Bryson. As a routine precaution, Reeder memorized its plate—Kentucky, 440 RHW.

Parking one door down from the security office, the hum of light traffic on Interstate 66 riding the chill wind, he made a threat assessment of the silent block. Just like Christmas—not a creature was stirring.

As if he belonged there, Reeder—in Burberry and gloves, his breath smoking—walked briskly to the security firm's door, whose handle he held as he prepared to work the key in the lock. That was when the door eased itself open an inch.

Apprehension coiled in his belly like a woken rattler.

His extending baton—which he preferred carrying over a gun—
was at home. He hadn't needed it for the meeting with Benjamin and
certainly not on his visit to the Bryson residence. He'd prefer having
the weapon in his coat pocket before entering, but running home for
it seemed out of the question . . .

Anyway, the unlocked door did not have to mean trouble.

Maybe Chris had fled in such fear-driven haste that he hadn't
made sure his office door was locked behind him. Possibly cleaning
staff had screwed up, or even the police, if they'd actually bothered
checking the place out.

Or Reeder might be walking in on an intruder, possibly an armed
one. His brain said, *Go back to the car, call 911, and just wait for the
cavalry.*

His gut said, *If there's a back door, the bastard could get away and
you wouldn't even know it!*

Gut trumped brains and he pushed the door open as slowly, as
quietly, as he could, leaving just room enough to slip inside. The
front window was tinted dark, filtering and lessening illumination
from outside, the outer office empty but for the part-time receptionist's desk and a few wall-lining chairs, one of which he used to pile
his topcoat and gloves. His eyes were on the inner-office door, no
light seeping around the edges. He moved cautiously closer to the
door, which like the front one was not closed tight. Not quite ajar,
but not really shut.

Carefully he nudged the door open a ways and peered into the
dark, apparently empty room. He opened the door halfway, stepping
inside, pausing to let his left hand search the wall for the light switch,
not finding it before the door shoved into him, squeezing him, wedg-
ing him there, half in, half out.

The pressure released but before he could either advance or

retreat, a hand grabbed him by the upper right arm and hurled him into the darkness, as if he were a toy flung by a bored child. The door slammed shut and what little light there had been was gone—*was the intruder gone as well?* The only advantage Reeder had, as he slid to the floor, having hit the edge of Chris's desk hard, was his knowledge of the office layout.

Then a shape he could more sense than see—the intruder, in black, still very much in the small office—was coming over to grab him and do God knew what, but Reeder kicked up and out, catching the ongoing shape between the legs with the hard toe of his right shod foot. Judging by the unmistakable yowl of kicked-in-the-balls pain, and the strength displayed by flinging Reeder across the room, the intruder was male.

Still sensing more than seeing, guided by his adversary's labored breathing, Reeder lurched to his feet and, figuring the man would be bent over, swung a right hand into where his head should be. Somehow his adversary sensed this and, in pain or not, threw up an arm and blocked the blow, throwing a short but powerful jab into Reeder's belly. Air whooshed from him, but Reeder struck out anyway, with a left that had less power than he'd have liked, but luckily caught the guy on his chin—the feel of flesh and bone on flesh and bone said the intruder wore no mask.

The attacker, upright now apparently, was wildly throwing lefts and rights in the darkness, swishing in front of Reeder, who had stepped back out of reach. Then the windmilling stopped and the guy growled and threw himself at Reeder in a mad tackle, sending him onto his back, hitting the floor hard.

Reeder lay there dazed for a moment, then the door opened and limited light came in to reveal the attacker already in the outer office. By the time Reeder got to his feet and staggered out there, it was too late—the black-clad man was gone.

So was the Nissan down the block.

Well, Reeder had the plate number, at least.

Something else was gone—any sliver of doubt that Chris Bryson had been murdered.

"The nation is only as strong
as the collective strength of its individuals."

Jeremiah A. Denton,
Retired Admiral, US Navy,
POW in North Vietnam for nearly eight years,
one-term United States Senator from Alabama,
1981–1987,
first Republican elected in his state post-Reconstruction.
Section 7, Grave 8011-B,
Arlington National Cemetery.

SEVEN

On her nightstand, Patti Rogers's cell did the vibration dance.

On call 24/7, like all FBI agents, she despised being wakened by a ring or ringtone, and the vibrate setting always roused her sufficiently. Her eyelids rose like reluctant curtains on a terrible play and she saw the clock face: 5:04 a.m.

Was it just four minutes ago that she'd hit snooze?

The alarm would go off again at five fifteen. The vibrating stopped. She would check the call first thing and return it, if it proved worthy. For now, she settled in for another eleven glorious minutes of that blissful state before the second alarm.

Then the phone began its dance again, and she sat up, wide awake, grabbed it, checked the caller ID.

LUCAS HARDESY.

What the hell did he want? Couldn't he wait till she came in to the office before being a pain in her ass?

"Yes?" she said to the phone.

"You may have been right," he said, biting off each word.

"How so?" *Did he need to sound so surprised?*

"Your serial killer theory. A cop buddy texted me about a DB he caught about an hour ago."

"Does the victim fit our profile?"

"We don't really have a profile," Hardesy reminded her. "But . . . yeah, the method at least. Two bullets to the head."

"Double-tap again."

"Yeah. Vic doesn't fit, though. Drag queen name of Karma Sabich."

"That's a new wrinkle."

"Yes it is. Somebody really wanted this motherfucker dead. Put him/her in the tub, popped her. Or him. Whatever."

"Hate crime?"

"Maybe." He took another beat. "Look, I know we sometimes, uh . . . grate on each other. But do you think you could trust my gut on this?"

"That all you have, your gut?"

"No. This kill has that professional touch we keep running into. Even though the vic doesn't match the others, you know, not a middle-class professional? It's just too . . . precise. Think you could come over and have a looky-loo?"

"Where?"

He gave her the address.

"Not far from me," she said, mostly to herself. Her apartment building was on Joyce Street in Arlington. "Give me half an hour to rejoin the human race."

"Appreciate this, boss."

First time he'd called her that.

She showered, dried her hair, did her makeup, dressed, and stopped at the lobby Starbucks for a to-go coffee—all in seventeen minutes. Then it was a quick two-mile drive to the corner of Columbia Pike and Oakland.

The once swanky enclave was a rectangle of buildings set up to look like row houses with a parking lot in the middle. Slowly getting gentrified after years of neglect, the complex was, by neighborhood standards, a perfect example of what locals termed "shithouse chic," where drug houses and hookers shared unlikely space with young executives and new families.

This morning, though, that center parking lot was alive with the blinking lights of an ambulance and police cars. Rogers parked to one side and got out into an ice cube of a morning, glad to be bundled in a gray Ann Taylor peacoat.

Despite the early hour, the neighbors were out to gawk. What primitive part of the human brain, she wondered, attracted the species to a scene of tragedy? If there was a one-car fatal accident in the Mojave Desert, hundreds of miles from supposed civilization, rubberneckers would still find their way to the side of the road.

The victim's house was immediately recognizable by the police tape cordoning it off. A uniformed officer, who looked like he'd driven here from his academy graduation ceremony, stood just inside the yellow-and-black border keeping people back. But the crowd was growing and he would soon need a hand.

Rogers displayed her credentials and the young cop leaned in for a look, then gave her an impressed little smile as he raised the tape for her. He really was new—hadn't learned to hate the dreaded "Fibbies" yet.

She rewarded his attitude, saying, "I'll try to get you some help, officer."

The rookie flashed a grateful smile. "Thanks, ma'am."

He was so young and helpless looking, she could even forgive him the "ma'am."

Up the sidewalk she found Hardesy waiting on the butcher-block front porch.

"In case you're wondering," he said, hands in the pockets of his dark-gray overcoat, breath pluming, rocking on his heels, "all these neighbors? Nobody saw shit. Nobody heard shit."

"Sounds unanimous. You talk to them yourself?"

He shook his head. "Didn't want to risk my amateur standing. Because I got a friend on the team, they've filled me in some."

"And what do they have?"

"Bupkus."

"How did your police pal happen to clue you in?"

"I'd told him, and a few other PD contacts, to be on the lookout for double-taps. You know, just in case."

She nodded. "Nice work, Luke."

He said nothing. Glanced away from her, uncomfortable with the compliment.

"So why are you changing your tune," she asked him, "where the serial theory is concerned?"

"I'm not, exactly. To me, this is one guy doing hits, and I don't consider that a serial. That's more like taking care of business."

"So you see a professional killing here. A drag queen among the young white collars."

Oddly, that thought fit the neighborhood.

With a shudder of cold, Hardesy said, "Like I told you on the phone—too precise, and not just this one. All these damn killings are just too damn perfect. No muss, no fuss, no mess. *Something* is going on here."

"But not a psychotic serial killer."

He shrugged, nodded. "Your behaviorist guy, Ivanek, is right— serial, you would expect more ritual or something. But these are so mechanical, so businesslike—and now five victims? Something's definitely goin' on, boss."

Boss again? Was she finally winning him over?

Her own breath pluming, gloved hands in her pockets, she asked, "Who's the detective in charge?"

"My in. Keith Ferguson—know him?"

She shook her head.

"Good guy. He'll play ball. If this *is* a serial, by any definition, he knows it's our deal."

"All right," she said. "He inside?"

"Yeah—finishing up with the friend. She/he is the one who found the victim."

"Both dressed as women?"

He nodded.

"Let's stick with 'she' then, okay?"

Hardesy gave her a what-the-hell nod.

Rogers was about to send her fellow FBI agent in to see when Ferguson would be available, when a heavyset, blunt-featured guy in an off-the-rack gray pinstripe came out on the porch and announced himself as that very person. No topcoat for him—he'd been inside working for a good while.

Like Hardesy, the detective in charge had a shaved head, which was about all the two had in common, other than likely shared second thoughts about going around hatless in this cold. Despite his boxer-battered features, Ferguson had easy eyes and an easier smile.

Hardesy made the introductions and the DC detective stuck out his hand.

"Heard a lot about you, Agent Rogers," Ferguson said.

"Don't believe everything you hear," Rogers said, giving Hardesy a sideways look. Then to Ferguson: "This is where you say, 'Not *all* bad.'"

The PD detective managed a tight smile. "Well, it isn't. Anyway, I read about you and your friend, Reeder—what you did last year, fine work. Brave as hell, too."

"Stop or I'll blush," she said, kidding on the square. "The friend you're talking to—is that who found her?"

"Yeah. Virginia Plain. Stage name. Same goes for the vic—Karma Sabich."

"I kind of guessed that."

"It's those kind of detective skills," Ferguson said cheerfully, "that makes the FBI so great. Anyway, Karma Sabich is really one DeShawn Davis. Virginia's real name, Kevin Lockwood . . . but if you wanna talk to Kev, call him 'Virginia' or 'Miss Plain.' He won't answer otherwise."

Rogers nodded. "Transsexual?"

"No. He made a point of saying he was a transvestite. But still wants to be referred to as a 'she.'"

"We'll honor that. Or at least SA Hardesy and I will."

Ferguson smirked. "What's that, some FBI political correctness directive?"

Rogers shook her head. "No. Not that a little human decency would hurt any of us. But you know how it is, Detective—respect runs both ways."

He grinned. "Not downhill, like shit?"

That seemed rhetorical, so she ignored it and asked, "Did Virginia tell you anything of interest?"

The big cop shook his bare head. "Nope, not really. Stays over sometimes. He . . . *she* . . . arrived, found Karma dead, upstairs, in the bathroom between bedrooms."

Rogers let out a smoky breath. "Mind if I talk to her?"

He gestured to the door. "Special Agent Rogers, I am a lot of things, but a proud man isn't one of 'em. About now, I'll take any and all the help I can get. Please."

She gave him half a smile. "Call me Patti."

"And I'm Keith."

"By the way, Keith, that kid at the cordon is looking a little over-whelmed. Might wanna get him some help before these neighbors stampede."

He nodded and went down the steps, talking into his radio.

"Luke," she said to her fellow agent, "you want in on this?"

He frowned in thought. "I do, but my gut says no."

"That gut of yours again."

He nodded. "I saw this guy, gal, what-have-you, being inter-viewed before, strictly by men, and whatever he/she/it is was clearly uncomfortable."

"All right. I'll handle it. By the way, did you attend that sensitivity seminar last quarter?"

Hardesy half smiled. "I hear you."

"Listen, why don't you head into the office. Take over the morn-ing briefing—I may be here awhile."

"Okay, boss."

He went away, and she went inside.

As Rogers stood in the entryway, getting her bearings, a uni-formed officer was coming down the stairs, headed for the front door. *Going to assist the crowd-control kid,* she figured. In front of her was the kitchen and a dining area. To her right, the living room.

The decor was like IKEA and a Salvation Army store had a baby. A newish blond coffee table, piled high with fast-food wrap-pers, squatted in front of a worn-out-looking sofa with mismatched replacement cushions, opposite which a medium-size flat-screen rode the wall. Most everything else, tables, lamps, chairs, looked like turn-of-the-century remnants. The upright La-Z-Boy recliner was newer but still looked frayed and tired.

So did its occupant, Virginia Plain.

Rogers had encountered her first transvestite in the service, back in MP days. After returning to Iowa, where she'd served as a deputy sheriff before getting the FBI nod, she had met a couple more. She learned a long time ago that people were just people—with all the good, bad, and ugly that went along with it. She could tell that the slender man—though he was seated—was a foot taller than her in those gold heels. Rogers could also see he . . . she . . . was in pain.

Virginia's dark hair was a glorious mountain of curls, her smeary makeup probably perfect before the tears. She clutched at a tissue, several more wadded on a small table next to her. She was still in her faux-fur coat, though it was fairly warm in here, her sequined black cocktail dress nicer than anything in Rogers's closet. Long neck, sharp nose, delicate cheekbones, wide fawn eyes red-rimmed from tears.

"Virginia, I'm Special Agent Rogers with the FBI. I thought we might talk. All right?"

A tiny nod.

Rogers pulled over a hardback chair and sat directly in front of her interview subject. "You found your friend?"

Virginia's eyes went automatically toward the stairs off the entryway, and began to well. She nodded again, head still turned that way.

"Look at me, please," Rogers said.

Slowly, tears brimming, Virginia faced her.

"Terrible thing," Rogers said, "making a discovery like that."

Virginia swallowed, nodded.

"You and Karma were close?"

". . . Yes."

Finally, a word.

Rogers asked, "How long have you been roommates?"

"Not roommates, not lately," Virginia said, in a warm alto-ish voice. "Karma took me in when I didn't have anywhere else to go . . . when I first moved to DC. I've got my own place now, but I still crash here sometimes."

"You could stay over whenever you wanted?"

She nodded.

"Karma sounds like a good person."

"The best. I have an early call at my other job, in the morning, so I stay here at Karma's those nights, because it's a lot closer."

"What's your other job?"

"Waitstaff. I take an occasional shift at Bob & Edith's. I'm supposed to work lunch today."

Rogers knew the diner, not quite a mile northeast from here on Columbia Pike. She ate there occasionally, but didn't remember ever seeing Virginia. It was the kind of all-night, no-questions-asked place where the late crowd would be . . . interesting.

She said to Virginia, "You better call in. You won't be done here for hours."

Virginia let out a tired sigh. "I will. I will. Just not right now."

"Okay. Did Karma have any enemies that you know of?"

"No. Everybody loved her."

That was a familiar refrain in homicide cases. "Can you tell me anything at all that might bear on what's happened?"

Virginia let out a long breath, wiggling fingers in front of her face, willing herself to get composed. She sat up a little straighter, shrugged out of her coat.

"I'm thinking," she said. "Gathering my thoughts."

"Take your time. I understand you worked together? Maybe we can start there."

"Yes. A club called Les Girls."

"I've heard of it. Highly rated."

Virginia nodded. "Last night, after work, I looked for Karma— thought we might grab a sandwich and coffee, which we do a lot. But she wasn't around."

"Didn't leave a note or tell anyone to tell you . . . ?"

"No, it's not like that. Sometimes we caught a bite, sometimes we didn't. She might have a date, so I didn't sweat it."

"She date a lot? Anybody steady?"

A bittersweet smile came. "Karma . . . whoa, *that* one, she did like to party."

"So, then—a lot of guys?"

"Some girls, too," Virginia said, with a shrug. "She had . . . varied interests? But mostly guys, and she had a couple who liked to . . . you know . . . buy her things."

"She was hooking?"

"No, not really. She just had friends, who, uh . . ."

Rogers said nothing.

Virginia shrugged again. "A little hooking maybe."

"You know any of the johns?"

"No! That is *not* my business, and not my thing. We keep that part of our lives separate. *Kept*, I mean. Hard thinking of her as something, someone . . . in the past."

"See anybody here, at her house, ever?"

"No. No, wait . . . I'm wrong. I *did* see an older guy here a couple of times."

"Can you describe him?"

"Older, white, nice suit, maybe even tailored. Successful. And, course, cheating on his wife."

"What's 'older'?"

Virginia gave a really elaborate shrug. "I don't know, you know, *old* . . . fifty, maybe?"

Rogers, in her midthirties, didn't think fifty sounded all that ancient anymore. How old was Virginia? Thirty maybe?

She gave Virginia a warm supportive smile, then stood. "I have to go upstairs. That's where she is, right?"

A nod, a trickle of tear. "Where I found her, yeah."

"You sit right here. I'll be back soon, okay?"

"Not going anywhere," Virginia said, softly, bleakly.

Snapping on latex gloves, Rogers trudged up the stairs, eased past two EMTs who were playing games on their phones, leaning against a wall on the landing.

Holding up her credentials, she asked, "ME been here yet?"

Without looking, the older of the pair said, "Still waiting."

She nodded. Not a surprise.

The bathroom was in front of her, two bedrooms on either side. She entered the bath, where Karma lay in the tub, clothed, with her back to Rogers. Curled fetally, the victim had two small nasty holes at the base of her skull; a trail of dried blood down her back; bits of skull, brain, and blood speckling the tile wall and far side of the tub.

Despite a close-cropped Afro appropriate for either male or female, Karma's wardrobe put to rest any doubt about her chosen identity. She wore a cocktail dress similar to her friend Virginia's, though hers was a hot-pink sequined number, her preposterously high heels a silver that matched bangly bracelets on both wrists and the rings on her every finger.

Her expression in profile seemed almost peaceful, makeup still perfect except for blowback teardrops of blood. Her wide brown eyes stared, her mouth seemed slightly puckered, as if about to kiss.

Why the tub?

Of the other four victims, none had been found in the bathtub. Rogers made a note to ask Ivanek about it.

Not a hell of a lot more to see. Crime scene unit would dust for prints and any other clues, probably to no avail.

But at least she now had no doubt there was a serial killer on the loose, or rather a multiple murderer, since Hardesy was likely correct that the shooter was a pro.

She went to the back bedroom first, larger of the two, likely Karma's as the permanent resident. The queen-sized bed had not been

slept in, a lavender comforter neatly in place, a stuffed unicorn leaning against the pillows. Next to a window sat a four-drawer dresser,
with framed photos of friends and family on top.

Rogers went over for a closer look, thinking the "old" john might
be among the photos; no candidates, though. She looked over Karma's
dressing table—a show-biz bulb-framed mirror, a ton of makeup, but
nothing jumped out as a clue. The closet was home to clothes that
ranged from thrift-shop blouses to higher-end dresses—courtesy of
the generous old john, maybe? Only that seemed even the faintest
clue to possibly identifying Karma's killer.

The guest bedroom where Virginia sometimes stayed was neat,
bed made, as anonymous as a motel room but for a pile of romance
novels on the nightstand. No help.

She went back downstairs where Virginia was still in the upright
La-Z-Boy, using another tissue.

"After these cops finish with you," Rogers said, "go home and climb
in bed. You're going to be physically ill for a day or two. Trust me."

Virginia managed a feeble smile. "Thanks. I'll do that. What was
your name again?"

Rogers told her, then handed her a card. "Anything else occurs to
you, anything at all, give me a call, okay?"

"Yeah," Virginia said. "Is . . . is this your case?"

"Right now it's the DC police's, but we'll be looking at Karma's
death through our end of the telescope, too."

"Good."

"Seriously, Virginia, I'm not going to bullshit you. Finding
Karma's killer is going to be tough. Everybody on this thing needs all
the help they can get—myself included—and right now you're the
most likely source. You and Karma were BFFs, right?"

"Right. Agent Rogers, if I think of anything, I'll call you. You
have my word."

"Good enough for me," Rogers said with a smile. "Listen, while you're waiting for them to dismiss you, do me a favor—make a list of all of Karma's friends. Maybe one of them can help. I'll send a cop in with paper and pen."

Virginia was nodding, all that beautiful dark hair bobbling. "Glad to. I need something *positive* to focus on, not just . . . what I keep *seeing* . . ."

"Give that list to Detective Ferguson. I'll have him send a copy to me at my office. Can you do that, Virginia?"

"Absolutely."

After a nod, Rogers turned, but the transvestite's voice stopped her: "Agent Rogers—thank you."

"What for, Virginia?"

"Treating me like a person."

"No problem," Rogers said, glancing back. "You didn't deserve something shitty like this happening."

"Neither did Karma."

"And neither did Karma. Stay in touch."

She found Ferguson on the porch and gave him a rundown of what she'd learned, requesting that he keep her in the loop, including that list Virginia was putting together. She gave him her card.

"If you don't get me," she said, "try Hardesy."

"You got it."

She was back in the car, about to pull out, when her cell vibrated again. *Now what?* Caller ID read: REEDER. She answered.

"We need to talk," he said.

"So talk."

"In person."

"Where are you?"

He told her.

"Okay," she said.

"Everyone is entitled to his own opinion,
but not his own facts."

Daniel Patrick Moynihan

EIGHT

Sitting outside Bryson Security in his Prius, heat on and engine running—which defeated the purpose of having a Prius at all—Joe Reeder steamed like a tin lizzie radiator about to blow. He had suffered both injury and insult, the aches of the brawl's aftermath followed by the affront of bystander status in his own case.

DC homicide detective Pete Woods, who Reeder had called to the scene, was finally buying into the probability of a staged "suicide" for Chris Bryson. That should have been cause for celebration; instead, Reeder boiled and brooded out here while Woods pursued the investigation inside the strip mall office.

Woods seemed even younger than Bishop had promised, somewhere barely north of thirty—short dark hair, steel-framed glasses, unimpressed green eyes, five ten, slender. His ensemble had a collegiate look—gray trench coat, maroon sweater barely showing the pale red-and-blue plaid shirt with navy tie, navy chinos. He struck Reeder as a refugee from a boy band back in daughter Amy's middle-school days.

"I can't allow a private citizen into an active crime scene," Woods had said. "That includes you, Mr. Reeder. Sorry."

"You're here because I called you," Reeder reminded him, with the fake calm he'd long ago learned to affect, "and one of the crimes committed here was an assault upon my person."

"Changes nothing."

"Well, something's changed anyway. Now you don't think Chris killed himself."

The boy detective raised a forefinger. "I don't *necessarily* think Mr. Bryson took his own life. You can wait outside or in your car. I'll have someone take your statement in a while."

Woods disappeared inside, leaving a uniformed officer to guard the door in case Reeder decided to storm the fortress.

That was when he'd phoned Rogers.

When she pulled into the lot, Reeder played traffic cop, directing her to a place several storefronts down from his Prius, away from Bryson Security, where the cop on guard looked on in confusion—his orders had apparently not included stopping Reeder from leaving his car and going over to another.

He got in and slammed the door behind him, saying, "The bastard won't let me in."

She was just unbuckling her seat belt. "Which bastard would that be?"

"The Doogie Howser detective."

"Who?"

Before her time.

He said, "That punk kid from DC Homicide."

"Take a breath. Take two. Remember who you are—the hard-to-read, unflappable Joe Reeder."

"Shit," he said, but he took the breaths.

"Isn't that better?" she asked. "Now tell me what the hell is going on."

He filled her in about getting jumped at Chris's office.

"Shoulda had the guy," he muttered.

"Shoulda coulda woulda," she said. "Then, what? You called Woods and he finally buys your theory?"

He grunted a laugh. "That Chris was murdered is a 'theory' like climate change or evolution. But yes, he pretty much buys it now."

"And?"

"And what?"

Patiently, she asked, "What makes him a bastard? Assuming his parents were married."

Reeder frowned. "He's a bastard because he won't let me into that office to, you know, help with the investigation. You know the investigation I mean—the one I started?"

"I do. Must I ask you to take two more deep breaths?"

"No. No, I'm fine. Peachy fuckin' keen."

"Is that a real expression?"

"Minus the middle word it is." He looked right at her. She was cool, calm, and collected—to invoke another old phrase everybody had forgotten but dinosaurs like him and his late friend Chris. He'd like to think part of her poise and self-confidence came from working with him. But he knew she was a natural.

"I need you," Reeder said, "to pull rank and get me in there, so I can help find whatever my attacker was looking for."

"Or," she said, "if Woods finds it first, to make sure he knows what he's found?"

"Right, only I don't think that kid could find a bee in a hive."

She shook her head. "Joe, that's what's called a crime scene. And, thanks to you, it's part of an active homicide investigation."

"Exactly, which is why I need in."

"No," she said.

He knew enough not to try to run roughshod over her. His back, where he slammed into the desk, nagged him. "You wouldn't have any naproxen, would you?"

She got him a couple from her purse. He took them down without water. He prescribed himself several more deep breaths, unbidden.

Then he said to her, "You're right."

"Don't play me, Joe. I'm one of the few people on this planet who can read you."

He managed a wry smile. "Guess I'm too good a teacher."

"If you're fishing for an apple, forget it. The naproxen is all you get, and that includes sympathy. Now, tell me, in detail, what the hell happened here. Back it up all the way."

He told her everything—a very brief rundown on the Benjamin meeting, then sending Christopher and Beth Bryson off to parts unknown, his arrival here to see if Chris's laptop was in his office, the fight in the dark. Even the license number of the Nissan that had apparently been the intruder's ride.

When he was done, she sat thinking, as expressionless as a bisque baby. Then a touch of Mona Lisa smile came to her lips.

"What?" he asked.

"Strikes me what we need here is a little interdepartmental assistance."

"That might get *you* in, but what about me?"

Now Mona Lisa was smirking a little. "You're a consultant to the Special Situations Task Force, remember? Don't tell me you forgot to mention that to Detective Woods?"

He grinned at her. "Slipped my elderly mind."

Getting her cell from a peacoat pocket, she silenced Reeder with a raised forefinger, then punched in a number and waited.

After a moment, she said, "Miggie? I need a couple of things . . . Yes, you can expect another bag of free-trade Sumatran, you pirate. What I need is the security footage from the Skyway Farer for Tuesday night . . . Right, that's the motel where Chris Bryson died."

She listened for the computer guru's response, which was brief, then said, "The other thing is more immediate—run a plate for me: Kentucky, 440 RHW . . . I can wait." She dropped cell-in-hand to her lap and asked Reeder, "Where's the box of evidence Mrs. Bryson gave you? And the home computer?"

"All in my trunk."

She gave him her keys. "Move it all to mine. I'll take it to the lab."

"Won't that piss off your about-to-be-interdepartmental pal, Detective Woods?"

She shrugged. "Valuable life lesson for him—shouldn't have jumped to a conclusion and jettisoned the evidence."

Reeder wasn't even out of the car before she got the return call. But he stayed on task, breath pluming as he went to the Prius and gathered from its trunk the box of bagged clothing and other effects, on top of which he piled the smallish computer tower. Then he lugged the box back to her Ford and put it in her trunk.

Again in the rider's seat, shut in from the cold, he handed the keys back to Rogers, already off the cell.

"Make me happy," he said.

"Well, of course retrieving that security footage is going to take some time."

"Of course. And the Nissan?"

"A rental. Avis. Picked up at their Dulles location. Cash transaction, but Miggie's got a photo ID and the rental form."

She showed Reeder the photo on her phone: guy in his thirties, brown-haired, long-nosed, sharp-chinned, somewhat blurry for an official photo. Had the guy moved on purpose a little, in front of the DMV camera?

"Name?" Reeder prompted.

"Henry Patrick."

He glanced at her. "As in, Patrick Henry backward?"

"As in."

"Funny." Reeder frowned at the photo on the phone. "This character even looks a little like Patrick Henry."

"I guess it's an honor, then."

"What is?"

"Getting your ass kicked by a founding father."

He smirked at her. "Well, *he* had the honor of getting kicked in the balls by a guy who saved a president. Still, let's get Miggie on facial recognition."

"Already in process."

Down at Bryson's office, the uniformed officer on guard was eyeballing them.

Reeder said, "How thrilled do you figure Woods will be with your offer of Uncle Sam's help?"

"Not at all. He'll know immediately you called me in. We're the brave duo who saved the Chief Justice, remember?"

"Vaguely."

She opened her door and cold blasted them. "You better just hang back and let me do the talking."

"You're the boss. I'm just a consultant."

Reeder stayed in the car as she walked over to the Bryson Security storefront. She showed her ID to the cop on the door and Woods came out to see what was up.

With the engine running and the heat going, Reeder couldn't make out anything they were saying. Rogers's back was mostly to him. The young detective threw the occasional glare Reeder's way, mostly listening to the FBI agent on his doorstep, his posture—lowered head, hunched shoulders, crossed arms—purely defensive. Reeder didn't need to see the guy's micro-expressions to know this wasn't going well. Clusters of gestures came quickly, defensive, aggressive.

Not good indicators.

The longer Rogers spoke, however, her posture firm but casual, expression pleasantly businesslike when Reeder caught glimpses of it, the more the young detective seemed to settle down. Hands went to his waist, chin came up, a looseness came in. Then he would nod now and then. Gesture clusters slowed, became more amicable.

Whatever Rogers was saying was having a positive effect.

FBI agent and homicide cop spoke another few minutes, then shook hands. Reeder waited to be waved over, but instead Rogers came over to him, moving neither fast nor slow. Woods stayed behind and was speaking to the uniformed cop.

She got in, bringing another momentary burst of cold with her. But her small smile had warmth.

Reeder said, "You turned him around, didn't you?"

"Somewhat. I wouldn't expect him to ask you for a signed photo."

"I can live with that, Patti. Where are we?"

"Well, Detective Woods knows he fumbled the ball, and at this point in his baby career, misreading the murder of an ex–Secret Service agent as suicide would hardly speed him on an upward path. If we—that's me and my consultant—can help him save face, he's up for some interdepartmental love."

"Patti, I always said you were cute."

"He didn't ask for a date. And you'll need to tread very lightly. You made him look incompetent. Save his bacon, though, and that all changes."

"Can we get inside?"

"Yes."

"Carte blanche?"

"Hardly. Now that this is a crime scene related to a murder, he's called for a CSI crew. When they show, we go. Should have fifteen minutes."

"We'll make that work," he said, and got out of the car.

So did Rogers.

As they walked over, he said, "Took a while selling him."

"I had to remind Detective Woods that our lab is both better and faster than his. I also said the Bryson family had turned his evidence box over to you, and retrieving it without a stink would be . . . problematic."

"We don't have to give it back?"

"Not till the FBI lab has processed everything."

At the door, a blank-faced Woods stopped them with a traffic-cop palm. But he tipped how pissed off he was by keeping his eyes on Rogers and never Reeder.

"Anything you find," Woods reminded her, "we share."

"I'm known for playing nice," she said.

Reeder said, "We're not looking for credit, Detective—we're after a killer."

Woods nodded at that, but still did not meet Reeder's eyes.

Rogers handed Reeder latex gloves; she had a pair for herself, and they put them on before she led the way inside. As she paused in the outer office to get the layout, Reeder said to her, "Chris wouldn't keep anything out here. Big window on the street, no computer, no filing cabinet or even closet."

"Still," she said, "I should check the receptionist's desk."

"Do that. See you inside."

He entered the inner office. A chair was overturned from the fight, and papers were scattered on the floor—obviously the work of the intruder, not the cops. Everything else seemed undisturbed. Reeder must have surprised the guy early in his search.

Rogers came in. "Nothing but some office supplies in that desk and not much of that."

"Receptionist worked a few half days a week," Reeder said. "Mostly Chris operated by appointment."

"Okay," Rogers said, hands on her hips, peacoat hanging open. "Here's the haystack. We looking for any needle in particular?"

"The needle that got him killed."

"Thanks for narrowing it."

"The only thing we know we're looking for is his laptop, but it's doubtful it's here. I figure his killers took that with them at the motel. But it's possible he left it behind . . . Take the file cabinet."

Rogers nodded and began going through the old-fashioned metal four-drawer file in one corner while Reeder took the desk. She started with the bottom drawer and said, "Bingo."

He looked over and she was holding up a bottle of bourbon by its neck.

"Heavy drinker, your friend?" she asked.

"Not really. That's probably as much a joke as anything. Typical Chris. Cliché from old detective novels."

"I know," she said with a little smile. "I've read Chandler, too, remember?"

"Listen, don't spend a lot of our limited time now on the files themselves. That stuff probably dates back, and this is likely something very recent. So be on the lookout for a flash drive or something, hidden away in there. Riffle the pages, don't study them."

"Right," she said. "Woods and his boys can go through this stuff thoroughly later. We'll keep looking for the needle."

Reeder checked a closet, found more work supplies, no laptop, then went through the desk and its drawers, no laptop there either. Then he stood in the middle of the area where not long ago he'd fought with that intruder.

He was studying the desk like it was a museum exhibit.

"Hey!" Rogers asked. "Tick tick tick—what, have you given up?"

He shook his head. "No."

"No?"

"We're doing this wrong."

She came over. "How so?"

"Chris was a careful guy. Cautious."

"Not cautious enough, obviously."

Reeder glanced at her.

"Sorry," she said. "Your point?"

He rubbed his chin. "It's just that . . . even if he ran? Chris wouldn't have left our needle just lying around. Not stuffed in a file folder, or taped under a desk drawer."

"If the needle is something on his computer," she said, "maybe he backed it up to the cloud. I can put Miggie on that."

"Do that," Reeder said. "But . . ."

"But?"

"He might have been dinosaur enough not to like the ethereal nature of the cloud. Might not've trusted something that insubstantial with his secret."

Rogers frowned in thought. "So something tangible, then. A physical object. We're back to a flash drive."

"Yes. Anyway, if we were to find a possible needle too easily, it might be a red herring he planted, or even a booby trap."

"You mean, don't drink the bourbon."

His eyebrows rose and fell. "If those CSIs get here too soon, I might do that anyway."

Reeder stepped back, tried to see the desk through his murdered friend's eyes.

The surface was relatively sparse. No monitor—Chris used the missing laptop. A cup held some pens, an open space the likely laptop home, a mouse and mouse pad, a notepad, framed pictures of Beth and Christopher, Scotch tape dispenser, Post-it notes, glasses case. Normal stuff, the same things everybody else had on their desk.

"Have a look inside the mouse," he said, "and look behind the photographs."

She started on that while he picked up the glasses case.

"This might be it," he said.

She glanced at him, curious.

"Chris has worn contacts for years," he told her. "I don't remember him ever to wear glasses."

"Maybe they're reading glasses."

"I don't think so. He wore graduated contacts. This would be a spare pair, for if he left his contacts in too long."

She shrugged and began taking the picture frames apart.

Almost to himself, he said, "I don't think Chris would leave his glasses case on top of his desk. It'd be tucked away in a drawer. Five bucks says there's a flash drive in here."

"You're on."

He opened the case and looked down at a pair of wire-frame glasses.

Rogers glanced over. "Glasses in a glasses case, huh? What will they think of next?"

"How long have we been here?"

"A good ten minutes. We'll have company soon."

"Shit."

"I'm an old-fashioned girl. I'll take the five in cash, or you can use PayPal, if dinosaurs know how to do that."

He removed the glasses from the case, studied its plush cloth lining. Felt along the inside with his latex-covered fingers. A tiny rectangular lump in the liner.

He slowly peeled back the cloth to reveal a SIM card.

She was looking at it and then him with big eyes. "So you don't owe me five dollars."

"Digital photos," he said, freeing the SIM card.

"But of what?"

"Let's go find out."

He was on his way when she was there beside him, touching his arm. "Joe, we're taking this to Woods. Double-cross him now and later there'll be hell to pay."

He paused, then nodded.

Outside, they showed Woods their discovery.

He held out a hand, also gloved in latex. "I'll take that, thank you."

Reeder closed a fist over the SIM card. "Why don't we all look at them together?"

Woods glared at him.

Reeder smiled sweetly. "You know—one big happy law enforcement family?"

"Somebody," the young cop said, "should let some of that hot air out of you."

"Now, Detective Woods," Rogers said, "we're operating on good faith. Your CSIs . . . where are they, by the way? . . . might or might not have found this. Also, we could have tucked that little gem away and walked out of here, taking along credit for ourselves and leaving any blame behind for you."

Woods thought he was looking back at Rogers blankly, but Reeder read one micro-expression after another, starting with anger but winding up with apprehension.

Reeder said, his tone devoid of sarcasm, "Derailing a promising career, this early on, would be a damn shame."

The CSI van was pulling in.

"Give me a few moments," Woods said, and went to deal with the techs.

Reeder and Rogers returned to the front seat of her car and she got the motor and heater going again. A minute or so later, her cell rang.

She was talking to her computer guy and, from the start of the conversation, looked unhappy.

She was asking, "Is that even *possible?*"

Her face tightened into a scowl as she listened, then she thanked Miggie, cursing as she clicked off.

She whirled to Reeder. "That photo ID?"

"Yeah?"

"Want to guess who Henry Patrick is?"

"No."

"Patrick Henry."

He frowned. "Either way it's an alias."

"That's not what I mean. The photo *is* Patrick Henry."

"A photo of Patrick Henry from the 1700s? Are Bill and Ted in it?"

The old film reference was lost on her, apparently.

She said, "Somebody took an oil painting image of Patrick Henry, changed the hair a little, and digitally tweaked the thing into looking like a photo."

"That can be done?"

"I can't do it, you can't do it, but some people can, and Miggie says it's not even that hard."

She was shaking her head, but Reeder was thinking.

Finally he said, "Why Patrick Henry do you suppose?"

"Why not Patrick Henry?"

"It's a lot of trouble to go to for an alias—I mean, it's an FU joke, granted, but was it supposed to signify something? If anybody figured it out."

She cocked her head. "Political maybe? Henry was the give-me-liberty-or-give-me-death revolutionary guy, right?"

"He was more than a revolutionary," Reeder said. "Twice governor of Virginia. We're in Virginia right now. Is it a state thing, then? Or a national thing? Some of what he said was considered outright treason—is this about somebody being a traitor? He was also a wealthy plantation owner—an anti-rich message? Something racial?"

"Or just," she said, "a dumb joke. You might be overthinking it, Joe."

"Maybe. But put your friend Miggie on it, anyway."

"He's probably already ahead of us, but I will."

Fifteen minutes later, Reeder, Rogers, and Woods were seated in a corner booth at a Denny's, having coffee. The Homicide man was using a tablet to run through the photos.

The detective found the file and they crowded around the screen looking at seven thumbnail photos.

"We'll start at the top," the detective said, clicking on the first photo.

They stared at a black plastic cube on a table. And it stared right back at them.

Rogers asked, "Anyone know what we're looking at?" Reeder said, "Looks like a Rubik's Cube in basic black."

"A what?" Woods asked.

"Never mind. Suffice to say none of us know what that is or why Chris Bryson had a picture of it."

Second photo.

Nondescript gray cement-block building with dirty windows, no signage. Parking lot in foreground, no cars.

"Anybody?" the detective asked.

Rogers said, "Just an anonymous building."

Reeder, still studying the image, said, "So far, seems like random pictures."

Third photo.

Well-dressed African American man in his thirties, formal-looking pose.

Reeder asked, "Could his name be 'Sink'?"

"No," Rogers said, sitting up. "That's Michael Balsin, congressional aide. My team is investigating his murder."

Woods perked. "Murder? When?"

"September. Two in the back of the head. No robbery, no clues, no apparent motive."

Reeder met Rogers's eyes with urgency. "What the hell is a vic of yours doing on Chris Bryson's SIM card?"

"No idea . . . but it's not like it's a surveillance photo, which you might expect from an investigator like Bryson." She nodded at the screen. "That's the photo that ran with Balsin's obit."

Photo four.

Blond guy, blue eyes, double chin, dark-framed glasses.

"Pattern's forming," Rogers said, frowning. "That's the obit picture for Harvey Carroll—an accountant. Our victim number two, double-tapped just like Balsin—in his home, no witnesses, no robbery."

Reeder felt that familiar combination of excitement and unease—the former because a pattern was indeed forming, unease because a brutal killer or killers had been revealed.

Photo five.

Latina, black hair, dark eyes, high cheekbones.

"Carolina Uribe," Rogers said, "a librarian, also double-tapped—our third victim. Died early November."

"Jesus," Reeder whispered.

Photo six.

Middle-aged white man with a receding hairline and an ugly cardigan.

"William Robertson," Rogers said. "Supervisor in the shop at Dunnelin Machine. Victim number four."

"A series of serial-killing victims," Woods said, quietly astonished, "on a SIM card Bryson hid away?"

"Maybe," Rogers said, "maybe not. The similarity of method got these killings onto our radar. We've been looking at them as a possible serial, yes. But the MO is execution style."

"*Contract killer* style," Reeder said. "And somehow, Chris got on a similar track. What do we think the building and the black cube might have to do with it?"

"No idea," Rogers said, shaking her head, shrugging.

They now all knew more, yet felt like they knew less.

Photo seven.

Blond man in his thirties, walking down a street. Shot from some distance.

Reeder and Woods turned to Rogers, but she said, "Not one of ours. Not yet anyway."

"Maybe *this* is Sink," Reeder said.

Woods frowned and almost snapped, "You said that before—who the hell is Sink?"

Reeder arched an eyebrow at him. "When you talked to Beth Bryson, she never mentioned Sink?"

Woods shrugged. "I don't remember that coming up . . ." Then the young detective's eyes tensed. "Wait. Damn. I *do* remember. She said her husband told her he shouldn't have looked into 'sink.' You think it's a name, Mr. Reeder?" He nodded to the tablet. "You think *that's* him?"

"You got me," Reeder admitted. "Could be anybody. Might be the guy I wrestled with tonight, back at Bryson's office. In the dark."

"Or," Rogers said, "could be the next victim."

A waitress came over with coffee. "Refills anyone? Anybody work up an appetite yet?"

"We know more about war than we know
about peace, more about killing than we
know about living."

General of the Army Omar N. Bradley,
commander of 1.3 million soldiers in World War II,
former head of the Joint Chiefs of Staff,
last to hold rank of five-star general.
Section 30, Lot 428-1, Grid AA-39,
Arlington National Cemetery.

NINE

The morning was cold and dreary and overcast, which seemed about right to Evan Carpenter, the way his week was going.

In parka, jeans, and work boots, his close-clipped blond hair under a shaggy black wig, blue eyes concealed by sunglasses, Carpenter walked along at an easy pace. He passed a few other strip mall shoppers pausing for a momentary gawk at the crime-scene-taped-off Bryson Security storefront. Cops and CSIs long gone now.

Finally, a break. Otherwise, you could have this goddamn born-under-a-bad-sign week, as far as he was concerned. From the moment Carpenter and his boys figured Bryson was onto them, the son of a bitch seemed to *know* he was blown, and blew. At least the bastard had been easy enough to track down, easier still to deal with. Tough guy in his time, but his time was up.

Carpenter alone had been dispatched to deal with the wife—first, to see what she knew and if she had anything of her late husband's that might lead back to his employers. Then the grieving widow would become a second tragic suicide.

Only the wife had company. Her son was with her, though that might be expected; wait for sonny to head home, and then Carpenter would call on mom. But the son wasn't the visitor that concerned him—it was the guy he'd seen being let into the house, who belonged to the candy-ass Prius in the drive.

The mercenary made a call, ran the plate, and *goddamnit!* The guy paying a visit wasn't just anybody, but Joe fucking Reeder himself.

Reeder, the ex–Secret Service guy who was a national hero these days. Just one man, yes, but a guy who could handle himself, despite the years he had on him, and whose death would ring bells all the way to the White House.

So his visit to the mourning family would have to be postponed.

In the meantime, he'd gone on to Bryson Security, figuring to come back later, after Reeder had gone, and tie up the loose ends that were the dead man's family.

At the security office, his key would work in either front or rear door; but with the strip mall so after-hours dead—his rental Nissan the only car in the small lot—he said what the hell, and went in the front.

If picking the lock had been necessary, he'd have gone in the back way; dressed all in black as he was, people driving or walking by just might get suspicious, seeing some ninja-wannabe asshole hunkered over a lock—even if only for the thirty seconds or so picking the thing would take.

He knew of no other key to the office, other than the one on Bryson's key ring, which would likely be in police custody. The key Carpenter used was courtesy of laser etchings one of his guys had made while their target dangled and died from that industrial-strength shower rod.

They'd taken the dead prick's laptop but the crew's computer guy hadn't come up with a goddamn thing. So last night, the mercenary meant to check that office and see if Bryson had left behind anything that could incriminate their employers.

But just a couple of minutes after Carpenter got inside, barely starting his search, some asshole came in on him. Either he had a key or Carpenter had screwed up and not shut the door tight.

And not just any asshole, but *Reeder*, who for an old fart put up one hell of a fight, rough enough that Carpenter had cut out soon as he got the chance.

From a vantage point half a block away, the merc had watched the cops show up for a search, and then Reeder and some woman joined in. He'd kept watch a long time, even after the CSIs showed up, after which a plainclothes cop, Reeder, and the female had gone off together. He'd used binoculars and was pretty sure he didn't see any evidence bags troop out of there into the crime lab van.

But he couldn't be sure.

And if something, anything, had been taken out of there, he had no way to know it. A thorough search would likely be pointless now. That left only one alternative—cleanse the place. If something was still in there, make it be gone.

He would come back and do that when the joint wasn't crawling with cops and CSIs.

At that point, he'd driven back to the Bryson residence, and *shit!* They were in the wind, Mommy and Baby Boy both, apparently having driven off in the dead dad's BMW. Now the Brysons were more than loose ends: they were a likely threat. The wife and/or son must know something.

Otherwise, why run?

Now, as sunshine peeked past dreary clouds, Carpenter strolled around the far corner of the strip mall sidewalk, on Bryson's end of the building, and circled around behind, in that not fast, not slow manner that said he belonged here.

He ambled into the alley, lighting up a cigarette, since an alley was one place in this damn restriction-happy country where a man could still catch a smoke. But catching a smoke wasn't what he was doing: he wanted to have a reason for being back here, should somebody ask. Plan was to lean against the wall and puff away till he had the alley to himself.

But he already did.

So he went directly to the Bryson Security back door stenciled PRIVATE—NO ENTRY. He used the key and went in. Last night, he'd been lazy and sloppy, leaving that front door unlocked. This time he threw the deadbolt.

The door opened directly onto Bryson's inner office. Carpenter briefly reconsidered searching the place, but then stuck to the plan. He removed the batteries from the smoke alarms in both inner and outer offices—the latter required caution and care, as the big window, tinted though it was, remained a hazard—then he disabled the sprinkler system.

He hadn't bothered acquiring an accelerant, because he'd seen one in the office last night, when he started his search by looking in the file cabinet. Bryson must have been a lush because the guy kept a bottle of bourbon in the bottom drawer.

That would do fine.

And with all the flammable stuff in here anyway, sprinkler system and smoke alarms down, it'd be tinderbox time.

Back in Bryson's inner office, he filled the wastebasket with paper, which he then doused with bourbon. He went to the desk and opened drawers and sprinkled bourbon on everything. Same for the desktop. He noticed something a little out of place—an insulated coffee mug with the Metro DC police badge logo. Probably left behind by that cop on guard last night.

In the outer office, keeping down low—that big window again— he filled that wastebasket, too. He splashed that with bourbon, as well as a stack of magazines on a little end table by the waiting-area chairs.

Returning to Bryson's inner office, he splashed what was left of the bourbon onto a wall. Then he pulled out his Air America lighter and went around lighting little fires, wastebasket, desktop, top drawer. He was heading toward the door to the outer office when the uniformed cop came through.

Not fucking again!

No weapon in his hands. He was bundled up for the cold and his eyes had gone immediately to the desk, and Carpenter knew. Last night's cop on the door—he'd left his coffee cup here, all right. Probably in his thirties, kind of heavy, cheeks rosy from the cold but maybe rosy anyway. His hand went toward his holstered weapon and Carpenter hurled the coffee cup at him, hitting him in the forehead. The cop winced and by then Carpenter had his .45 out of his parka pocket.

"Hands where I can see them," Carpenter said.

Around them the little fires crackled and smoked and popped.

The cop held up his hands, swallowed. "What is this, anyway?"

"This is where you turn around and face that wall. Do it."

Like a big blundering beast, the heavily winterized cop turned to the wall. Smoke was getting thick now, each little fire sending its fumes to meet other fumes. The desktop was entirely consumed by dancing orange and blue.

"I don't care about you," the cop said. "All I want is to get the fire department out here, protect the people in these stores. There's a back door. Use it. Go!"

Carpenter was holding his breath, smoke thickening.

But he let some breath out as he said, "I don't care about you, either."

And put two holes in the back of the cop's head.

"Everyone wants to go to heaven,
but no one wants to die."

Joe Louis,
Heavyweight Champion of the World, 1937–1949.
Section 7A, Grave 177,
Arlington National Cemetery.

TEN

Patti Rogers, in a gray suit with a white blouse, stood before her assembled team in a small conference room, with a sixty-inch wall monitor looming behind her.

Joe Reeder, in a camel-hair sport coat with a light-blue shirt and navy-and-black striped tie, was the closest thing to casual in a room of FBI agents in suits. Immediately to Rogers's right, Reeder sat next to Miguel Altuve (blue suit, darker blue tie) with the rest spread around the oblong table—attractive African American Anne Nichols, dark-haired handsome Jerry Bohannon, former college hoop star Reggie Wade, skeletal Trevor Ivanek, and of course resident cue ball Lucas Hardesy, who was more up to speed than the rest, having been the one who'd called Rogers to the Karma Sabich crime scene the day before.

Arrayed on the big flat screen were all seven of Chris Bryson's SIM card photos, as well as a glamorous head shot of Karma Sabich, pulled from the website of the club where the transvestite had worked.

"I trust you all know Joe Reeder," she said, "or at least know of him."

Nods and murmured hellos from the team, a nod and murmured hello from the new face at the table.

Rogers made a slow scan of the faces looking up at her. "Did any of you ever meet Chris Bryson? Or even just hear of him?"

Head shakes and a few "No" responses.

She paced a few steps. "Does anybody know how a one-man strip mall security outfit could get ahead of us in our serial investigation?"

Silence.

Which finally was broken by Reeder.

"Agent Rogers," he said, in that flat manner he used in public, "if I might respond?"

She nodded to him. "Certainly. For the record, Mr. Reeder has signed on with us as a consultant."

"Pro bono," he said with a slight smile. "I know Agent Rogers has provided you with the basics. But let me reiterate: Chris Bryson was a friend. And I need to make a point about him. He was ex–Secret Service, so he wasn't just some storefront PI. He was also a Medal of Honor winner. He was as good as anybody in this room. So we don't need to beat ourselves up about him getting out ahead of us."

If anyone else had said that, Rogers would have felt undermined. But Reeder was right, both in what he said and in gently guiding her onto the right track with her people.

Reeder continued: "That someone took Chris out of the game, before he could do anything about it, is worth our careful consideration. My guess is that those photos don't represent an investigation for a client. Working on something else, Chris tumbled onto a situation that got his Spidey senses tingling. So he took a few pictures."

Roger gave Reeder a tiny gesture that told him to join her. He rose, came up and stood beside her. Without a word, they were now sharing leadership of the team.

The four field agents traded looks, understanding very well what had just happened. Everyone seemed focused, even calm, except maybe Miggie, a chronic fidgeter due to his jones for imported coffee.

Ivanek was looking past Rogers and Reeder. "Have we identified that building?" the behaviorist asked, nodding toward the screen.

"No," Rogers said.

Bohannon, in a well-cut gray suit probably picked out by partner Wade, said, "Small factory of some sort. Job shop, maybe."

"Whatever it is," Miggie said, "it's not in DC. I've got software searching for it in concentric circles. Bryson may have downloaded it from the web—he took screenshots of the obits to get the victim photos. I'm searching, but with so little to work with, it may be a while."

Wade, typically stylish in a tailored dark-green suit, looming even when he was sitting down, asked, "And the black cube?"

"No idea," Miggie said with a shrug. "Nothing around it to provide context or perspective. No clue how big it is, where it is, what it is."

Lovely Nichols—in a dark-taupe suit with black V-neck blouse (an ensemble Rogers would never have risked)—asked the computer guru, "What about our blond boy there?"

"Photo's from the side," Miggie said, "at a distance—a shot Bryson grabbed on the street. Facial rec no help so far."

Ivanek asked, "What's the story on the transvestite?"

Rogers nodded at Hardesy, saying, "Luke, take that, would you? You made the connection."

"You got it, boss," he said.

The other team members goggled at each other—though the behaviorist only allowed himself an arched eyebrow—as they tried to process this unlikely exchange between a pair of coworkers who to date had been adversarial.

Hardesy said, "DeShawn Davis, twenty-four. Worked as a dancer at Les Girls under the stage name Karma Sabich. Lived in Arlington. Night before last, found dead by a friend. Double-tapped. Sound familiar?"

"Familiar," Ivanek said, "but not familiar enough. However scant the profile we've developed, it doesn't leave room for a transvestite victim."

"Why not?" Reeder asked offhandedly. "Agent Rogers says the other victims were all professionals."

Now both of the behaviorist's eyebrows went up. "You're calling this person a professional?"

Reeder shrugged. "Did they pay her for what she did? And the comments at the Les Girls website are very favorable. She was a pro."

"In the broadest definition."

Reeder allowed himself a smile. "I hope that wasn't a pun, Agent Ivanek."

"No pun intended, or disrespect either. But also no apparent connection to previous victims, other than mode of death."

"Mode of death," Reeder said, "or mode of execution? The other person who's a pro here—besides Karma Sabich and the other victims—would seem to be the killer. You can call this a serial killing if you like . . . and it's useful labeling in that it allows the FBI to look into these crimes . . . but these are almost certainly contract killings."

"A *series* of them," Ivanek said, almost bristling.

"A series grouped close enough in time," Reeder said, "to indicate a connection between victims."

Rogers said, "A connection that we haven't made yet. So let's go over it again."

The agents arranged their materials in front of them, ranging from field notes and printouts to tablets or laptops. No one bitched about going back to square one—that was common in any big case—but the team seemed especially alert, game faces on, perhaps because the celebrated Joe Reeder was present. Or maybe it was the additional victim, which seemed to say more bodies would be coming if they couldn't stop this.

Whatever "this" was.

Bohannon was first to speak. "Still no ballistics match on the rounds. If one shooter is responsible for all these kills, he's using a different gun each time."

Reeder said, "I understood that these were all .45 double-taps."

"They are," Bohannon confirmed, "but from different weapons apparently."

"Changing out the barrel maybe?"

"One possibility. A pro might do that routinely."

Wade asked, "How about multiple shooters?"

Bohannon shrugged. "We have five known victims now. Do we think we have five killers, each using the same two-slugs-in-back-of-the-head MO? That's a hell of a coincidence."

Nichols asked, "What about a gang initiation? Five new members, five random victims?"

Wade said, "Bullet pattern is so closely placed, feels like one guy."

Reeder asked, "Any shells found at the scenes?"

"Nope," Bohannon said with a disgusted smirk. "He collects his brass."

"So," Rogers said, "most likely one shooter."

"One very careful shooter."

Still at Rogers's side, Reeder said, "Let's say this isn't a professional assassin. For the sake of argument. Let's say it's a serial killer who saw a movie or a TV show with the double-tap thing and thought, wow, that's cool. Now he's randomly assassinating people."

Ivanek leaned forward a little. "Random isn't part of the serial killer playbook. There's *always* a pattern."

Pleasantly, Reeder said, "Random can't be a pattern?"

"I couldn't give you an example of one, Mr. Reeder."

"Make it 'Joe' . . . Trevor, isn't it?"

"It is," Ivanek said. "And I'm the guy who should be able to give you that pattern, but so far—unlike our killer—I'm shooting blanks.

The victims don't work in the same fields, they don't live near each other, they're not close in income, they're not one race or gender. We just don't have a bead yet."

"*Sounds* random, anyway," Reeder said.

The behaviorist said, "'Natural selection is anything but random.'"

"You know your Richard Dawkins," Reeder said with the slightest smile. "You think this is some kind of screwed-up social Darwinism?"

"No, but it's *not* random. We just haven't seen the pattern yet. Maybe as we accrue information on the new victim, it'll finally become clear."

"Okay," Reeder said. "So we go back to contract killings."

"In some respects," Ivanek said, "that does make sense. In others, it doesn't."

"How so?"

"All the victims, prior to the transvestite, were good citizens, squeaky clean, no gang ties, no organized crime ties, no loan sharks in the mix, just plain nothing. And Karma Sabich or DeShawn Davis . . ."

"Rose by any other name," Hardesy muttered.

". . . may well have been a solid citizen, too, in the context of her, or his, world."

Rogers said, "Trevor, take us through them one at a time, will you?"

All eyes returned to the faces on the big monitor.

Ivanek said, "Victim number one, September 12 of last year— Michael Balsin, congressional aide. Thirty-four years old, shot to death in his apartment, lived alone. No sign of struggle."

Reeder asked, "Aide for . . . ?"

"Congressman Silas Denton from New Jersey."

"Liberal."

"Yes."

"Michael have a significant other?"

"No. Nor did he have much of a social life. A very work-driven individual. Representative Denton was extremely upset about the murder, said the young man was going places."

Wade said glumly, "Which he did."

"Victim number *two* is no liberal," Ivanek said. "Harvey Carroll, CPA, Springfield resident, had his own small business in Fairfax Station. Killed at home, no struggle—October 7. Divorced, father of one girl, who lives with her mom. Conservative voter, churchgoer. A good guy, by all accounts."

Reeder asked, "A good guy, but was he the accountant for somebody bad?"

"Not that we've found," Ivanek said. "Mostly, he worked for Christian charities and a few small companies. He did very little work for individuals. We haven't found anybody who's had a bad word to say about him—well, except his ex-wife."

Anticipating Reeder's next question, Rogers said, "And the ex-wife's bad words are limited to how boring ol' Work-Work-Work Harvey had been. Not exactly the kind of complaints that lead to two bullets in the back of the head."

Reeder's eyebrows made a little shrug. "You should talk to my ex before you make that assumption."

That got a few chuckles.

Ivanek picked up: "Victim number three—a reference librarian from Burke. Carolina Uribe worked at the Burke Centre Library, lived alone, killed November 15."

Reeder asked, "The only female victim?"

Hardesy said, "Depends on how you count this Karma character."

Rogers said, "Luke, let's not spoil our new friendly relationship by you making inappropriate cracks about one of the victims, whose murder we're trying to solve."

All heads turned to the ex-military man, anticipating flying fur. None flew.

He held up his hands. "My bad, kids. My only question is whether we refer to this vic as Karma or DeShawn, her or him. Not bein' snide, boss—just practical."

Rogers thought about that. "Legal name is DeShawn, and gender on the autopsy is male. We'll go with DeShawn and 'he.'"

Nobody disagreed with that assessment.

Hardesy did say, "I understand this individual preferred to be referred to as female. But we'll make it up to the vic by bringing in his goddamn killer."

Nods and even some applause.

Ivanek resumed his rundown. "Victim number four, William Robertson. Floor supervisor at Dunnelin Machine in Bowie, Maryland. Married with two kids, only vic—including DeShawn Davis—not killed at home. December 17."

Reeder asked, "Where did the shooting go down?"

"Men's room of the shop where he worked."

Nichols said, "I covered that one. Perfect place for a murder. Twenty employees who mostly run machines and don't talk except at breaks. Office is separate, away from the workers. Trucks bring material in, take product out, mailman, FedEx, UPS, people in and out all the time. If you're a killer, here's the beauty part—no security cameras. They have no problem with theft, so there's no need."

Reeder asked, "Robertson got shot twice in the head and nobody saw or heard *anything*?"

"Factory noise there is pretty intense," Nichols said. "Plus, the killer might have used a sound suppressor—some damn good ones available these days."

Rogers asked, "But would a pro do that? A hit at a busy workplace?"

Reeder said, "A pro who has done his homework would do that sooner than some serial killer might."

"There are exceptions," Ivanek said, "but most serials operate under conditions they've thoroughly stage-managed—they like things wholly in their control."

Reeder glanced back at the screen, then said to Nichols, "You went to this factory?"

"I did."

"I take it Dunnelin Machine's not the building in the Bryson SIM card photo."

"It's not." She smiled, mildly embarrassed. "Sorry, I should have said that right away. No, Dunnelin is a smaller building, brick."

Rogers could see Reeder's wheels turning, though his expression itself was typically unreadable. But everyone seemed to sense he was mulling something, and all eyes were on him.

Finally he said, "Rule out serial killer."

Ivanek frowned. "Mr. Reeder, it's too early for that. We still can't know that—"

"You can rule it out. Narrow your focus. This is a professional killer. This is a killer with a list. Your job isn't so much to find the connections between these victims as it is how they got on the same kill list."

Rogers asked, "Was Chris Bryson on that list, do you think?"

"A late addition."

Ivanek sat up so straight he almost stood. "But the mode is completely different. A faked suicide by hanging is hardly a double-tap execution."

"Chris was a special case," Reeder said, "and required more than a lone killer to carry out the execution. The others got themselves on the list for reasons as yet unknown. But we do know how Chris got on there."

Rogers said, "We *do?*"

Reeder nodded. "He stumbled onto something that he recognized as something big, something bad. Possibly these murders you've been looking into . . . but I think it's more than that. Chris was a fine investigator, with the same kind of top-notch training everyone here has had. If he'd run into a possible serial killer, he'd have gone to you guys at the FBI. Not pursue it himself."

Bohannon said, "So what the hell *are* we dealing with then?"

"I'm not sure," Reeder admitted.

Wade was shaking his head. "I don't see how we can rule out a serial killer yet. Maybe your pal Chris didn't come to us or the cops because he wasn't sure what he had."

"Agent Wade—Reggie?" Reeder's smile was barely there. "Why would a serial who killed four victims in their homes—counting DeShawn Davis—break the pattern for this one vic, Robertson, and kill him at work?"

"Because Robertson had a family maybe."

"Okay, but why not take out the whole family?"

Wade shrugged. "Not his deal."

"All right . . . but why not choose a victim who *was* his 'deal'? Not strike at the vic's workplace, where the possibility of getting caught was exponentially greater?"

"No idea," Wade admitted.

"Trevor," Reeder said, turning to the behaviorist, "I don't mean to tread on your specialty. But nothing's been taken, no trophies."

Ivanek said, "Serials don't always take trophies."

"Granted. But if this *is* a serial, how did he get so goddamn good, right out of the gate?"

Nobody had an answer.

Reeder turned to Bohannon. "You've said the entry-wound groupings are damn near perfect." Then to Ivanek: "Does someone killing out of a need to fulfill a compulsion usually display that kind of skill?"

The behaviorist let out some air. "That bothered me, too. Most serials perfect their craft over time and out of experience. Assuming he hasn't been operating elsewhere . . ."

"FBI computers would have picked that up," Miggie said.

". . . this guy is already good at his killing craft."

"*Professional*-level good?" Reeder asked.

Trevor nodded.

Rogers said, "Which brings us back to a professional killer with a list of victims."

"It does," Reeder said, and gestured to the flat-screen. "If Chris somehow tumbled into whatever these pictures add up to—and started looking into something suspicious—then we'll find the answer in the three photos that he left behind for us."

All eyes were on the screen.

Reeder continued: "We need to figure out what the black cube is . . . and what and where that building is . . . and who our blond man-on-the-street is. A potential victim . . . or Chris Bryson's suspect? And it follows there is indeed a connection between these five victims . . . and my late friend's murder."

Luke Hardesy, who had mostly just been listening, said, "Mr. Reeder . . . Joe . . . we *have* been digging. What we have so far mostly falls into the negative column—victims who didn't know each other or frequent the same places or live in the same towns. No work similarities, no social connections."

"Understood," Reeder said. "But something *is* there. And now with DeShawn Davis and, yes, Chris Bryson, we have two more victims to look at."

"We?" Rogers said with a smile. "Sounds like you plan to do your typical brand of hands-on 'consulting.'"

He grinned at her. The others in the room were almost surprised, because Reeder was usually so deadpan, and his smiles barely visible. Not this time.

"Patti," he said, "you were looking for a possible serial killer, and I was trying to find Chris Bryson's murderer. Those inquiries have clearly converged."

She grinned back at him. "Should I say 'welcome aboard'?"

Looking around the room, he said, "I was thinking of saying the same thing to all of you people."

That got smiles and a few laughs.

Reeder and Rogers took seats at the conference table and they dug in, beginning with their new member briefing the team on Chris's murder, concluding with the possibility that the blond man might have been last night's attacker at the Bryson Security office.

Rogers said, "Even when our unknown subject deviated and killed Robertson away from home, he used the double-tap method. The faked suicide is an entirely new one."

Reeder said, "Chris was ex–Secret Service. You don't execute a former agent with two bullets in the back of the head without calling undue attention to the crime. Make it a suicide, and it goes away."

"And doesn't get connected," Hardesy said, nodding, "to the double-tap killings."

Nodding back, Reeder said, "And the 'suicide' buys the killer time to search out and find . . . and destroy . . . anything an investigator like Chris might've come up with."

"It's a workable theory at least," Rogers said. She slapped the table. "So we see what we can find out about Bryson's activities in the week before his death, and DeShawn Davis, too. Got to be something."

Miggie chimed in: "Maybe I can help . . . Mind if I take your pictures down?"

"Go ahead," she said.

Miggie used his tablet, tapped some virtual keys, and the photos were replaced by a grainy video image of a man in black walking down a corridor, doors on either side.

Ivanek frowned at the screen. "What's this?"

"Security footage," Miggie said, "from the hotel the night Bryson died."

Nichols asked, "How did we get this so fast?"

Rogers said, "When Joe told me he was looking into his friend's suspicious death, I had Miggie get that footage for him. As a favor."

"Do we get a better look at this guy?" Bohannon asked. "Working pretty hard to keep his face a secret."

Miggie said, "At the very end, we do."

A few seconds later, a hand came across the lens, then a forearm, and the picture went to snow.

Hardesy frowned. "*That's* the better look?"

"Tattoo," Reeder said.

"*Gesundheit,*" Wade joked, but he was staring at the snowy screen.

Reeder said, "Run it back slow, Miggie."

Rogers had seen it, too, a hint of something on the wrist where the shirt and coat sleeves tugged down as the arm reached up.

Miggie froze the image, the inked skin still half-hidden under the cuff of the shirt.

"What is it?" Wade asked.

Bohannon said, "A banner of some kind . . . ?"

Nichols said, "Lettering, but I can't tell . . ."

Hardesy stood with a suddenness that startled everybody a little. He took off his jacket, unbuttoned the cuff of his shirt, folded it back and showed his own tattoo: a sword pointed upward, two arrows crossing it diagonally, a black banner, the ends touching the tip of the blade on either side, forming a shield. Within the banner, in white, the words *De Oppresso Liber*.

It matched the one in the video.

"Finally we have a suspect," Wade said. "Somebody put the bracelets on Luke here."

A few laughed; most didn't.

Rogers had seen that tattoo plenty of times back in her days as an MP. She said, "United States Army Special Forces."

Hardesy nodded. "That's the Special Forces motto—loosely translates to 'liberate the oppressed.'"

Rogers sighed, nodded, and said, "It's a beginning."

Ivanek said, "It is, but not enough to tell us if our guy is current military or a mercenary."

"Almost certainly a merc," Reeder said in a quiet way that brought all eyes to him. "Currently serving Special Forces guys aren't running around DC over a period of four months committing executions."

Wade said, "Guy in the video's blond, and so's the guy in Bryson's photo. Are they one and the same? Before, I thought the SIM card blond was our next possible victim. Now I'd vote for suspect."

"If," Reeder said, "they're the same guy."

Ivanek was shaking his head. "Hard to say. Video's worse than the crappy picture."

"I'll take a swing at a comparison," Miggie said to Rogers, "and get back to you."

Rogers's cell phone rang. She would have preferred to ignore it, but caller ID said it was Woods, the DC homicide detective.

"Shit news," Woods said.

"What?"

"Somebody torched Bryson's office."

"Damnit."

"It gets worse. The uniformed officer we left on the door last night? He went back this morning, looking for a coffee cup he left behind.

Walked right in on the guy torching the place, apparently. Wasn't expecting anything, so the arsonist got the best of him somehow."

"When you say 'the best of' . . ."

"Shot him. Execution style. Two in the back of the head."

She sucked in breath, the news hitting her like a blow. "I'm so very sorry, Detective Woods. We'll do everything we can for you. I'll have agents out there ASAP."

"Well, I appreciate that, Special Agent Rogers," he said, his voice conveying the opposite. "But this is *our* case. Please keep that in mind. I'm just calling as a courtesy."

"I do understand. You've lost one of your own. But we're in this together now. You take lead on this aspect, okay?"

"Fine," he said, in an I'll-believe-it-when-I-see-it manner, and clicked off.

She did the same, then answered the question that every face in the room was silently asking.

"Bryson's office has been torched," she said.

"Good," Reeder said.

Rogers suddenly recalled how cold he had at first seemed to her, on their case last year.

She said, hollowly, "Joe, an officer's been killed," and filled them in on that, leaning hard on the double-tap that made this part of their case.

"I'm sorry to hear about the officer," Reeder said without apparent emotion. "But we've picked up a valuable piece of the puzzle."

"Well, I'm glad there's a silver lining to an officer's death."

He ignored that. "The killer doesn't know that we found what he was looking for—the SIM card that gave us those photos."

Rogers frowned. "How do you figure that?"

"Well, if he'd known, he wouldn't have gone back there this morning. No reason to."

Getting it, she said, "Instead he did go back, finished his search, unsuccessfully, then burned the office, so that nobody could find whatever-it-was."

"Exactly," Reeder said. "Remember, if what we have is a serial killer, this would go on till we catch him. People would die, but eventually the killer would lead us to him. But a pro, killing names on a list? He stops when he gets to the bottom. And then he's gone."

Rogers said softly, "That could be at any moment."

"Which means," Reeder said, slowly scanning the faces at the table, "we need to catch him fast."

"'Tis the business of little minds to shrink,
but he whose heart is firm,
and whose conscience approves his conduct,
will pursue his principles unto death."

Thomas Paine

ELEVEN

The Special Situations Task Force worked through the weekend, but their efforts produced no new leads. Plowing through security footage—from both the Skyway Farer motor hotel and various businesses in the Bryson Security strip mall—made for tedious, eye-strain-inducing work; but that had been Reeder's assignment.

The task force boss, Patti Rogers, was doing the same shit duty herself, while Miguel Altuve had taken up a desk in the bullpen to work his computer magic (somewhat surprisingly, no goats were sacrificed). The two teams of agents—Lucas Hardesy and Anne Nichols, Jerry Bohannon and Reggie Wade—were out talking to friends, neighbors, and work associates of both Chris Bryson and DeShawn (aka Karma Sabich) Davis.

Behaviorist Trevor Ivanek had begged the day off, having worked the weekend before, and got it. With the serial killer theory pulled out from under him, Ivanek seemed to Reeder frankly a little lost.

So far, Monday morning had been taken up by another conference-room meeting where everybody reported in on what they'd found, which was the same thing: nothing. Or at least nothing that seemed to move them even one move ahead on this chessboard.

With his head in the investigation, Reeder had all but forgotten he'd agreed to join Adam Benjamin at the big "A Citizen's State of the Union" event; and until his cell vibrated, Benjamin's private number on caller ID, he'd lost track of how fast the speech was coming up.

Tomorrow night, in fact.

"Joe, Adam Benjamin. Sorry to interrupt if you're working. I hoped we might chat briefly about tomorrow night."

Benjamin, in good assume-the-sale salesman form, hadn't asked if he was still coming.

Reeder was searching for a diplomatic way to decline an invitation he'd already accepted when the billionaire said, "Joe, your support is extremely important to me. Not to embarrass you, but you're an American hero. Admiration for you crosses party lines, which is a perfect fit for the Common Sense Movement."

"Not so long ago," Reeder reminded him, "I was a pariah on the right."

"Yes, because you had the balls to criticize the president you saved."

"If by 'balls' you mean poor judgment, yes."

Benjamin snorted a laugh. "That's forgotten and forgiven by the American people. Your approval rating is 92 percent—do you know what any presidential candidate, hell, any *president*, would do for that level of public approval?"

"Who's taking *my* approval rating, anyway?"

"Well, frankly . . . I am. Or my polling people, anyway. Look, your presence at the rally would be comforting to voters. Not necessarily seen as a seal of approval, but would lend me credibility."

"You already have plenty of that, Mr. Benjamin."

"None of that 'Mr. Benjamin' crap. Adam. Okay, Joe?"

"Okay."

"Then I can count on you?"

"You switched up questions on me, Adam. You *are* a politician now."

The chuckle lost none of its warmth over the phone. "Perhaps I am. But it's a necessary evil. I *know* we think alike in the need to wrest this country out of the hands of special interests, and back to the hands of real people."

"Are you reading that?" Reeder asked lightly. "If not, write it down. It's pretty good."

Another warm chuckle. "Joe. I'm counting on you."

"Adam, I don't view myself as someone who can . . . deliver votes."

"It's not how you view yourself, Joe—it's how the people view you."

"I'm just a guy who got hot for a couple of news cycles. Which I'm glad cooled down."

"Don't kid yourself, Joe. No cooling off, according to my pollsters. The vast majority of Americans respect you, and consider you the kind of old-fashioned hero we haven't seen in a very long time."

"Just doing my job."

"Which is what every great hero says . . . but usually that job is something most people can't, won't, or wouldn't do. I'm not asking for your endorsement, just your presence. Come listen to the speech, be seen there, and if the media sticks a mic in your face, and you want to say I'm a huckster or a fool or a fraud, well . . . that's your privilege. At least they haven't taken our freedom of speech away yet."

Maybe he was *reading some of this stuff . . .*

"Joe, I've reserved good seats for you and a guest. Join us, please. This might . . . just *might* . . . put you on the ground floor of something historic."

Of course Reeder didn't need to attend this rally, or hear the speech, to know what Benjamin had to say. He'd read the man's book, heard him give interviews. But Reeder remained curious to see how this Midwestern populist would play in front of a crowd in a frankly political setting. It was just possible this *was* history in the making.

Or maybe it was just another fart in the wind, like Ross Perot.

Either way, should make for good theater.

"Joe . . . ?"

"Yes, Adam. You can count on me being there."

"Well, that's just wonderful. Call this number when you arrive at Constitution Hall. My man, Frank Elmore, will have this phone. He'll make sure you get in and get to your seats. *Thank* you, Joe."

Reeder paused, not sure whether to thank the man back, or say "You're welcome"; but then Benjamin clicked off.

Rogers came over to Reeder's desk, toward the back of the bullpen, and leaned in. "That seemed fairly intense. Breakthrough on the case?"

"No. Pull up a chair, though."

"That sounds ominous."

"It isn't."

She pulled a chair over.

He said, "Whose turn is it to buy?"

"Mine. Unless you don't count the barbecue the whole team went out for last night where you picked up the check."

"No, that's its own thing. *Your* turn to buy. But how would you like to get off cheap and yet have a unique evening of entertainment?"

"What, are we checking out Les Girls?"

He smiled. "No," he said, and invited her to be his plus-one at the "Citizen's State of the Union" rally.

She immediately said yes.

"Really?" he said. "I thought I'd have to twist your arm."

"No, I'm a Benjamin fan. You may not realize it, but you and I don't usually vote for the same side of the ticket."

"Oh, I know you're a Republican."

That surprised her. "Really? More 'people reading'?"

"Betting that an FBI agent is a Republican is not exactly long odds."

"Hey, I'm not one of these crazy right-wingers or anything, like that Spirit bunch. But some of the changes that President Bennett made—you remember him, right, guy you saved?—are just *fine* by me."

"I know. You're the kind of traditional Republican that my father was. Which makes you a Commie pinko in the eyes of that Spirit crowd."

She smiled a little. "You're overstating it, but kind of, yes."

"They'd feel the same about Ronald Reagan, if they actually studied his presidency. So—you like what Adam Benjamin has to say?"

"Based on what I've picked up, yeah. It's like he says, common sense. Joe, I'd love to be your date. Finally a *real* date, huh?"

"We're going to have good seats, I'm told, probably down front, so that leaves out necking. And you can take me to a Wendy's drive-thru after."

"No way! I do have *some* class, Joe Reeder."

"Do you?"

"Sure. Wendy's, yes. But we'll eat inside."

Chill January wind from the west greeted Reeder and Rogers as they walked from a parking lot to DAR Constitution Hall on D Street NW. Built by the Daughters of the American Revolution one hundred years ago, the auditorium was still a much-used concert venue, and served Benjamin's political purposes well, practically set as it was on the south White House grounds.

"Nothing like thumbing your nose at the President of the United States," Rogers said, "from his own front lawn."

She was in a gray sweater coat over a black ensemble—turtleneck with jacket, slim skirt, tights with boots.

"Benjamin wasn't the first," Reeder said, "and certainly won't be the last."

Reeder was in his Burberry trench coat over a Brooks Brothers navy suit and (what the hell) red-white-and-blue striped tie.

They paused at the foot of the short series of steps to the front doors. Reeder got out his cell, turning east onto a view of the Capitol and the web of scaffolding that surrounded it. Even during renovation, the building had a classic beauty that stirred the patriotic kid in him. He punched in Benjamin's number.

"Frank Elmore," a rough-hewed voice replied.

"Frank, Joe Reeder. We're here." He told Elmore where exactly.

"Our security chief will pick you up," Elmore said curtly.

"Thanks," Reeder said, but Elmore clicked off halfway.

Rogers picked up on that. "Benjamin's majordomo?"

"Real sweetheart. Somebody you might consider dating."

She crinkle-smiled and elbowed him.

Perhaps a minute later, a tall man in a navy suit approached, earbud in, mic attached to his cuff. Short dark hair, brown eyes, angular no-nonsense features, the security man was someone Reeder knew well: former Secret Service agent Jay Akers. Akers, usually affable, wore a vaguely troubled look that few but Reeder would have picked up on.

Still, Akers managed a smile. "Peep, how the hell have you been? Been too long."

They shook hands. Reeder wondered if perhaps Akers sensed he was on his way out as security chief, the Benjamin spot that Reeder had turned down. Too bad for Akers—he was a smart, decent guy and an able agent.

"Jay, meet the FBI's finest," Reeder said, gesturing to his companion. "Special Agent Patti Rogers. Patti, Jay Akers—he and I worked presidential detail together, a lifetime or two ago."

Akers smiled, said, "No need for an introduction, Agent Rogers. You're almost as famous as Peep here."

"Almost," she said with her own little smile.

Akers let out some air. "Better get you two inside."

As they headed up the steps, Rogers on his left, Akers on the right, Reeder said to the ex-agent, "So you're head of security, huh?"

"That's the job description."

"Do I detect discontent?"

"No, no. Everything's fine."

Something in the man's voice, however, said just the opposite to Reeder. So did the anxious micro-expressions that Akers never would have guessed he revealed.

They were inside now, past the metal detectors, the crowd all around them as they made the shuffle toward the auditorium. He and Rogers had both dressed up somewhat for the evening, but around them was everything from near formal wear to baseball caps and running pants.

Keeping his voice low, but up over the crowd murmur, Reeder asked, "Jay, what's wrong?"

"Who said something was wrong?" Akers said with a smile that said something was wrong.

"Don't shit a shitter, my friend."

The smile disappeared. "Call you tomorrow—we'll get a drink. Catch up."

"Don't blow me off, buddy."

"No. We *should* talk. We *will* talk."

Akers led them into the auditorium and the three went down the center aisle toward the stage.

Reeder said, "Jay, if there's something pressing we should . . ."

"It'll keep," Akers said.

The hall was festooned in red-white-and-blue bunting, seats filling up fast with such a cross section of Americans, the attendees might have been selected to represent every segment of American life. Had they been? Those pollsters of Benjamin's at work, maybe?

On stage, a simple podium was adorned with a seal not unlike the presidential one, but saying "Common Sense." The backdrop of satin-looking curtains of red, white, and blue were draped elegantly. Between the patriotic curtains and the podium were risers arranged with chairs, which (with the front row on the stage floor) added up to five rows. That was where the rich friends would be seated, Reeder knew, and any true-believer celebrities in attendance.

The hall had the political-extravaganza feel of a major political party convention. Above were nets brimming with balloons, as if Benjamin was about to win the nomination of some party or other. In a sense, maybe he would, since this appeared to be the de facto coronation of Benjamin as the Common Sense Movement candidate for president.

The speech would be broadcast by all the news channels, and the networks, too—the latter had declined to interrupt their programming until Benjamin bought an hour of prime time. Adding in live Internet streaming, the expected audience was in the double-digit millions.

In twenty-four hours—if Benjamin was as convincing a public speaker as he'd been in private at the Holiday Inn Express—everybody in America, and many worldwide, would know he was a serious political player. Those who hadn't heard the speech live would catch YouTube highlights and hear water-cooler conversations and be caught up in the Big News that the Common Sense Movement had become.

Impressive what a down-to-earth small-town former professor could pull off with a persuasive, folksy gift for gab . . .

. . . and billions of dollars.

Hell, at least Benjamin had earned them. And the bill of goods he was selling was, for a change, a damn good one.

Akers led Reeder and Rogers over to a half flight of stairs up onto the stage at left. Looming over them was Frank Elmore, at the edge of the stage apron; he wore a dark-gray suit and a somewhat oversize American flag lapel pin, the scar on his cheek shining pink under the bright TV lights. On left and right, taking up some audience seating, were platforms on which were positioned manned TV cameras on tripods, the space also home to reporters seated at banquet tables.

Reeder touched Akers's sleeve. "Jay, we're not seated up there on stage, are we?"

"Why, yes."

"I'm not comfortable with that. My presence will be taken as an endorsement."

"Those are the seats reserved for you, Peep. Look, take it up with Frank. I have to go see if these amateurs they gave me to work with are at least correctly positioned . . . We'll talk tomorrow at the latest."

"Counting on it," Reeder said.

Akers nodded and headed back up the aisle.

Reeder said to Rogers, "Are you okay with this? They're playing off who we are."

"We're here," she said with a shrug. "If we don't like what we hear and see, there's not going to be a muzzle on us. We can speak our mind."

"Okay."

They climbed the five steps and were met by Elmore.

"Joe," he said, shaking Reeder's hand, with a smile that looked like it hurt, "Mr. Benjamin is very pleased you're here with us tonight. We all are."

"Thank you, Frank. This is Patti Rogers, the FBI agent I worked with last year on the Supreme Court case."

He gave her a crisp nod but did not offer a hand. "Pleasure, Ms. Rogers. If you'll come this way . . ."

Elmore led them to the nearest two chairs, in the front row of those set up on the stage.

"I don't know about this," Reeder said.

Elmore shrugged, gave up another forced smile. "Mr. Benjamin said to make sure you had good seats. These are assigned to you, and we start in less than ten minutes, so making a change isn't really possible."

Reeder flashed Rogers a get-me-the-hell-out-of-here look, but she only shook her head gently and took him by the arm. She deposited him in the seat nearer the podium and took the chair on the end for herself.

Elmore said, "Some last minute things to do—if you'll excuse me."

The majordomo didn't wait for a reply, leaving so quickly Reeder half expected a vapor trail.

Reeder said to Rogers, "At least we're on the end. Maybe we won't be taken for major supporters."

"Right," she said, amused. "Really low profile."

A crowd this size—he'd estimate well over three thousand, near capacity—turned individual chatting among attendees into a roar, an ocean-worthy tide threatening to wash over the stage. His old Secret Service juices were flowing as he tried to look out into the hall, particularly the seating toward the front, but the TV lights were so bright that the audience was mostly a blur.

Even finding spaces between bursts of brightness, he was not positioned to see much of anything, not there on stage, risers climbing behind him. Up on the top row, he'd have had a much better view of floor seating, which lacked the slope of a more modern theater— from here, a short person seated behind a tall person became invisible.

From a security standpoint, especially from the stage, Constitution Hall had always been a nightmare venue. No wonder Akers seemed troubled—Reeder would be, too, if he were among those in charge of Benjamin's safety.

Around them now were wealthy donors, few of whom Reeder recognized; they tended to be former backers of conservative candidates. In more prominent evidence were some A-list TV and movie stars known previously as supporters of liberal candidates.

The house lights went down and the applause came up, and within seconds, the hall was on its feet, including those around them, which forced Rogers and Reeder to their feet as well. Rogers didn't seem to mind, but Reeder felt manipulated.

But he applauded anyway. Despite the bright lights, Reeder could make out waving signs with such slogans as COMMON SENSE FOR AMERICA and BENJAMIN FOR PRESIDENT. As the seconds dragged into minutes, the audience only intensified its applause.

Finally, just as the thunder seemed about to diminish, Adam Benjamin, in a blue off-the-rack suit with white shirt and red tie, strode out from the wings, beaming to the crowd and waving, walking right by Rogers and Reeder. Now the applause rose to its former apex and beyond.

Akers emerged from the wings, close on Benjamin's heels, and took position at the top of the stairs just to the right of Rogers.

A spotlight followed Benjamin and stopped with him as he paused to stand and wave, poised between Akers and Rogers, the speaker nodding to the crowd in humble acceptance of their adoration.

Just as the applause began to diminish, Benjamin turned, nodded to Reeder, then strode to the podium. He patted the air to silence the crowd, which of course only inflamed them further.

Benjamin stepped away from the podium, smiled at the crowd, shaking his head, finally putting a big show of putting his finger to his lips. They laughed, and applauded even more, the crowd well aware of its costarring role in the spectacle.

Finally Benjamin moved to the podium and the crowd took their seats.

"*Usually,*" he said, in his casual way, "*a speech like this begins: 'My fellow Americans.' But the politicians who address you that way don't view you as their 'fellow' anything. They view you as, well, I guess . . . a kind of obstacle. Those hypocrites calling you 'Americans' is almost an insult, because these politicians . . . not all, but many . . . don't really believe in America. At least not the Common Sense version that the founding fathers had in mind.*"

He paused to let them applaud again and seemed flattered when the crowd again got to its feet. When those on the stage did the same, Reeder reluctantly joined them. Just because he liked what this guy had to say didn't make him any happier about being played like this.

With a palm, Benjamin quieted the crowd and the applause gradually thinned and seats were again taken.

But one man was still on his feet.

One man was in fact coming down the left outside aisle, quickly, applauding as he came, as if his enthusiasm couldn't be contained. The spotlight on Benjamin meant some of the other bright lights were off now, and Reeder could see the guy pretty clearly.

Akers apparently hadn't seen the man, his eyes on the front row where two audience members were on their feet and coming toward the stage, applauding, maybe just wanting a closer look. One of Benjamin's security staff cut in front of them and the pair backed up to their seats.

At the podium, Benjamin was saying, "*Our two once-great political parties have been driven to the far left and far right, leaving the rank and file among us alone in the middle, without representation.*"

The two at right taken care of, Reeder swung his attention back to the guy in that outside aisle, who was now almost to the stairs onto the stage at far left. Surely security near the stage would grab him—*but where were they?* The audience member approaching, applauding, looked respectable enough—navy blue suit, white shirt, shades of red-striped tie, echoing the speaker's own wardrobe. A thirty-something profes-sional, sandy hair cut short.

"*Everybody tells me,*" Benjamin was saying, "*that it's impossible for a third-party candidate to win. But what if that third-party candidate represents the vast majority of Americans in the common-sense middle?*"

Could this be Reeder's attacker at Bryson Security?

Was it the blond from the SIM card?

At this distance, and with the bright lights, Reeder couldn't be sure. Half out of his chair, he was about to yell to Akers, to alert him, but the security man was turning toward the left side of the stage, hav-ing apparently spotted the guy, so yelling might only distract Akers, who had this.

Then the approaching figure's hand slipped under the suit coat and came back with something.

"*Gun!*" Reeder yelled.

A collective gasp came up from the crowd, sucking the air from the room and silencing the speaker as Akers reached for his own piece on his hip under his unbuttoned suit coat . . .

. . . but too late.

The sandy-haired figure pointed a sound-suppressed automatic at Akers, who fell to his knees as if pleading to the man not to shoot.

Only Akers had already been hit, the silenced shot inaudible over the noise of the crowd, who were now reacting in screaming horror and yelling amazement.

But Reeder had seen the reduced muzzle flash and, instinct tak-ing over, he leapt from his chair, Rogers rising, too.

Gun still in hand, Akers was trying to get up, the bullet having hit him in his Kevlar vest, but the sandy-haired man—up on the stage now, at Reeder's far left—leveled what was probably a .45, wearing the bulky extension of a sound suppressor, right at the agent, hitting Akers twice in the side, under the arms, where the Kevlar didn't cover.

Then the sandy-haired man (not the SIM card blond at all) wheeled toward Benjamin at the podium, the big automatic with its extended snout pointing the speaker's way.

Three thousand–plus were on their feet shrieking now, like a hellish choir, while members of Benjamin's security force were coming toward the stage, too little, too late.

This time Reeder heard the cough of the silenced weapon, and the crunch of metal meeting wood as the bullet slammed into the podium just as he threw himself at Benjamin, taking him to the floor, onto his side, covering him as he would a president, bracing for the impact of any rounds from the assassin that might try to get through him to their target.

Reeder flinched at the whipcrack of a round, fired nearby, but not a silenced one, a Glock round, and knew he was all right.

Confirming that came: "*Clear!*"

Rogers.

Staying on top of Benjamin, who was still on his side, face to the crowd, Reeder shifted enough to see the would-be assassin sprawled on the stage, eyes open wide and a black-rimmed, scarlet-dripping hole in his mid-forehead.

Rogers, on stage, Glock gripped in both hands, swiftly scanned the crowd for other shooters. The hall was half-empty now, many having fled, others frozen on their feet at their seats, some recording the pandemonium with their cells, while the camera crews on their platforms left and right kept rolling. The reporters, on both the left and right of the hall (and politically as well, for that matter), were to a man and woman hiding under their tables.

Frank Elmore materialized and leaned in to say, "Mr. Reeder, we'll take it from here," and Reeder rose while four security men in "COMMON SENSE" windbreakers helped the stunned Benjamin to his feet, and formed a phalanx around him, hustling him offstage.

Reeder rushed to the fallen Akers, where Rogers was already down at the man's side, trying to staunch the bleeding with her jacket. As Reeder knelt opposite her, Rogers lifted her bloody jacket so Reeder could appraise the red-gushing entry wounds under the man's other arm.

She gave Reeder a look.

He gave her one back.

She returned to keeping pressure against the fallen man's side with the jacket, for what good it would do.

Akers, his flesh now a wet-newspaper gray, grabbed Reeder's wrist with surprising strength.

"Cap . . ." Akers said. "Cap it . . . all."

"Cap it all? You mean, Capitol?"

Akers swallowed and nodded once. ". . . Senk."

"You mean 'sink'? What about sink?"

The grip on Reeder's wrist was limp now. "No! No . . . *Senk.*"

"Senk. Is that a *name*, Jay? Is that—"

But Akers was gone, eyes rolled back as if staring at the ceiling, where netted balloons awaited a celebratory release not to come.

Uniformed police were moving quickly down the aisles now. Soon FBI and Homeland Security agents would descend on Constitution Hall. Rogers stood guard over the dead security man while Reeder went over to where the sandy-haired shooter lay dead as hell on his side, a mere trickle of red out the puncture of a forehead entry wound, while the larger exit wound had puked blood, brains, and bone onto the stage.

Reeder knelt and had a closer look at the man's face—no, this was not Bryson's blond, but could possibly be the attacker from the security office. He pulled back the man's shirt and jacket cuffs, both arms—no Special Forces tattoo. So this wasn't the man recorded on the Skyway Farer motel security cam.

So who *was* the man who wanted Adam Benjamin dead?

Elmore was coming over to him again. Reeder stood and met him halfway, near the bullet-pocked podium. Rogers came over and fell in at Reeder's side, two DC uniformed men huddling around the fallen Akers now.

"Thanks to the two of you," Elmore said, as if he were reporting the weather, "Adam Benjamin is alive and well."

Rogers said, "Just doing my job."

Reeder said, "Instinct kicks in. You know."

"Mr. Benjamin would very much like to thank you both person-ally."

Rogers said, "That won't be necessary," just as Reeder was saying, "No need."

"He's quite insistent."

Bohannon and Wade, from Rogers's team, were coming swiftly down an aisle. Just behind them, trench coat flapping, came DC homi-cide detective Pete Woods.

Reeder asked Elmore, "Where is Mr. Benjamin?"

"Heading back to the hotel."

"What hotel?"

"The Holiday Inn Express in Falls Church, of course."

Rogers gave Reeder a wide-eyed, you-gotta-be-kidding-me look. He shrugged.

Elmore was saying, "We can arrange a limo for you."

Detective Woods, approaching, overheard that and said, a little louder than necessary, "Mr. Reeder and Ms. Rogers won't be needing a limo tonight! We'll be having conversations with them that may last some time."

Reeder gave Elmore a shrug. "You'll have to convey our regrets."

The majordomo nodded curtly, then disappeared into the wings.

Reeder said to Woods, "Let's have a look at our dead would-be assassin."

Woods didn't argue as Reeder led the way, Rogers falling in behind the homicide detective, perhaps not eager for a closer look at the man she'd killed.

"Watch your step," Reeder said. "Little messy right over there—see it?"

Woods looked a little pale around the gills. Homicide man or not, he was still new to the job.

Reeder knelt near the corpse and Woods crouched near Reeder, who said, "This isn't the blond from the SIM card. Agreed?"

"Agreed."

"By the build, it might be the guy I mixed it up with at Bryson's, so it could also make him your uniformed officer's killer. Might even be one of the guys who murdered Chris."

Woods frowned at Reeder. "'One of the guys'?"

"Detective, Chris Bryson could handle himself—former Secret Service agent, armed, not a small man. Our failed assassin here, all by himself, could hardly incapacitate Bryson and hang him with his own belt."

Opposite them, Bohannon had squatted next to the shooter; with a latex-gloved hand, he pressed the dead man's thumb to his smartphone screen, utilizing its fingerprint ID app. A moment later, the screen displayed the results.

Bohannon said, "Thomas Louis Stanton." He scrolled through a few screens. "At first glance? A solid citizen . . . until tonight."

Rogers asked, "Prints on file because of military service?"

"Yep. Honorable discharge twenty years ago."

She frowned. "How does a 'solid citizen' turn into a political assassin?"

Bohannon gave her half a smile and said, "This app just does fingerprints."

Over the next twenty-four hours, they would surely come to know Thomas Louis Stanton inside and out. For now, though, Reeder and Rogers had hours ahead of them of police interviews, and after that FBI debriefings.

But it could be worse. It was a bad night to be a rank-and-file cop. This had been a hall filled with up to 3,500 eye witnesses, many of whom had beat it out before the boys in blue showed, though enough remained that a staggering number of names would need collecting for later interviews. And all of that news footage would have to be collected and looked at closely.

"Shit," Reeder said, aloud, something occurring to him, then turned to Rogers. "I have to call Amy and tell her I'm all right."

"Did your daughter know you were going to be at the event tonight?"

He put a hand on his forehead as if he were taking his own temperature. "No, but this is going to hit the news and is probably already all over the net. Don't you think those TV crews uploaded everything they caught right on the spot, before the cops could seize it?"

Rogers grinned. "Amy's the least of your worries."

"What do you mean?"

"Those cameras caught you throwing yourself on Adam Benjamin, ready to take another bullet for a great man. Joe Reeder, welcome back to the twenty-four-hour news cycle—you're a hero again."

"Shit," he said.

"All of us might wish at times
that we lived in a more tranquil world,
but we don't.
And if our times are difficult and perplexing,
so are they challenging and filled with opportunity."

Robert F. Kennedy,
64th Attorney General of the United States,
Senator from New York, 1965–1968.
Section 45, Grid U-33.5,
Arlington National Cemetery.

TWELVE

Patti Rogers had expected to be answering questions for hours either at Convention Hall or DC Homicide, but that changed in a hurry when—on the phone she'd just rescued from her bloody jacket—she got a call from the Director himself.

"Special Agent Rogers," came the deep rasp of a man she'd rarely spoken to, much less seen, "you need to report here to Assistant Director Fisk as soon as possible."

She swallowed. "Sir, at this juncture, this is not our investigation. Detective Peter Woods from DC Homicide is on the scene, as are several of his men."

"Put him on the phone."

She was still near the fallen Akers; Woods with Reeder and Bohannon were across the stage by the dead shooter. Uniformed men swarmed the hall, but right now the stage itself was limited to a handful of law enforcement officers—and Reeder, of course.

She summoned Woods with a flip of her fingers and he frowned but came over.

"What?"

"Not what," Rogers said. "*Who*—the Director of the Federal Bureau of Investigation."

The young cop's eyebrows went up and he took the cell and said, "Detective Peter Woods, sir."

Soon Agents Wade and Bohannon were leading Woods, Reeder, and Rogers (backed up by several uniformed men) through the wings. No sign of Benjamin and his people, who by all rights should have stayed but essentially took advantage of the confusion to leave before anything official kicked in.

They were whisked past dressing rooms, stage gear, backstage crew (herded by two uniformed cops), and out a rear door into a waiting black SUV, which the Director had apparently dispatched before Rogers had even been called. The driver, a solemn male agent she didn't recognize, gunned the vehicle and they sped away from Constitution Hall. The interior of the vehicle was almost as cold as outside—heater hadn't even had the chance to warm up yet.

An incident like this, so close to the White House, meant the entire DC area was heading into lockdown. The chance that any media could follow them was fairly remote—those in attendance were being held at the hall—and, anyway, the driver was rocketing through city streets with blue and red lights flashing.

She shared the backseat with Reeder. Detective Woods was in the front passenger seat, her guys Bohannon and Wade remaining behind at the crime scene.

Rogers phoned Anne Nichols to assemble the team in their office, then called Miggie—not an official task force member—to join them. Both already knew what had gone down, the shooting all over TV and the net.

Woods, with just a little edge, craned to ask Reeder, "So you've saved another political figure from assassination. How does that happen three times?"

Reeder said flatly, "Just lucky I guess."

Woods frowned but turned back around, as they slowed to pass security before entering the J. Edgar Hoover Building's underground garage. Rogers was not surprised to see news vans lined up out front.

"Welcome to the media shitstorm," she said to Reeder.

"And me without my umbrella."

"I don't envy you."

Reeder gave her a sideways look as they speed-bumped into the concrete catacombs. "Are you kidding? You're the one who took down a wannabe assassin. You're the star here."

Rogers said, with a shiver, "Hell, I hope not."

She had enough to contend with just for discharging her weapon, however righteous the reason—there'd be a board of inquiry and almost certainly desk duty until a ruling confirmed a justified shoot. No worries about the decision, just the time it would take away from the Bryson investigation.

Though private-citizen Reeder hadn't fired a shot, the Bureau—due to the inevitable media attention—would surely want to distance itself from him. In stopping this crime tonight, had she and Reeder lost their ability to solve a series of crimes already committed?

The SUV slowed and stopped twenty feet from a bank of elevators. Waiting there like a classy tour guide—her charcoal suit immaculate, her helmet of dark hair perfect, her mouth a thin straight line, arms folded—stood Assistant Director Margery Fisk.

They clearly rated. Not all condemned prisoners were met at the gate by their executioner.

"Fuck me," Rogers muttered under her breath.

Reeder said, "Not on the first date."

She managed a grunt of a laugh and he gave her a little supportive pat on the shoulder. After climbing out on the driver's side, she took her time coming around the vehicle, composing herself.

Reeder and Detective Woods, having gotten out on the passenger side, were already approaching the AD. To Rogers's surprise, Fisk smiled as she extended her hand to Reeder.

"Joe, good to see you," the AD said, putting her left on top as they shook, a surprisingly warm gesture. "Mr. Benjamin is very lucky you were around."

"You can take the man out of the Secret Service," he said with a small smile, "but not the Secret Service . . . you know the rest."

"I do," Fisk said.

Rogers fell in at Reeder's side, nodding to Fisk, saying, "Assistant Director."

Fisk's smile was tight but seemed genuine. "Well done, Special Agent Rogers."

"Thank you, ma'am."

The AD turned a businesslike smile onto Woods, who was beside Reeder. "Detective Woods?" she asked, extending a hand. "Thank you for coming."

Woods nodded, shook her hand and smiled back, obviously a little flattered by such attention from a high-ranking FBI official.

"Would you mind," she said pleasantly, "giving us a few moments in private?"

The young detective shrugged, perhaps too intimidated to feel offended, and walked halfway down a row of mostly empty parking places, out of earshot.

Fisk returned her gaze to Rogers. "This is the first time you've taken a life?"

"It is," Rogers said, somewhat surprised that Fisk seemed already to know that.

"How are you with it?"

"Necessary action, ma'am. I'm fine."

"You'll have to undergo counseling."

"Understood." That wasn't optional.

"Of course," Fisk said, "you'll work that in and around your duties."

That rated a *Huh?*

But Rogers just said, "Of course."

"Good. There'll be a board of inquiry, naturally, but with positive media reaction and social media trending so highly in your favor, the Director will encourage a prompt decision. After all, almost everyone in this country has seen, by now, what you did. You're a hero. In my opinion, you made the only decision you could."

"Thank you, ma'am."

"My *off the record* opinion, that is. In the meantime, I need you to keep a low profile for a while."

Rogers nodded dutifully. "If I'm to be temporarily reassigned to desk duty, might I request input into which task force member steps in for me?"

Fisk's smile actually showed some teeth. "Special Agent Rogers, I think you're quite capable of continuing to lead your task force. I would avoid fieldwork, when possible . . . but if that should prove necessary, avoid media contact. For now."

"Uh, understood, ma'am."

"Good."

Fisk turned in the direction of Woods and called, voice echoing, "Detective, if you'd join us please?"

Woods clip-clopped over and resumed his place next to Reeder.

Fisk said, "Detective Woods, thank you again for coming. We have an unusual situation in that you were already working with Rogers and Reeder on a series of related murders that may include the faked suicide of a former Secret Service agent."

"Yes, ma'am."

"And you understand that we will be taking the lead in this attempted assassination of Adam Benjamin."

His brow furrowed. "That would seem to be a DC *police* matter, ma'am."

"Not when a major political figure, on the verge of running for president, is nearly killed within yards of the White House. And not when the assassination is prevented by the actions of an FBI agent and one of our consultants."

"Excuse me," Reeder said.

Everyone looked his way.

"There's a possibility these investigations could converge. The assassination attempt and the string of murders might possibly be related."

Fisk asked, "Why do you say that?"

"Start with a .45 automatic being the weapon of choice tonight as well. And while the attempt on Benjamin's life was hardly execution-style, the use of a sound suppressor seems a professional's touch."

Fisk gave him a single, narrow-eyed nod.

He continued: "Who needs a silencer in a room that size? But a professional might have one handy and feel the silenced shot in the noisy hall could give him a few seconds before the realization of what happened kicks in."

"Making an escape," Rogers said softly, "more possible."

Reeder nodded. "To pull it off, he had to get close—but still wanted a way out of the hall."

"A possibility," Fisk granted.

"There's something that *isn't* just a possibility—before he died, Jay Akers uttered the word 'senk.' And shortly before *his* death, Bryson told his wife that he was worried about what she *thought* was 'sink.' If this isn't one case, I'm surprised."

His irritation finally showing, Woods said, "I don't care how many cases you think this is—these are DC Homicide's jurisdiction."

"No, Detective Woods," Fisk said. "The Benjamin investigation is ours—we'll keep you in the loop, work with you—but it's ours."

He frowned, a child fighting back a tantrum. "I need to interview your agent and Mr. Reeder."

"We will conduct our own interviews with our agent and our consultant, and keep you apprised. Thank you for your cooperation. We'll give you a ride back to the crime scene, where our agents Bohannon and Wade are now in charge."

Woods flushed, and seemed about to say something he shouldn't, when Rogers cut in.

"Director Fisk," she said, "I don't know how closely you're following the task force's investigation into the Bryson 'suicide,' and the murders that appear tied to it . . . but Detective Woods lost an officer when that security office got torched."

"I *am* aware of that."

"We thought it better to have him spearhead the segment of the investigation relating to the officer's murder, while we concentrate on the other shootings."

Fisk considered that, then nodded. "Makes sense to me. What do you say, Detective Woods? Does that sound reasonable?"

Woods was frowning, but he said, "It does, Director Fisk."

"Good. Why don't you head back to your crime scene and get to work with Special Agents Bohannon and Wade."

He let out air, not quite a sigh. "I will, ma'am. Thank you."

Fisk offered her hand again, and they shook.

When he was gone, Fisk said, "My apologies for conducting a meeting in a parking garage like this. But it's a longstanding Washington tradition for matters best spoken of discreetly."

The AD rode up in the elevator with them, saying only, "You'll find your task force waiting," and when they got out at that floor, Fisk stayed on—her office much higher up, in several senses.

They found the corridors as busy as if this were midday. Busier. Fire a shot anywhere near the White House, and the Washington law enforcement world scrambled.

Luke Hardesy and Anne Nichols were at their desks, drinking coffee, waiting for marching orders. But Miggie was already at work on his tablet with behaviorist Trevor Ivanek at his desk watching the computer god's progress on the wall monitor. Everyone was rather casually dressed—no ties on the men, pretty Nichols in a silk blouse and slacks—having been called from home for this session.

Rogers and Reeder took positions by the monitor.

Nichols asked, "Can I assume Jerry and Reggie are at Constitution Hall?"

Rogers said, "You can. I'm sure you know the media's version of what happened, although frankly Joe and I don't—we've been in a law enforcement bubble since it happened. But here's how it went down."

She told them, asking Reeder to pitch in here and there.

Sitting forward, Luke Hardesy asked, "Reeder, how well did you know this Akers?"

"Very well. And here's a possible connection to our double-tap case—for a couple of years, Jay Akers, Chris Bryson, and I were on presidential detail together."

The shaved head shook solemnly. "Sorry to hear about a good man going down."

"And Jay *was* a good man," Reeder said. "A good man who wanted to talk to me because he'd caught wind of something bad."

"Like Bryson had wanted to tell you something," Hardesy said. "Another possible link between investigations?"

"I'm already convinced it's one investigation."

Nichols asked, "Is that why we're here?"

Rogers said, "This is just a typical 'all hands on deck' following tonight's incident. Who knows what else will pop up around town? In the meantime, we're here."

With a slow scan of faces, Reeder said, "Are we getting anywhere at connecting our double-tap victims?"

Ivanek said, "Miggie and I've been going over every aspect of their lives. No connections so far."

"Miggie, how about the 'sink' search? Narrowing that any?"

He nodded. "To a couple of million possibilities."

Reeder gave the computer analyst a look.

"No, really," Miggie said. "We started with over a *billion* and a quarter." He shrugged. "I said this would take time."

Reeder said, "I'm afraid it's going to take more."

Miggie's eyes widened, then narrowed. "How so?"

"Before he died," Reeder said, "Akers's last word was 'senk.'"

Pin-drop silence.

Reeder went on: "He said it more than once, and I even asked if he meant 'sink.' He didn't. We can assume Mrs. Bryson heard it wrong."

Ivanek asked, "Is that a word, 'senk'? A name?"

Miggie—face in his tablet, fingers flying—said, "Give me a second . . . it *can* be a name . . . Not a word, unless it's phonetically the French word *cinq*."

Reeder asked, "How many hits for 'senk'?"

"Not quite 800,000." Miggie grinned. "But that's an improvement, anyway."

Nichols asked, "How does an attempted assassination of a presidential hopeful link up with our murder victims? Including Chris Bryson?"

"Answering that," Rogers said, "is where *we* come in."

Reeder said, "Akers also said the word 'Capitol.' I assume he meant the capitol city—Washington, DC—or the building itself. The word, depending on how you spell it, has other meanings, obviously."

Nichols said, "None that immediately resonate."

Reeder went on: "That 'capitol' and 'senk' were his two last words indicates a connection between them."

Hardesy said, "But how the hell could taking Benjamin out have anything to do with that?" He held up surrender hands. "Rhetorical question."

Frowning, Ivanek asked, "Why didn't Benjamin have Secret Service protection? And that *isn't* rhetorical."

Reeder said, "He hasn't announced his candidacy yet. It's possible he intended to do that before his speech was cut short."

The Secret Service provided protection for official candidates only, a policy that had been in place since the attempted assassination of George Wallace in 1972. Bobby Kennedy hadn't had Secret Service protection, either, when he was shot and killed in 1968.

Reeder said, "Had Benjamin announced his candidacy at that event—and my bet is he would have—any later attempts on him would become far more tricky. The Secret Service would be in place."

Nichols asked, "Out of all the potential presidential hopefuls . . . why kill Adam Benjamin? Whose idea is that?"

Ivanek opened his palms. "Any psychotic with less than a billion dollars, whose envy has run amok. Any fringe figure, right or left, who might consider a centrist a threat. Certain traditional liberal or conservative politicians might fear the loss of money that a middle-of-the-road populist might generate. Who knows, maybe forces on the left and right pooled their money to take him off the ballot before he's even on it."

Reeder said, "He's bad for business for both sides."

Miggie brought the shooter up on the monitor—on stage, gun in hand. *Not,* Rogers was thankful, *a shot of the dead man after her bullet had plowed through his brain.*

"Pulled from an audience member's posted cell phone photo," Miggie said. "Front row, I'd say." Fingers flew again. "Now, here our man is, as they say, in happier times."

A smiling head-and-shoulders shot took the screen. Sandy haired, glasses, unremarkable. *He was such a nice man,* the neighbors would say. *Quiet, nice to dogs and children.*

"Photo from the church where he was a lay minister," Miggie said. "Thomas Louis Stanton—our late shooter."

"Church," Hardesy muttered. "Jesus."

Reeder asked, "Does the media have this yet?"

"Don't think so. Bohannon sent me the name, from Constitution Hall, and I did some preliminary digging. Honorably discharged from the Army, divorced, father of two boys, who live with their mother. And you'll love this. Ohio state trooper."

All around the room, heads were shaking.

"*Former,* I should say," Miggie said. "Retired last year on disability—stage-four cancer."

Ivanek asked, "Brain cancer maybe?"

"Much as I'd like an easy explanation," Miggie said, "for a former cop turning political assassin? I can't help you. Not brain cancer—appendix."

"That's a new one," Hardesy said.

"Not new, just rare. Occurs in about one half of one percent of those diagnosed. But it's as good at killing you as any other cancer."

Reeder was studying the image on the monitor.

Rogers said to him, "What?"

No response.

Then finally he turned to her and said, "Two things."

"Start with number one."

"You're a good guy," Reeder said, looking up at Stanton's smiling image. "You have a good job. Okay, then you get divorced, which is a possibility in any marriage, but higher odds in law enforcement."

"We're still on number one?"

"Still on number one. You get dealt the cancer card. Sucks. Tragic as hell, and maybe enough to unhinge you some. But why does it make a 'good man' want to travel from Ohio to DC to shoot Adam Benjamin? Which brings us to number two."

Rogers squinted at him. "Does it?"

"Ohio is Adam Benjamin's home state. More than that, it's where our unpretentious billionaire still lives. And if Benjamin has acquired any under-the-radar enemies, what better place than Ohio to find them? Also, an Ohio enemy might hire somebody from around those parts to do this thing."

Rogers said, "Murder for hire?"

Reeder didn't answer, instead saying to Miggie, "Did you check Stanton's financials yet?"

Miggie nodded. "At first look anyway, nothing special. Checking account with about two hundred bucks in it, savings account with a couple of grand, and an IRA that hasn't seen a deposit since our ex-trooper went on disability."

Reeder said, "Keep digging to see if he was sending hate mail to Benjamin, or spouting off around town about the man. If not, then maybe it's just a case of somebody local hiring somebody local."

Ivanek said, "If so, where's the big money a job like this pays? No way this guy breaks that bad and trades everything in, including his life, for a few thousand bucks."

"He was dying," Reeder said. "The money wasn't for him, and it'll not likely be found in any domestic bank account. Safety deposit box, maybe."

A sad smile on her lovely face, Nichols said, "The money's for his boys."

"My bet," Reeder agreed. "So we need to look at the ex-wife's financials."

Hardesy laughed. "Thank you, Joe."

"What for?"

"Saving President Bennett's ass. Without that beefed-up Patriot Act of his, we'd be *weeks* trying to get warrants for this shit."

"You're welcome," Reeder said.

Miggie's fingers danced. "Be a minute," he said, barely audible.

They waited.

Then: "Money's not with the ex-wife, at least not anywhere I can touch. No trust fund for the kids that I can find. Mom's remarried, new husband makes a decent living. Nothing to write home about, but decent."

Rogers's cell vibrated. Caller ID read: WADE. She took the call.

"Boss," Wade said, "it's Clusterfuck City here. Gonna take days, even weeks, to interview everyone. A crime lab team of ours is collecting evidence. We don't even know what became of the intended target."

She said, "Sorry, I thought you knew. He's at the Holiday Inn Express in Falls Church."

"Adam Benjamin? Holiday Inn Express?"

"You better talk to Joe."

She handed her phone to Reeder, who filled Wade in on the whereabouts of Benjamin, Frank Elmore, and their so-called security staff. Then he handed the cell back to her.

Rogers told Wade, "I understand you and Bohannon will be tied up with this awhile."

"We feel like we're letting you down in the middle of something big."

"You aren't. The assassination attempt appears to tie in with our double-taps." She filled him in on that score.

When she was off the phone, Miggie said, "I ran facial rec on Stanton against the SIM card photo of our blond, but no match. Anyway, no tattoo, right?"

Reeder said, "No tattoo. So not the guy from the *Skyway Farer* video, either. Anything yet on our black cube or that anonymous building?"

"Nothing on the black cube, but maybe something on the building."

Rogers said, "Maybe?"

"'Maybe' because, weirdly enough, I've got two buildings that match the photo Bryson took."

Reeder said, "Seems like a list we could run through easy enough."

"Not from here," the computer guru said, "although they're both on the same property in an industrial park . . . on the outskirts of Charlottesville."

Rogers said to Reeder, "What the hell was your friend Chris doing in Charlottesville?"

"One way to find out."

She smirked at him. "What, drive to Charlottesville to look at two buildings in the middle of the night?"

"Or," Reeder said, "we can wait till morning when the media platoon is an army, who can clearly see that it's us."

She thought about it.

"Road trip?" she asked.

"Road trip," he said.

"Wars are . . . often the products
of conflicting intentions of decent men
who have lost the patience to negotiate."

Vance Hartke,
Senator from Indiana, 1959–1977.
Section 5, Lot 7043-A,
Arlington National Cemetery.

THIRTEEN

Joe Reeder had never harbored any sexist notions about women drivers, but tonight he might have asked Rogers to drive in any case.

The old shoulder wound from the bullet he'd taken for Bennett was really acting up. Earlier, when he'd tackled Adam Benjamin, getting him out of harm's way, Reeder had landed hard on that shoulder. He'd already taken a double dose of Patti's over-the-counter naproxen.

Anyway, she had a heavier foot than he did, and once the media was no longer an issue, the flashers had come on and she had gone for it.

They were in a Bureau car from the motor pool, since Reeder's Prius was still back at the Constitution Hall parking lot. The unmarked gray Ford Fusion was anonymous enough–looking that the camped-out media paid little or no heed when it had emerged from the underground garage.

As they headed south on snow-cleared I-95, Reeder adjusted his position in the passenger seat, trying to find a spot his shoulder liked. He hadn't said anything to Rogers and felt sure she hadn't noticed.

"How's the shoulder?" she asked.

"Like new."

"Like hell."

The woman didn't miss much. It pleased but also mildly annoyed him that she'd picked up so much from him. Not that she hadn't come equipped with formidable skills from the start.

"Too bad I'm driving," she said.

"Why's that?"

"It'd make a great drinking game, the way you've moved that seat belt around since we left."

"I spy with my little eye," Reeder said, "a big pain in the ass."

She grinned at the road, taking one hand from the wheel to flip him off in the dashboard glow.

"So that was the first time for you," he said, after a while. "Taking a life."

She nodded.

"How are you doing?"

"Fine. If I could skip the damn counseling, I would."

"Don't."

She glanced at him. "Oh?"

"It's going to hit you. Maybe when you try to sleep next, maybe in a month or two, when your guard's down."

"Joe, really. I don't relish killing that man, but the circumstances made it necessary."

"Different issue. That shooting board would clear you, even without the Director nudging them. All I'm saying is, don't blow off the counseling. And when this *does* hit, don't think less of yourself. Nothing to do with mental toughness."

". . . Does it get easier?"

"With luck, you'll never find out."

Even though I-95 was more direct than, say, veering over to I-81 and down the west side of the state, this route was usually slowed by traffic and what seemed like endless construction.

But tonight they'd gotten lucky and Rogers had made good time, only having to drive on the shoulder twice, a major victory, even with flashers going.

Off the interstate now, she wound around to Virginia 20, hurtling south toward Charlottesville. She hadn't slowed much for the two-lane, but he was fine with that—no sign of ice, just snow lining the shoulders—and he trusted Rogers implicitly. She was a hell of a driver.

Just before Charlottesville, two vehicles in the oncoming lane, less than a car-length apart, caught Reeder's attention, the rear one getting ready to pass perhaps. He figured Rogers might slow a little, but she didn't. She blew by them and he had just enough time to make out two black SUVs with tinted windows. Not a passing situation, but a two-car caravan.

"I'd say those boys were going just under the speed limit," he told her.

"Yeah? So?"

"Kind of a rarity here in *Dukes of Hazzard* country."

"Dukes of what?"

In the side mirror, the taillights of the two SUVs were barely blips in the night, then gone.

Reeder said, "Counterfeiter I busted early on told me, 'Never commit a misdemeanor while committing a felony.' We'd just tracked him down on unpaid parking tickets."

"What are you talking about?"

"Maybe nothing."

Rogers made the last turn onto the two-lane to the industrial park.

"Should be coming up on the left," she said, slowing to something less than the speed of light.

They passed a service road lined with trees. A car was parked along there, lights out, pluming smoke, condensation from the exhaust on the cold night. Reeder looked back but the row of trees blocked his view.

She turned into the industrial park. A cluster of buildings were on the right side of the road, but only two on the left, their silhouettes in the moonlight tallying with Bryson's photo of one such building. She swung into a drive that took them into a snow-covered parking lot between the pair of concrete bunker-like structures. These buildings didn't seem to get a lot of traffic, but tire tracks said someone had been here, and recently.

She shut off the engine.

He asked her, "Did you see a car parked back there?"

"Where?"

"On that service road—just sitting there in the dark. Engine running?"

"What service road?"

"Never mind."

"Joe, we can go back and check it out if you like."

He considered that. "No, just me being jumpy, I guess. I get that way after ducking bullets."

She half smirked. "Then maybe you should stop jumping into the line of fire."

"I'll try to remember that."

She opened her door and crisp cold air came in. But she glanced at him and asked, "You're sure you don't want to go back for another look?"

"What," he said, opening his own door, "and interrupt some kids playing hide the salami? Let's do what we came for."

He joined her on her side of the Fusion, a building on their left and right. There was a compact battering ram in the trunk but first he and Rogers would check the buildings out. By current rulings, they had enough probable cause and needed no warrants.

"Which one first?" she asked, patting gloved hands, her breath visible. "Joe?"

That parked motor-running car he'd seen—*what kind was it?* He'd gotten just a glance, not even a glimpse of plates . . . but was it a Nissan? An Altima, like the rental he'd seen at Bryson's office? He grabbed Rogers by the arm and threw her to the snowy cement and fell on top of her.

"What the hell?" she said, from under him. He would have explaining to do, if he was wrong; one minute from now, he would seem some aging letch or maybe paranoid over-the-hill former man of action, on edge from what had gone down at Constitution Hall.

"Joe!" she said into his coat. "Goddamnit, what—"

The two buildings exploded.

Two buildings but one big blast, the first concussion wave from the right hitting the car and shaking it like a brat before the wave from their left struck them, flopping them back against the driver's side door; they slid down as blasting heat came from both sides at once, Reeder doing his best to protect Rogers as fiery debris rained down on them.

The main blasts were over in seconds that felt much longer, and when he finally uncovered his head, orange and blue flames were dancing madly in both buildings, mirror-image conflagrations, flickering limbs reaching skyward through blown-off roofs.

He rolled off her and she sat up, leaning on her gloved palms.

"You okay?" he asked. With his ears ringing like that, he must have been shouting, but she'd be experiencing the same temporary hearing loss.

"Yeah," she said, just as loud, getting to her feet, brushing off snow and debris.

The all-encompassing sound of buildings on fire always struck Reeder as oddly similar to a rainstorm, even generating its own thunder.

Wild-eyed, she asked him, "How did you know that was going to happen? You're not a damn *building* reader."

He brushed himself off. "I didn't know, and I could have been wrong, and God knows how I would have explained jumping you like that. But it came to me that car I saw could've been the Nissan at Bryson's office that night."

"The missing rental?"

He nodded. "The BOLO we sent out didn't turn it up, so he must have switched plates."

"You think he made us and waited till we were close before hitting a detonator?"

"I do. Or else the explosives had been set shortly before we got here, and we were just in the wrong place at the right time."

But halfway through that she stopped looking at him, in fact staring past him, and he was about to turn and see for himself when she took off at a dead run for the building on their left.

They'd both survived twin explosions, and now she was running into one of the burning buildings? Was she crazy? Was he crazy, too?

Because he found himself instinctively dashing right behind her . . .

Covering his mouth and nose with his bent, Burberry-clad arm, he followed her through what was left of glass doors that were only a scorched framework with not even the shattered remains of their panes in sight. Smoke rushed to greet them as they stepped into a furnace at least equal to the explosion's heat waves.

While what remained of the post-blast concrete structure itself wouldn't burn, plenty of flammable material had been in here, judging from the flames licking all around them. Despite thickening smoke, he could make out the twisted remains of a sort of lab-cum-machine shop. That meant chemicals in here might any moment ignite into secondary explosions; he shoved that thought away as he went to Rogers's side, just a few feet into the hellish sauna that had been a building.

Covering her face with her coat sleeve, Rogers knelt over a body on the floor. If it hadn't been near the exploded doorway, neither of them would have noticed it from the parking lot. The blackened thing that had been a person lay on its stomach, and the only way Reeder could tell this had been a male was the body's size and its work boots.

Rogers gripped a hand under one arm of the charred victim, and Reeder grabbed the other one by the forearm. The blackened limb came off at the elbow. That sent both Reeder and Rogers off balance, almost falling, but then Reeder discarded the limb and got a better hold on the body's shoulder and dragged the remains well out into the middle of the parking lot, next to the Fusion, where an oasis of air existed between where plumes of black and gray smoke surged into the sky and met each other, creating a terrible roiling storm cloud that held no moisture at all. Both Rogers and Reeder were coughing now, and the corpse fell from their grasp, onto its side.

Reeder looked toward the service road, but the tree line blocked his view—not that the Nissan was likely still around.

Breathing hard, intermittently coughing, Rogers plopped down, sitting in the snow, her back against the driver's side door. Reeder's own breathing was labored, too, smoke mingling with cold air to burn his lungs.

Reeder asked, "What were you thinking?"

"I knew he was probably dead, but with him there, on the floor . . . just inside the door? Had to try. If you'd seen him first, you'd have done the same thing."

"Hell I would."

"Oh, you didn't follow *me* in there?"

"You weren't dead. Yet." His breath was beginning to slow. "Those two SUVs? Guys in them set the bombs. Their leader was in that Nissan, giving them time to get well away before he detonated the charges."

"Then . . . then we showed up."

"If he recognized me as we drove past—this was likely our blond perp—he knew he'd scored a bonus round. If you and I hadn't chatted a while in the car, we'd have already been inside when he hit the detonator."

"We . . . we'd have been . . . scattered all over this parking lot . . . with the rest of the debris."

Sirens sang their distant song. This was the boonies, but somebody had seen the flames rising into the sky, and/or heard the big boom.

Their breathing slowing, the air clearing some, the smoke on its upward trajectory, the two got up and had a look at their rescued corpse. Only the figure's back was charred black, the front of him appearing relatively normal—his expression almost serene, as if he'd slept through the other side of him getting cooked.

"Dead before the explosion," Rogers said.

Reeder pointed out the two punctures in the blackened back of his neck—barely visible but the indentations were there, all right.

"Double-tapped," Rogers said.

Reeder nodded and looked back toward the trees on the other side of which was the service road. Just then flames illuminated something over that way, and glass winked and blinked at him.

A sniper scope.

"Gun!" he said, and then came the muzzle flash.

They both hit the snowy cement, sending up puffs of white, then each scrambled around behind the car, Reeder around front, Rogers around back. The shooter had seen that action through his scope, because two more rounds slammed into the car, and then another took the back left tire, which hissed as if a villain had come on stage, and hadn't he?

Each sat with their backs to the passenger side of the Fusion. Breathing hard again, Reeder said, "You got extra magazines?"

"Yeah. Two."

"Good. Keep him busy."

"What do you mean, keep him busy?"

"Do it."

From around the rear of the car, Rogers threw shots into the line of trees. She had a handgun and the shooter had a rifle and the advantage of firepower and distance were his. But she kept it up, the sharp cracks of her Glock rising over the rumbling murmur of the burning buildings.

She was shooting as Reeder took off, very low, right toward the facing fires, running between them and skirting around the building at left and staying parallel to it. He couldn't remember the last time he'd run on snow. He was trying to be careful in the dark, trying not to trip over any chunks of debris, and was grateful for the minimal moonlight and even fire glow, assuming it didn't give him away.

As he reached where the building ended and concrete parking lot yawned to a strip of snowy landscape with the line of trees waiting, he climbed out of his Burberry and left it behind, his dark suit better suited for his purpose.

With the night alternating pops of the Glock and resonant reports from the rifle, Reeder headed over to where the service road curved around behind the buildings, the line of trees ending where that curve began. As the shooter exchanged shots with Rogers, the rifle's scope would not be swung way the hell over here. Or so Reeder told himself as he kept very low on the asphalt, as low as possible and still run.

Any other Tuesday night, this industrial park would be all but silent. An occasional car would thrum by, the odd owl might hoot, tree leaves might rustle with wind; but tonight was a cacophony of howling flames, screaming sirens, crunching snow, all punctuated by the bellows of his own labored breathing.

Reeder wanted to surprise the shooter, and if he made it to that stand of trees, he just might do that. One small detail, though: he was unarmed. He rarely carried a gun and his extending baton was back in his car at Constitution Hall, where he'd left the weapon before passing through metal detectors and security.

And in the midst of his unarmed pursuit of a man with a rifle, it came to him: *the would-be assassin had gotten a .45 into the event! How the hell had he managed that?*

That thought he filed away for later use, should he survive this lopsided encounter.

But as he reached the row of trees lining the service road, he tucked himself behind the nearest one, peeking around to see what his options were . . .

. . . and the guy, all in black, including a stocking cap (blond under there, he'd bet), was leaving his position between trees to jog to the parked Nissan. With sirens growing ever louder, the guy was bailing, just getting the hell out.

That was a kind of break, because the unarmed Reeder could pursue the shooter, since a rifle was a poor weapon to try to use on the move. With some luck he could come up behind him and take the man down; but the black-clad figure heard Reeder's running steps in back of him, glanced over his shoulder, and kept going, even faster.

Reeder summoned more speed somehow and was closing the distance when the shooter reached the car, spun and raised the rifle to his shoulder like a hunter who just spotted a very stupid deer.

The night-shattering report was in his ears as Reeder dove for the asphalt, then rolled onto snowy ground and scrambled into the trees, ducking behind the nearest one, which took a shot meant for him, spewing fragmented bark and splintered wood.

When Reeder eased out for a look, red brake lights signaled the Nissan's hesitation just before the vehicle turned onto the road, and was gone.

For perhaps thirty seconds, Reeder—his shoulder screaming louder than the sirens—leaned forward with his hands on the knees of legs whose muscles were burning with an intensity to rival the buildings, and he breathed slowly, slowly, slowly, trying not to die.

Rogers came trotting up through the trees. "And you gave *me* shit for trying to save somebody in a burning building?"

"You can't . . . can't . . . save . . . a . . . corpse."

"Yeah, but I didn't know it was a corpse. And you knew that was a guy with a rifle. You aren't armed, are you?"

He stood erect. Shook his head.

She came over and took his arm and squeezed. "You okay?"

"Let me ask you something," Reeder said.

"What?"

"Metal detectors, security people, how did our ex–Ohio state trooper get into Constitution Hall?"

"This came to you now?"

"Just now."

Her eyebrows lifted as her breath smoked. "Well, I imagine Bohannon and Wade are all over that. We can check with them. But let's deal with this first."

Walking between trees, Rogers supported Reeder by the arm, and back across the snowy ground and then snowy cement to where fire trucks and police cars were parading into the lot.

Rogers had her cell out. "I'll make sure Bohannon and Wade are as smart as you are, and then I'll let Miggie know what happened here."

While she did that, Reeder went over to speak to the first uniformed policeman on site. He still had the FBI consultant's ID in his billfold from last year, and he hoped that would suffice.

The cop climbing from the first squad car was well scrubbed and wore a navy-blue winter jacket with a Charlottesville badge on the left and "CHANEY" on a patch on the right.

As Reeder approached, the young cop's eyes grew wide and his steamy breath came more quickly.

"You're Joe Reeder!" he said, amazed, extending his hand.

As gloved hands shook, Reeder thought, *About damn time this hero crap paid off.*

"It's an honor, Mr. Reeder."

Reeder nodded. "Officer Chaney. First name?"

"Tim, sir."

"Tim," Reeder said, jerking a thumb toward the destruction around him. "You've arrived in the middle of an incident relating to a federal investigation. It's going to be a very long night for all of us. But first we need a BOLO out on a Nissan Altima. And I have plates for you."

As he continued to fill Chaney in, firefighters were hard at it, spraying down the twin blazes. The fiftyish chief—an obvious veteran, cool and in command—supervised and quickly called for reinforcements. EMTs were putting the corpse on a stretcher, with no pretense of trying to save an obviously dead body. Rogers was with them, getting pictures of the deceased with her cell.

"You need your detectives out here, Tim," Reeder advised the young uniform. "The FBI will be handling the investigation, but your people will be in on it. This is arson and murder, for starters."

The kid was doing a good job tamping down the celebrity worship. He said, "Yes, sir," and called dispatch on his shoulder radio.

Her pictures taken, and seeing Reeder was no longer talking to the cop, Rogers headed back over, shaking her head.

"What?" he asked.

"Bohannon and Wade had the same thought you did, only about four hours ago. They've been watching security video."

"Lucky them."

"Not a single damn frame of Stanton coming through the metal detectors."

Reeder thought about that, briefly. "If he didn't come in the front, then he came in the back."

She nodded. "Inside job, then."

"Was the security a mix of Constitution Hall's own people and Benjamin's?"

"Yes, but mostly Benjamin's." She frowned. "Did one of them let somebody in to take out their own boss?"

"That's a good solid maybe," Reeder said. "Nasty as that is, at least we have somewhere to start."

Rogers's cell phone vibrated in her hand. She looked at the caller ID and put it on speaker so Reeder could hear.

She said, "What do you have, Miggie?"

"Like to know why those two buildings blew?"

"We're on the scene, standing in the glow of two fires, and *you* know why the buildings blew?"

"I do," he said with a smile in his voice. "We got lab results on Bryson's clothes. Either of you ever hear of something called Senkstone?"

She gave Reeder a raised eyebrow look.

He said, "That's *s-e-n-k* Senkstone?"

"Surely is," Miggie said. His voice was crisp and confident coming from the tiny cell speaker. "Five years ago, Senkstone was a failed plastic explosive—real next-gen stuff, but unstable as hell. So the company responsible shut down. Well, there were traces of the stuff on Bryson's clothes."

"Judging by the fires around us," Rogers said, "it may *still* be unstable."

"More likely," Reeder said, leaning in for Miggie to hear, "someone figured out how to stabilize it, and for some as yet unknown reason, decided to cover up that discovery."

Rogers said, "I'm sending you some pictures, Miggie. See if you can ID the guy before we get back."

"Can you send me his prints?"

"Can't. Burned off."

She sent the pics and ended the call. Then she looked at Reeder and said, "So this is what date night is like with Joe Reeder, huh?"

"Now you know why my ex divorced me," he said.

She shrugged. "At least it's not boring."

"Those who make peaceful revolution impossible
will make violent revolution inevitable."

John Fitzgerald Kennedy,
35th President of the United States of America,
Senator and Representative
from the Commonwealth of Massachusetts,
1947–1960.
Section 45, Grid U-35, Arlington National Cemetery.

FOURTEEN

Dawn arrived with them as they hit DC, the sun making picture-perfect postcards of the Capitol and its majestic neighbors. Rogers, behind the wheel, thought about nudging Reeder awake, but decided against it, though she knew he had a sentimental streak for the city and its history.

After a long night into wee-hours morning, dealing with efficient but dogged local cops, she'd caught an hour's catnap while Reeder spelled her; snoozing in the passenger seat, arms folded, he seemed to have finally found a comfortable compromise between his sore shoulder and the seat belt.

He asked from behind closed eyes, "Who knew we were going to Charlottesville?"

"We made the decision in the conference room, remember," she said, "and left from there."

His eyes remained closed. "So most of the task force team knew . . . including Miggie."

"Right. Excluding Bohannon and Wade, over at Constitution Hall."

He opened his eyes, tasted his mouth, didn't like it, straightened, grimaced, readjusted his seat belt, asked, "What about the motor pool guy?"

"I signed out the car without a destination."

"That narrows the suspect field by one, anyway."

"You think we were set up?"

"You don't? Our best lead, so far, blows up in our face, and not metaphorically. You can't think that's a coincidence."

She was a few blocks from the Hoover Building. "I don't, but I trust my team. I vetted them personally."

He gave her a sideways glance. "You and I have less than spotless records in that regard."

Rogers didn't need to be reminded that the Supreme Court task force had included a betrayer.

"I was very damn careful," she said, "when I put this team together."

"You didn't select Detective Woods," Reeder said.

"He's not one of us."

"In a way he is."

"But Woods wasn't around when we decided to go to Charlottes-ville."

He shrugged. "Maybe somebody on the team filled him in about our road trip. Maybe somebody called Bohannon and Wade, just keeping them up to speed, and then *they* told Woods. We need to check, first opportunity."

"All right."

"And even if Woods *didn't* know about Charlottesville, what do we know about the man? Just that he's new, was assigned the Bryson investigation, initially bobbled it, and then was on the scene right away at the security office break-in."

"You might be reaching, Joe."

"Probably am. But just the same, let's have Miggie check him out—discreetly."

"Then you *do* trust Miggie?"

"Yeah, I do."

"Even though he sent us to a couple of buildings that exploded in our laps?"

Half a grin cracked his placid mask. "You're starting to sound like me."

"Paranoid you mean?"

"Patti," he said, "if after all we've been through together, you *aren't* paranoid? You're just not trying."

She laughed. "Okay, you've made your point. But looking at our team, and its extended family? It's hardly the only possibility."

"I'm listening."

"Miggie says whoever removed Bryson from the equation had skills enough to turn on the GPS on that burner phone, and track him with it, with your friend none the wiser."

He gave her a sharp look. "Then they weren't *following* Chris—they were *ahead* of him."

She nodded. "I think we're up against some seriously professional big-leaguers who we need to get a bead on, before we start accusing our own."

He thought about that.

Then he said, "Consider me on the same page."

She smiled, trying not to look too proud of herself.

"But, Patti, let's still be careful about what we say in front of our people . . . till we know who your big-leaguers are."

The number of media vehicles outside the J. Edgar Hoover Building had tripled by the time Rogers pulled into the underground garage. Some were waiting on foot next to the ramp, catching Rogers and Reeder arriving on camera; but uniformed officers kept the reporters and camera crews back and out of the garage.

Upstairs in the Special Situations Task Force bullpen, she and Reeder found every desk vacant but for the one that had recently been assigned to Miggie. Before they'd left for Charlottesville, Rogers had encouraged her team to work for another hour and then go home for some rest and cleanup; it would be late morning before they'd be back in.

As for their Latino computer expert, he had obviously been glued to his chair all night, no doubt mainlining free-trade Sumatran, at least judging by the way his fingers were still flying at the virtual keyboard.

Reeder went right to him and pulled over chairs for himself and Rogers.

He said to Miggie, "Once upon a time there was something called Senkstone . . . do you know the rest of the story?"

Miggie grinned, obviously ready to be asked. "Okay if I skip the fairy-tale framework and stick to the facts, Mr. Reeder? 'Cause there's no happily ever after."

"Make it 'Joe.' A coffee guy like you oughta be able to remember that."

Another grin. "Let's start with the SIM card pic of that black what's-it. I'm pretty sure Senkstone, Senk for short, is what our solid-black Rubik's Cube consisted of. Now, from the outset you need to understand something—*none of the net hits we got on 'senk' referred to any kind of explosive. Not one.*"

Reeder's smile was faint but there. "So how is it you found out that's what it was?"

"I'll get to that. But next let's look at Chris Bryson and Jay Akers—two smart guys who used to be in the Secret Service, both of whom had long since developed a good, experienced feel for big-time dangerous."

"Fair statement."

"*Both* of them are concerned about Senk. Both of them got recently made *dead*—the first after expressing concern about Senk to his wife, the other killed on the job, but making Senk one of his last words."

Rogers asked, "What do we make of that?"

"We come up with two smart guys who mention a word that refers to something that, I think we can safely extrapolate, both of them considered incredibly dangerous."

Reeder said, "Let's so extrapolate."

"Fine," Miggie said, sitting forward, "but this incredibly dangerous thing called Senk doesn't exist . . . at least, not if you ask the net about it."

"Everything that exists is on the net."

"Right, Joe. That's why I started searching places that *don't* exist."

"Miggie," Rogers said, half smiling, "maybe you need to knock off for a while. Catch some sleep like the other humans."

He waved her off. "Joe . . . Patti . . . there are entire networks not open to the public: the Silk Road for illegal drugs, the Armory for guns, dozens of others on the Dark Web. Nucleus, Agora, a slew of 'em used for all kinds of illegal activities."

Reeder said, "And that's where you found out about Senkstone."

"Not quite. I found *rumors* of a compound that was said to be the next generation of plastic explosives . . . but at first it was like a sea creature said to inhabit a certain loch in Scotland—lots of talk, no proof. Then, at the Armory site, I found a chat room where guys were talking about how cool this compound would be if it *did* exist."

"What would make it 'cool' to a chat room like that?"

The lightness went out of Miggie's tone: "For starters, it could be made into *anything.*"

"Molded," Rogers said, "like plastic explosives?"

"No," Miggie said. He tapped his desk. "I could use Senk to make this desk or that tablet or *anything* in this office. The chairs you're sitting on could be fashioned from this explosive material, and you'd never know it . . . till it went off." Miggie's eyebrows went up, then down. "Well, actually, you still wouldn't know, because you'd be dead."

Reeder's brow furrowed. "Sounds like a geek fantasy. How could that even be possible?"

"Because," Miggie said, "you could theoretically put liquid Senk into a 3-D printer and just 'print' yourself a desk, a chair, *whatever,* and it would also be a bomb. A very lethal one."

"How lethal?"

"A pound of the stuff would take out a three-story building."

Reeder and Rogers exchanged slow glances.

"And," Miggie was saying, "because Senk was deemed unstable, and never went to market, there are no dogs trained to sniff it. Airport-style puffer machines don't work on it. It's plastic, so metal detectors won't pick it up. There's just no good way to know for sure what it is you're sitting on."

Rogers shifted in her chair. "If this Senk stuff got out into the world," she said, feeling a little sick, "it'd make terrorists unstoppable."

Miggie just nodded.

"But you said it was unstable," Reeder said, "and research was shut down . . . ?"

The computer expert's excitement, at sharing what he'd discovered, had vanished. He was coldly serious now, even somber.

He said, "After I left the Armory site, I got into some secure DOD files . . ."

"*What?*" Rogers said.

". . . which might, technically, be above my clearance and pay grade."

"You hacked the Department of Defense?"

Miggie shrugged, smiled sheepishly, but Reeder gave him a grin and a nod and said, "Good man."

Rogers knew that Miggie's actions could come back on her, but—like Reeder—she cared more at the moment about moving forward than worrying about trifling repercussions, like losing her job or going to prison.

She asked, "What did you find?"

Very quietly, Miggie said, "A company called Senkian Chemicals developed Senkstone eight years ago, on a DOD contract, working on it for three years and a few months. Five years ago, the DOD shut down Senkian's research when an explosion killed three employees, including one of the company's main partners."

"If they were shut down five years ago," Rogers said, "why is Senk a topic of discussion now? Even if it's just limited to the Dark Web."

Miggie said, "For a year after the Pentagon shut them down, Senkian was in limbo. The company was built strictly around that one area of research—this new breed of explosive. Then, four years ago, an obscure firm called Chemical Solutions, Inc., bought Senkian out."

Reeder frowned. "And the DOD didn't stop it?"

Miggie nodded. "Why that's the case, I haven't found out yet—it's all very hush-hush. Payoff to someone high up to sign off, maybe. An elaborate black op, possibly. Anyway, after that, Senkian dropped off everybody's radar."

"Absorbed," Reeder said, "into Chemical Solutions."

Rogers asked, "What do we know about Chemical Solutions? What's the ownership?"

"That's just it," Miggie said, with a shrug. "They're a shell within a shell within a shell—if the trail has an end, I haven't found it yet."

Reeder asked, "A shell that owns the two buildings that blew up in Charlottesville?"

"No—that's a company called Barmore Holdings. Who and what that is, I don't know yet."

"Any sign of Barmore Holdings in the ownership chain of Chemical Solutions?"

Miggie shook his head. "Not that I've found. Haven't tracked down the actual owners of *any* of these companies, but this kind of entity is created to protect the anonymity of owners. These aren't exactly publicly held companies. I know it's a familiar refrain I'm singing, guys, but it's going to take time. I could have a team on this for months, and it would still take time. Doing it by myself, it's slow going."

"Stick with it," Rogers said. That had been a lot to absorb, and in truth she hadn't absorbed it yet. But she pressed on. "Anything else, Mig?"

"Yeah," he said, and turned to Reeder and said, "Your instincts were right about our friendly neighborhood would-be assassin, Thomas Stanton."

"How so?"

"Stanton's sons have Cayman Islands trust funds—each with one hundred K in them. Opened two days ago."

"By whom?"

"That's still murky," Miggie said. "These people clearly don't want to be found out. Let's face it, they were paying for an assassination."

"Keep an eye on those accounts," Reeder said. "Since Stanton failed, maybe whoever paid him will try to renege. Might provide a path."

Rogers said, "How about the body Joe and I hauled out of that building? Any luck with facial recognition?"

"Yes!" He summoned a front-on mug shot–type photo on his tablet screen of a man Roger immediately recognized as their half-charred, all-dead rescue. "Our latest double-tap is one Lester Blake."

Leaning in for a look, Reeder asked, "Did he work for Barmore? Or whatever the business in those buildings was calling itself?"

"No, surprisingly. Actually, Lester Blake was employed in the maintenance department at the Capitol."

"The *US* Capitol?"

"The one and only."

"Maintenance," Rogers said, frowning. "A janitor?"

"Limited information on that so far. But I'd say, probably, yes."

Reeder said, "Jay Akers's last words weren't limited to 'Senk'—he also said 'Capitol.' And now a Capitol Hill maintenance man winds up dead in a building that exploded *after* he was killed? A building that may have been a site of manufacture for a highly dangerous, impossible-to-find plastic explosive?"

Rogers said, "Sounds like we better get over to the Capitol and find somebody to talk to."

Reeder was already on his feet.

She said to Miggie, "While we're gone, we need you to run a discreet background check on Detective Woods."

"Oh, that's already done," Miggie said. "You have to multitask when you're running these searches, or you'll go gonzo waiting."

"What do you have?"

"Detective Peter Arthur Woods," Miggie read. "BS in criminal justice from Virginia Commonwealth, high marks, spotless record, citations, youngest on DC PD to make detective in twenty-five years. Seems like a really good guy."

"So," Reeder reminded him, "did Thomas Stanton."

Miggie shrugged. "I'll dig deeper."

Rogers said, "Incredible job all around, Miggie. Uh, did Lester Blake have a family?"

"Wife and three kids."

She sighed. "I'll have Hardesy and Nichols make the survivor visit. While Reeder and I go over to the Hill, make the same level search on Blake that you gave Stanton—okay?"

"No problem."

"But, Miggie—when did you sleep last?"

". . . Day or two ago?"

"Go take a nap on that nice couch in your office. That's an order."

Miggie's expression was just a little mocking. "Technically, I'm just helping out here. You're not my boss, you know."

"Then it's not an order. It's an earnest request from a caring friend."

"Now you're making me sick."

"Then maybe you better lie down."

In the hallway, Rogers and Reeder ran into AD Fisk, still in yesterday's apparel, meaning she'd been here all night as well, though she looked typically perfect. The AD had been on her way to the Special Situations bullpen, having been alerted that Rogers was back in the building.

After a quick update from Rogers, Fisk said, "I'll call ahead and set up a meeting for you and Joe with the chief of the Capitol police. I'm going to make it for this afternoon, so the two of you can go catch some sleep. But first, there's something I need Joe to do."

Reeder frowned a little. "What would that be?"

"I've been dealing directly with the media, under the guidance of our top PR officer, of course."

"Okay."

"But here's the thing—I can protect our agents, to some extent, but you're a consultant, Joe—not technically an employee—and there's only so much I can do to keep the press away from you."

He chuckled. "Thanks, but I can handle myself."

"I know you can. But the reporters did not get the chance to quiz you after the Constitution Hall incident. I spoke to a large group outside the building, not long ago, and they're already asking questions about Charlottesville—the local police there seem competent enough, but haven't exactly been discreet."

"We drove in the building," Reeder said, "we'll drive out the building."

"I prefer you wouldn't. That same group is waiting now in the press room. I indicated I'd ask you if you were willing to talk to them."

Reeder's eyes and nostrils flared like a rearing horse's. "A press conference?"

"That sounds more formal than I mean it to."

"Director Fisk," he said, "as a dollar-a-year man, I reserve the right to pick and choose my assignments."

"Joe, you and Special Agent Rogers are running our most important current FBI investigation. The media's going to dog your heels and impede that investigation at every turn, unless you get out ahead of it."

He turned to Rogers, who said, "You're on your own. I can't talk to the media before I deal with a shooting board. Two shooting boards, now."

Fisk said, "She's correct, Joe."

"Okay," he sighed. "I don't suppose you could find me a shaver, safety or electric, and somewhere I can throw some water on my face? Unless you enjoy having somebody who looks like a homeless guy representing the Bureau."

"Give me your sizes," Fisk said with a smile, "and I'll get you fresh clothes as well."

"You're a full-service operation, I'll give you that."

All of that was done, and quickly. Rogers took advantage of freshening up, too, and she had extra clothes in her office closet. As she'd pointedly told Reeder, she would not be taking questions, but would have eyes and cameras on her.

Soon she, Reeder, and Fisk were in a room the size of the task force bullpen, filled with chairs, all taken by reporters who looked as harried and sleep-deprived as Rogers felt, with TV cameras along the side walls and in back.

The AD introduced Reeder, then joined Rogers behind him at his podium. When Reeder stepped to the microphone, Rogers half expected the press to leap to their feet and frantically pelt him with questions. They leapt to their feet, all right, but what they gave him was applause.

"Thank you," he said, looking surprised and frankly humbled, and said, "I'll take a few questions."

Rogers smiled. He knew how to silence their applause. They resumed their seats and hands shot up.

Reeder pointed.

"Mr. Reeder," a Fox News reporter asked, "some years ago you took a bullet for your president. Last year, you saved the life of the Chief Justice of the Supreme Court. Now you've prevented the assassination of a possible candidate for the presidency. That's an impressive trifecta."

Some laughter.

"Would you care to comment?"

Reeder said, "I prefer to call it a hat trick. It depresses me to think I made a trifecta and didn't put any money down."

More laughter.

"Frankly," Reeder said, in the affable yet unreadable manner he reserved for the media, "I didn't prevent an assassination last night. I played a secondary role, but my friend and associate, Special Agent Patti Rogers, really prevented the tragedy through her quick-thinking action. And, no, you can't talk to her, because there are internal FBI procedures that must be addressed first."

No laughter at all.

"In the case of President Bennett, I was doing my job. As for the Chief Justice, I was working at the time as a consultant with the FBI . . . hired through my ABC Security, if I might inject a brief commercial message . . . so that was doing my job as well. Last night, I was attending a political rally as a private citizen, and I also did my job, as any citizen would—I saw someone in trouble and tried to help. And really, that's all I'd like to say about it at this time. I've been up for some hours and, in fact, I'm pretty sure I'm hallucinating this press conference. Thank you."

He began to step away from the podium and a woman from MSNBC called out: "Mr. Reeder, is it true you're working with the FBI on another case?"

He returned to the mic. "I'm working with the FBI as a consultant on a matter, yes."

"Could you elaborate?"

"No."

Another reporter asked, "Were you in Charlottesville at the site of an industrial explosion last night?"

"Yes."

"Is that part of the FBI investigation you're attached to as a consultant?"

"I was at the scene in my consultant role. Now if you don't mind—"

A voice called out, "Are you a supporter of Adam Benjamin's assumed bid for the presidency?"

"My politics are private. I made the mistake of going public with political opinions, once, and decided never again."

That got a few laughs, particularly from older members of the press.

Another shouted question: "Mr. Reeder, you were right there, on that stage—anyone watching could easily take that as support for Mr. Benjamin."

"I was there because I was invited. I was interested in hearing what Adam Benjamin had to say. But it's not my practice to endorse candidates for office."

From the back came: "Do you think your implied support played a role in Benjamin's surge in the presidential polls?"

"I wasn't aware of any such surge. I was busy last night."

Rogers was also unaware of that. Of course, she'd been busy, too . . .

"Yes," the reporter said. "Polls have Benjamin pulling even with all the major potential Republican candidates and only a few percentage points behind President Harrison."

"Meaning no disrespect," Reeder said, "these political matters are not of much interest to me right now. My friend Jay Akers, a former Secret Service agent, a good man, was killed last night. My thoughts, like my prayers, are with his family during this terrible loss."

Apparently unmoved, another reporter called out: "Do you think Mr. Benjamin will announce his candidacy at his press conference?"

"I didn't even know he was holding a press conference."

"Yes, on the Capitol steps this afternoon."

Finally Fisk stepped in, Reeder stepped back, and the Assistant Director said, "Thank you, everyone. That's all for today."

Reeder gave the reporters a nod and went out. Rogers followed.

As they walked quickly down the corridor, Rogers said, "You did fine. What's the idea of making me out a hero?"

"You are one. Anyway, maybe it'll get some of the heat off me."

They went their separate ways, to go home and get a few hours sleep.

Looked like date night with Joe Reeder was finally over. With more fun soon to begin.

"Those who expect to reap
the blessings of freedom
must, like men,
undergo the fatigue of supporting it."

Thomas Paine

FIFTEEN

Walking with Rogers along First Street SE, the Capitol on their left, their breaths sending smoke signals, Joe Reeder looked up at the dome and wondered how much longer the scaffolding would be part of the view. The dome was cast iron, so fixes didn't happen overnight, and of course cosmetic work would follow. The 2014 renovation had run over schedule and he assumed—relentless as the winter had been—this one would, too.

"What are you thinking, Joe?"

"That we finally have a connection between victims, though it's goddamn vague."

"A maintenance man from the Capitol and a congressional aide."

"Right. Murdered months apart, in what seems to be the same series of crimes."

Rogers nodded. She was in her gray peacoat. "No mistaking it for serial killing now, not with attempted political assassination and arson in the mix."

Reeder gestured to the imposing building they were approaching. "But these two victims are tied to the Capitol, where our others—librarian, accountant, transvestite—aren't."

"Don't forget our factory supervisor."

Reeder's gloved hands were in his Burberry pockets. "I haven't. William Robertson. He provides a possible tie to the exploded buildings where our maintenance guy was dumped. An operation like that can always use a good factory supervisor."

"Joe, Robertson already worked at a manufacturing plant in Bowie, Maryland. And he was hardly moonlighting at a shop almost three hours away."

"Rough commute," Reeder admitted.

Rogers, thinking, mused, "Of course that plant in Bowie might be related somehow to the Charlottesville shops . . ."

They made the turn onto the wide sidewalk that led up to the Capitol's east front. Coming toward him was a very pleasant sight: his daughter Amy, in a navy-blue parka in keeping with her Georgetown school colors, walking head down, in conversation with a distinguished-looking fifty-something blonde, Senator Diane Trempe Hackbarth. Reeder had never met the attractive congresswoman, but she was a familiar face from TV.

His daughter glanced up, beamed upon seeing him, and came over quickly and gave him a hug and a kiss on the cheek. She gave Rogers a hug, too—they weren't close but had become friendly after the dramatic events of last year.

Amy introduced them both to Senator Hackbarth.

"An honor to meet you, Mr. Reeder," the senator said, smiling warmly, shaking his hand. "I admit to being a fan . . . although I assure you that your daughter has never played upon that weakness."

"An honor here, too, Senator. Amy seems to really enjoy working with you."

Another warm smile from the senator, whose cheeks were probably rosy even when the wind chill wasn't below freezing. "Amy's been fairly successful in not bragging you up too much . . . until just recently. You're making a noticeable habit out of this hero business."

"Not my intention, I assure you. Anyway, this Benjamin thing, my partner Special Agent Rogers was the real hero."

Rogers suddenly had rosy cheeks, too.

Amy said to her, "Partner? Are you and Dad working together again?"

"Yes, he's consulting with my task force."

Amy knew not to ask anything further, saying, "Sounds like you're the boss. Good luck getting him to do what you want."

"Tell me about it."

His daughter turned to him. "Have you heard from Mom?"

"Not for a few days."

Her smile was gently mocking. "Well, she's probably trying to figure out what to say to you."

"Oh?"

"She's very proud. And truly furious . . . Sorry to air our mildly dirty laundry in front of you, Senator."

Hackbarth said, "I can understand your mother's mixed emotions." She turned a faintly amused smile on him. "If you were *my* husband . . . even my *ex*-husband . . . we'd be discussing your propensity to jump in front of bullets."

Reeder grinned. "Amy's mother and I have had that discussion."

"But speaking not as a hypothetical wife, ex or otherwise, rather as United States Senator . . . I am grateful for your bravery, Mr. Reeder."

"Make it Joe, please. And thanks."

"Dad," Amy said, uncharacteristically bubbly, "Senator Hackbarth just invited me to be her guest at the State of the Union speech—did you ever hear anything more cool?"

"Short of this weather we're crazily out talking in? No. Thank you, Senator, that's generous."

"You have a very intelligent daughter, Joe, who works hard."

"Great to hear," Reeder said. "But credit her mother."

Amy gave him an amused smile. "If you're expecting me to report that remark back to Mom . . . I will."

He smiled back at her, then said to the senator, "You're on your way somewhere and so are we. We'd better get going before we all freeze into just so many more DC statues."

Everybody laughed a little—politely, he thought—and they made their good-byes, he and Rogers repeating their gloved hand-shakes with the senator, then going their separate ways.

Reeder and the FBI agent took the stairs down to the lower entrance where all visitors passed through security, beyond which a dark-blue-uniformed Capitol Police officer waited to walk them through the labyrinth of corridors to the chief's office. Wordlessly the officer led them through a small reception area with a currently unmanned reception desk and a handful of empty chairs, and right up to the frosted-glass door, where he knocked twice.

This was a modest satellite office of the chief's—the main HQ of Capitol PD was over on D Street NE—reserved for meetings like the one AD Fisk had scheduled for them.

"Come," a voice within said, and the officer opened the door for them, giving them a nod as crisp as his dark-blue tie; when Reeder and Rogers were inside, their escort pulled the door shut behind him.

"Chief Ackley," Rogers said with her own crisp nod. "Special Agent Rogers. This is—"

But the big man at the desk in the small, nondescript inner office was already on his feet and coming around. "How the hell are you, Peep?"

"Old and hurting, Bob," Reeder said with a grin, as the two men shook hands. "But then you know the feeling."

Chief Robert Ackley, in uniform from badge to dark-blue tie, the pepper of his black hair heavily salted, was around Reeder's age but looked older, the price of decades of tough, challenging police work.

The chief got behind his desk again, and Reeder and Rogers took two of a trio of waiting visitor chairs.

Before they got to it, Reeder asked about Ackley's wife, Margie, who'd been fighting breast cancer. Ackley said everything was fine now.

"We just try to find a way to enjoy every day," Ackley said. "Easier to do that at home, on a day like this."

"When is it ever easy in this building?"

"There isn't always *this* bullshit," Ackley said, gesturing to a medium-size monitor on the wall.

Adam Benjamin, in a red, gray-trimmed Ohio State letter jacket, stood with a hand mic on the stairs of the West Front, a cadre of reporters before him with rows of supporters in back of them. Positioned behind the speaker, fanned on the stairs, were a quartet of hard, tough-looking men in black suits and black ties, with ear mics and sunglasses, suggesting Secret Service minus any sense of discretion.

"The *biiiiig* announcement," Ackley said with quiet sarcasm. "Was saving that clown really necessary, Peep?"

"He's a good man, Bob. Very down-to-earth for a billionaire. Anyway, I have to do *something* to keep myself out there."

"Wouldn't buying commercial time be easier?"

Reeder grunted a laugh. "So he's running for president, huh?"

The chief said, "What a shock."

"Let's hear it."

Ackley used a remote to unmute the sound.

Benjamin was saying, "*I know many of you here today are expecting me to announce my candidacy for the presidency of the United States. If so, I'm afraid you're going to be disappointed."*

Moans, groans, and no's from the crowd. Reeder and Ackley shrugged at each other.

Benjamin held up a hand, as if being sworn in to office. *"I will let the Common Sense Movement dictate who their candidate will be, and if they choose to draft me, well, we'll see. For now, I am here to offer my humble thanks to the brave man who died protecting me at Constitution Hall—I would rather it have been me."*

Ackley said, "Now we've moved from bullshit to horseshit . . . Apologies, Agent Rogers."

"Not necessary, Chief."

"On this day of mourning," Benjamin was saying, *"our thoughts and prayers should be with the family of Jay Akers, former Secret Service agent and a patriot who gave his last full measure of devotion for the Common Sense cause he believed in. Thank you."*

The solemn man in the letter jacket strode away, even as questions came fast and heavy from the reporters. He answered none of them, his bodyguards in black surrounding him and hustling him away.

Ackley muted the TV. "I didn't see that coming."

"I'd call it well played," Reeder said.

"For building his poll numbers, I guess," Rogers said. "But with the spotlight on him, why *not* announce?"

Reeder shrugged a shoulder. "He's playing the long game. There's no Common Sense Movement convention, but he can create the illusion that he's been 'drafted,' when the numbers are right."

Rogers cocked her head. "I thought you liked the guy, Joe. Everything you say about where this country's heading, he says, too . . . better, of course."

"Thanks. Don't read my pragmatism for cynicism."

Ackley said, "But, Peep, you *are* cynical."

"Oh yeah."

A knock came to the door. Apparently the whole world hadn't been watching Adam Benjamin's big moment.

"Come!" Ackley said.

A birdlike man in his late forties entered, widow's peak hair combed straight back, its brown invaded by gray. He wore a work jumpsuit with a Capitol crest, but the creased pants and spotless appearance indicated these threads had never seen a real day of blue-collar work—the same could be said for its wearer. The walkie-talkie in a belt holster, however, had seen plenty of action.

Ackley said to Reeder, "This is Ronald Murton, Lester Blake's supervisor . . . Ron, have a seat. This is Joe Reeder, who's consulting with FBI Special Agent Patti Rogers, here."

Reeder and Rogers stood, hands were shaken, and then everybody sat down.

Murton, perhaps slightly intimidated by FBI presence, asked, "Bob, what's this about?"

The chief said, "Special Agent Rogers, would you like to handle that?"

Murton turned to her.

Rogers said, "I'm sorry to inform you, Mr. Murton, that Lester Blake, of your department, was murdered."

"You said . . . murdered?" Murton said, frowning, obviously trying to turn the abstraction of the word into something real. "Of all things. How? Where? This was last night?"

"His remains were found last night. We don't know the time or even date of death as yet, and the specific cause has not been released."

"That doesn't make *sense* . . ."

"All I can say is, we've positively identified Mr. Blake, and murder is strongly indicated."

Reeder just sat staring through the blank mask he gave the world, reading Murton's body language. On hearing that Blake had been murdered, the supervisor had crossed both his feet and his arms, as if it were cold in this toasty room. Going into a defensive posture because he had something to hide, possibly; or perhaps just shielding himself from the sad news.

Rogers was asking, "Do you know anyone who might have wanted Lester Blake dead, Mr. Murton? Work conflicts perhaps, someone with a grudge that Mr. Blake may have mentioned . . . ?"

Murton shook his head. "Lester was a good employee, a hard worker. Make that a *great* employee. Quiet but friendly, everybody liked him."

Didn't they always, Reeder thought.

"I'd go so far," Murton said, uncrossing his arms, "as to call him a friend."

"Close friend?"

"Well . . . close for a workplace friend. He's been on my crew here at the Capitol for, oh, almost twenty years. We went out for a drink after work, now and then—maybe once a month? But then, so did most of the crew."

"No other socializing?"

"No. Well, our respective kids' weddings. That's about it."

"He get along with the rest of the crew?"

"Yeah, like I said—everybody liked him."

"What were his duties, exactly?"

Murton uncoiled a bit. Work was a more comfortable subject than murder.

"Recent years, with all his experience, he got the most important maintenance jobs. When something needed to be done right, I turned to Lester. Things break down in the Capitol, you know—it's a beautiful building but it's old. Anything we can fix ourselves, we do—hardly ever contract outside workers. So, Lester, he was usually busy."

Reeder asked, "Was he in on repairing the dome?"

"No, that's the kind of job we *do* bid out."

Reeder nodded.

Rogers asked, "What was Lester's most recent project?"

"A big one—he oversaw the installation of a new furnace."

Could you construct a furnace out of Senkstone?

Miggie had talked about desks and chairs, but they didn't have moving parts, like a motor-driven machine. Mig mentioned making a computer of Senkstone, too, but that was only an object that *looked* like a computer, right? A 3-D rendering?

Could something mechanical be built entirely out of plastic explosive?

Reeder said, "We'd like to have a look at the new furnace."

Murton frowned so hard, it was like all of his features had converged on the center of his face. "Why would you—"

Rogers, staying right with him, said, "It may have a bearing on our case."

Ackley was frowning, too, but in a different way. "Is this something I need to worry about?"

Reeder said, "We're just doing some due diligence, Bob. I'll let you know if the threat level goes from green to blue."

"You do that," the chief said, hard-eyed. "Ron, you wanna show our guests our brand-new furnace?"

The supervisor, confused as hell, shrugged. "I can do that."

Everybody got up but Ackley. Reeder and Rogers left their topcoats behind in the chief's office and followed the maintenance supervisor into the corridor. Soon Murton was leading them down into the vast, well-lit Capitol basement, roaring with the merged vibrations of what looked like an underground city of machines.

Wide concrete aisles were on either side of an M. C. Escher design of pipework, furnaces, air conditioners, water heaters, and more. Pipes of metal, PVC, and copper snaked everywhere—upward to provide heat, air conditioning, water, downward for drainage.

Murton stayed in the lead, taking them on a guided tour of an underground world civilians never got to see.

"The Capitol Power Plant provides electricity and natural gas for us," Murton said, working his voice up over the din, "in addition to almost twenty other federal buildings in the Capitol Hill area."

Reeder, nearly shouting, asked, "Is replacing a furnace routine or rare?"

"We've been installing new furnaces in the basement for most of the last ten years, part of the Capitol working to shrink its carbon footprint."

"How many furnaces replaced recently?"

"Two in the last year—this one, and one under the Senate." He paused. "No, *three*, now that I think of it. The one Lester put in? That was a replacement for one that failed its test run."

They kept walking.

Reeder asked, "How long has the plan to change out the furnaces been on the schedule?"

Murton laughed but it got lost in the din. "For fifteen years, anyway! Each year, the budget either allows us to continue, or not. The last couple years, under Harrison, things have improved. This replacement furnace? Lester just finished that job a week ago. Here it is."

Murton was gesturing to a sleek new furnace: big, black, geometric, boxes on boxes. *Had one of them been in Bryson's SIM card picture?*

Reeder and Rogers stood staring at the thing, like Ahab spotting Moby Dick lounging in the sun, shooting spray from its blowhole— *What are* you *gonna do about it, you one-legged asshole?*

"It's running," Rogers said, sounding surprised.

The thrum of the black furnace was like an aircraft about to take off.

"Of course it's running," Murton said, with an are-you-crazy smirk. "It's winter!"

While Rogers tried to explain to Murton that the furnace might have been sabotaged—without getting into the Senkstone aspect—Reeder moved off a little ways to call Miggie. He tucked into a recess that cut the machinery noise somewhat, but still kept his mouth close to the phone—he wanted to be heard, but only by Miggie.

Reeder asked, "Could you 3-D print a working Senkstone furnace?"

"Hell no," Miggie said. "But . . . well, you could print each part separately, and then assemble it."

"Thanks," Reeder said, not sure he knew much more than before he called.

"What's up, Joe?"

"Fill you in later, Mig."

He clicked off, and stepped out from the recess just as somebody bumped into something to his right. Rogers and Murton were down to his left, and he turned toward the sound.

Just another Capitol worker in no hurry, in that same jumpsuit uniform, in the opposite aisle, barely visible through the crowded pipes and furnace. Headed back the way he, Rogers, and Murton had come.

No big deal, Reeder thought, and then the guy glanced his way.

The SIM card blond.

Give the guy credit—he didn't react at all. Maybe that was what removed any small doubt from Reeder's mind, since most people, even meeting the eyes of a stranger, would nod or even smile. Not this guy, though again to his credit, he did not pick up his pace. Just looked ahead as if nothing special had occurred, as if he hadn't recognized Reeder.

But Reeder knew the blond had made him, and moved along with the man, mirroring his pace, separated by the mechanical hum-and-clank snarl of the bowels of the Capitol.

Reeder considered trying to work his way through the clustered pipes and PVC and coils and boxy metal units, but better to wait for a cross aisle—one would have to be coming up. The blond picked up speed, still walking but briskly now.

Rogers had apparently not noticed any of this, talking with Murton, and Reeder cursed himself for not yelling to her before he took up this bizarre chase. She could have cut across and come up behind the blond.

But it had gone down too quickly, and to yell now would spark his prey into a full-on run. He fished for his cell—he could at least send a text to Rogers—and maybe the blond saw that, because he broke into a run and Reeder had no choice but to give damn-the-torpedoes chase.

Reeder and the blond were both running now, footfalls eaten up by the mechanical noise, like they were figures in a silent movie. Someone behind him was running, likely Rogers finally figuring something was up; but he didn't look back, keeping his head down as he charged forward, well aware he was in a race with a younger man.

The blond guy cut from the aisle into the nightmare jungle gym of pipes and Reeder automatically slowed, peering through the PVC and metal maze, searching for any small glimpse of the intruder. *Had he passed the guy?* Had Reeder kept moving forward and now the guy was behind him? Then the son of a bitch jumped out of a cross aisle fifty feet in front of him.

They were in the Capitol and yet the guy somehow had a gun in his hand, a .45. Made of Senkstone, perhaps, one moving damn part at a time.

"Gun!" Reeder shouted, for the third time in two days, and threw himself against the pipes as the guy planted himself and aimed, Reeder bracing for the shot.

"Ow! Shit!"

Rogers!

He turned toward her, twenty feet behind him in his aisle. She was dropping to her knees, pistol clattering to the cement. He glanced back to make sure he wasn't in the line of fire, and the blond guy was gone.

A door slammed.

He went quickly to his partner's side and knelt beside her. She was on her back, moaning.

"How bad?" he asked.

"He . . . he got me in the . . . vest. The *vest!* Then why, why . . . why does it hurt . . . like a mother?"

Murton, not far away, had crammed himself behind a furnace, walkie-talkie out as he barked into it, though he too was in a silent movie, drowned out by machines.

Reeder went down to quickly check something about the black furnace. When he returned in a minute or so, Rogers was in a sitting position and her gun was back in her hip holster.

"Shit!" she said again, the word handball-careening off the hard walls.

"We'll get the bastard," Reeder said.

"Yes we will," she said, massively pissed, "and when we do, I'm going to kick his ass around this grand old building for shooting a hole in my best silk blouse. That's *two* blouses ruined in twenty-four hours. Does this prick think I'm made of money?"

Reeder smiled, an arm around her shoulder. "You FBI agents aren't usually so colorful. But could I have a slice of that ass kicking? Son of a bitch owes me for a suit, too."

"Why the hell are you smiling?"

"Two things. First, you're alive, and second, we saw our blond here—at the Capitol. That confirms it—*this* is the target."

"Domestic terrorism?"

"If it needs a name."

"Is that . . . that *furnace* made of Senk?"

"Probably not. I scraped paint off a side and got sheet metal. Anyway, it's been running for a week. Miggie says every moving part would have to be printed separately, and there could still be stability issues."

"Should we call the bomb squad?"

He shook his head. "If it's Senk, they wouldn't know what to do about it. We need that furnace off-line and disassembled for the lab guys to test it, run 'em through the gas chromatograph."

Soon Capitol cops were swarming the basement, and—while a medic cleared Rogers—the Capitol PD explored the mechanical jungle. Others were searching the rest of the building, using the SIM card pic of the blond that Reeder provided via his cell. Nothing so far.

Chief Ackley approached and said grimly, "First shooting inside the building since 1998—I don't love it happening on my watch."

"Building's on lockdown?"

"Why didn't I think of that? Thank God a hero like Joe Reeder is around to—"

"Screw you, Bob," he said pleasantly. "Didn't you ever ask a stupid question?"

"Sure. Here's one—what the hell's this about?"

"Filling you in is over my pay grade. Patti will do that, after AD Fisk clears it."

One by one, Ackley's subordinates reported in: nothing on the blond so far.

Rogers, surprisingly steady on her feet, came over and joined them, wincing as she put her jacket back on.

"Sure you're okay?" Reeder asked.

"Hurts like root canal, but I'll live."

"Good to hear."

"You caught a round once," she said, "that *missed* the vest."

"Thanks for reminding me," he said. "My shoulder forgot to ache for a while."

"Why the hell would you jump in front of a gunman for Adam Benjamin? Now that I've been shot in the vest, just the *vest* mind you, I sure don't want to do that again."

He shrugged. "I wasn't wearing a vest."

Into his cell, Ackley was yelling, "How the hell did *that* happen?" Scowling, he listened for a moment. Then: "Keep looking, goddamnit!"

Thirty minutes later, back in Ackley's office, coffees all around, Rogers asked, "Just *disappeared*?"

The chief shrugged wearily. "It's a big building with hundreds of doors, loading docks, about a thousand or so people in the corridors at any given moment, plenty to get lost in. Losing track of one person isn't that hard to do, especially one *trying* to get lost."

Reeder said to the chief, "Why was he down here with a gun? It's not the kind of place you shoot your way out of."

Rogers added, "And what was he here to do?"

"Good questions," Ackley said tightly. "Here's my favorite—what the hell is going on in my building?"

Rogers glanced at Reeder, who said, "He deserves an answer. See if you can get through to Fisk."

She tried and did.

With the AD's blessing, she gave Chief Ackley a broad-strokes rendition of what they were working on, what they knew, what they suspected, what they feared.

Finally, Rogers said, "I think you should probably shut down this building until that new furnace has been thoroughly checked, and till we know for sure what the intruder was doing in the basement."

Ackley's laugh was mirthless. "Shut down the United States Capitol, Agent Rogers? It's like turning the *Titanic*—in mud."

"What if you had time to turn before you hit the iceberg, mud or not?"

Ackley shook his head and said, "In 1954, four Puerto Rican nationals fired shots from the gallery of the House of Representatives. That was before any of us were born. Three men and a female fired thirty shots, wounded five congressmen . . . but the Capitol didn't stop running that day. Trust me, *nothing* we say is going to shut down this place."

"You have it locked down already."

"Right, and I guarantee you, at least five hundred members of Congress don't think that pertains to them . . . like half the laws they pass. Right now, you'll see them strolling between offices, some heading downstairs for a late lunch. Then there's the tourists who don't have anywhere to go during a lockdown."

"Damnit," Rogers said.

Reeder said, "She gets grouchy when somebody shoots her. Tell her what you *can* do, Bob."

"Agent Rogers, my people will go through that basement inch by inch, using human eyes and every high-tech tool. I *will* find out why our interloper was down there, and how he got through security with a weapon."

Rogers's cell vibrated. She rose and went out into the outer office to take the call.

Ackley said to Reeder, "You think this Senk stuff is a real threat?"

"I do," Reeder said. "But that new furnace isn't what we're looking for."

"But the target is this building?"

"Maybe, or the White House, or even something nonpolitical—I don't know. Remember Guy Fawkes?"

"The Gunpowder Plot," Ackley said.

In 1605, in London, Guy Fawkes and his coconspirators planned to blow up the House of Lords with gunpowder they stashed beneath Parliament.

"Hell, Peep—you think that's what's going on here?"

"Certainly is possible, and you don't need hundreds of pounds of this Senk stuff. Ten pounds would shuffle the deck from here to the Washington Monument."

"You want to be free, don't you?
And how can you if you are scared?
That's prison. Fear's a jailer."

Audie Murphy,
most decorated soldier of World War II,
Medal of Honor winner.
Section 46, Lot 366-11, Grid O/P-22.5,
Arlington National Cemetery.

SIXTEEN

Patti Rogers, in the otherwise unoccupied outer area of Chief Ackley's satellite office, did not immediately recognize the name in her cell phone's caller ID window—KEVIN LOCKWOOD—but something about it was so frustratingly familiar that she took the call.

"Patti Rogers."

"Agent Rogers, it's . . . it's me. *Virginia*."

The transvestite friend who'd found DeShawn Davis aka Karma Sabich: Kevin Lockwood.

"Virginia," Rogers said. "What can I do for you?"

That came out like a salesperson and Rogers immediately regretted it.

"Can you meet me?" The next was whispered: "I'm . . . I'm *scared*."

"Virginia, are you in immediate danger?"

"Not this second, but . . . *please,* I really need to see you."

Holding the hand of a jittery drag queen was probably not the best use of Rogers's time, but Virginia sounded terrified, and was a part of this case, after all. "Where are you?"

"Bob & Edith's," she said. "The diner where I work sometimes? There are enough people here to make me feel *fairly* safe."

"It may be as much as an hour. Are you all right for that long?"

"I . . . I think so."

"Good. I'm in the middle of something, but I'll get there as soon as I can."

"Thank you. Really, thank you."

They clicked off.

Leaving Reeder behind to participate in the Capitol search, Rogers got to Bob & Edith's on Columbia Pike in Arlington in just under an hour—a small miracle in that kind of traffic.

The cozy diner stayed open 24/7, and most people seemed to be eating breakfast, no matter the time of day. Stools at the counter alternated blue and yellow seats, a color scheme continued with the blue tabletops in booths.

As usual, the aromas of comfort food welcomed Rogers—Bob & Edith's was a place where she often brought visitors from her native Iowa, the fare making them feel at home and the clientele reminding them they weren't. The families bringing their kids here for Mom-style cookin' did so as part of a shifting Fellini-esque cast of transvestites, junkies, and alkies. Yet there were no fights, no robberies, not even misdemeanors at Bob & Edith's, the Switzerland of the DC map.

Not spotting Virginia, Rogers settled into the nearest booth. A handful of patrons were scattered around the place, at what seemed to be an off time; and what few customers were here appeared to be in groups of at least two.

A waiter came over, took her order for coffee, went away. She didn't even look up, her concentration going to her cell as she retrieved Virginia's number. She punched it in but it went to voice mail.

Had Virginia been in real trouble? Was Rogers too late? Too late for what?

The muted sounds of "It's Raining Men"—Virginia's ringtone?—came from somewhere, the timing making it clear this was Rogers's call. Had someone grabbed Virginia, and she left her phone behind, on a nearby booth maybe?

The ringtone continued as her waiter returned to her table, poured her coffee, then said over his shoulder to a middle-aged henna-haired female cashier, "Pinky, I'm going on break."

Then Rogers's waiter sat across from her in the booth. The sample of "It's Raining Men" started up again, third time through.

"Part of the persona," he said with a shy shrug. "My ringtone, I mean."

She hit END on her phone and the song stopped playing.

Kevin Lockwood had short dark hair and tortoise-shell-framed glasses behind which Virginia's fawn eyes gazed at her. He was impossibly handsome in that *GQ* model manner, making even his waiter's white shirt and black bow tie look fashionable.

Still, she found herself asking the one-word question: "Virginia?"

The young man smiled. "Yes, Agent Rogers," he said quietly, "there *is* a Virginia . . . but best call me Kevin in here. Virginia has the waitress job, but sometimes Kevin takes a shift for her."

For a few moments, she just studied him, getting used to this new person. "Is it just an act? *Virginia,* I mean?"

He shrugged a shoulder. "It's more than that. The best way I can explain is, I'm at my most comfortable when I'm her."

"Why is, uh, Kevin taking her shift today?"

"Because Virginia is afraid." The fawn eyes narrowed. "And I don't think the person following me knows what Kevin looks like."

"You've been followed? You're sure of that?"

He nodded. "*Was* being followed, anyway. I shook him, I think."

"Him."

"A dangerous-looking blond man."

Their SIM card blond again.

Rogers asked, "This was when?"

"Just last night, or really today, because it was past midnight. I saw him sitting at the bar in back, when I was on stage—at Les Girls? He had a nice build, and kind of a Beach Boy grown-up look. Cardigan, chinos, shades of tan. And he was still there, when I came from the dressing room to go home."

"Still as Virginia?"

"Still as Virginia."

"Did you get a good look at him?"

"As I left, I did—I passed right by the bar. He was watching me, but of course a lot of guys at Les Girls do that, on and off the stage. Really, it was the *way* he was watching me."

"What way was that?"

"Stealing looks. Pretending not to."

"Isn't that common, too?"

"It wasn't in the way *most* guys do, where you get that . . . checking-you-out kind of look. Something else. Can't explain much more than that. Not sexual."

Rogers nodded. "You got a good look, you said."

Kevin nodded back. "Light-blue eyes to go with the blond hair— you know the expression, 'ice-blue eyes'?"

"Those kind of eyes."

"Those kind of eyes," Kevin said, "but not in a good way. And the Beach Boy features, that kind of chiseled California thing, closer up they looked hard. Rough complexion."

Rogers got the SIM card picture up on her phone. "Could this be him?"

"Not *could*—that's him. That *is* him. Who is he?"

"We don't have a name yet, Kevin, but he's wanted."

"Not by me! I got Ronnie, one of the bartenders, to drive me, I was so shaken up."

"And he followed you home?"

"Somebody was following us, I thought. I kept looking back. Ronnie said I was being paranoid, but just when I got dropped off outside my place, that blond creep drove by."

"Do you know what he was driving?"

"A Nissan. An Altima? And, no, I didn't get a license plate. I was in a hurry to get inside behind a locked door."

"So, what then? How did you lose him if you just locked yourself in?"

Kevin leaned forward in a sharing secrets way. "After Virginia went inside, I did the big cleanup. Makeup off, wig, clothes, showered, shaved again . . . then I came back out of the building as Kevin. I haven't seen him since."

Rogers sipped her coffee, thinking. Then she said, "Kevin, I'd like to get you into a safe house for the next few days."

"Is that like . . . protective custody?"

"Yes. You may be a material witness in this case. The blond who followed you is someone who doesn't just *look* dangerous. And what we're investigating isn't merely one crime, but a series of ongoing crimes."

"Like Karma's murder."

She nodded. "That reminds me—would you mind sitting down with a forensic artist, to come up with a likeness of Karma's older gentleman friend?"

"I could do that. Anything for Karma." He smiled and it was a dazzler. "Anything for *you*, Agent Rogers."

Was he flirting with her? And was she liking it? She didn't even know for sure what this guy was—gay, straight, bi—and then Reeder kidding her on the same subject flashed into her mind and she shifted gears back to business, where she belonged.

"Shouldn't be tough," Kevin said, "getting a decent likeness."

"Oh?"

"Yeah. He was pretty distinctive looking."

"Tell me."

"Well, he had this scar. Not very long, maybe an inch and a half or so—right here?" Kevin indicated his right cheekbone.

She did a quick Internet search on her phone and brought up a photo of Adam Benjamin's majordomo, Frank Elmore, whose scar she'd noticed at Constitution Hall.

"A scar like this one?" she asked, holding up her phone screen.

Kevin's eyebrows rose. "You *are* good. That's him."

"Karma's generous john?"

"No question. Swear to it in court."

"Let's not get ahead of ourselves. What do you remember Karma saying about him?"

"Just that he had plenty of money, but was somebody we could *never* talk about."

"So . . . money and power."

Kevin shrugged. "That's typical in this town. Anybody tricking, like Karma, knows to be discreet, or . . ."

"Or it might get you killed?"

Kevin paled. "I never thought of it like that. Just that this was a sugar daddy, probably up the political food chain, with a wife and kids, and . . . you know, the old story."

Rogers's mind went from zero to bullet train in milliseconds. *Did Adam Benjamin have a traitor on his staff?* A man with the kind of background that made hiring a mercenary for a professional killing a no-brainer?

Or was this just a well-off guy having a sketchy hookup with a transvestite hooker, a misjudged affair that led to having the hooker killed? In this cruel town, that scenario made sense.

But not when Karma was just one in this unending line of double-tap professional killings.

Rogers wanted to get this in front of Reeder, but right now getting Kevin to safety was the priority.

She said to him, "Tell the cashier you're going."

"Pinky already knows that's a possibility."

He took a moment with the henna-haired gal at the register while Rogers left a five for the coffee. Then she and Kevin went out into the tiny parking lot where Rogers slowly scanned the sidewalk out front (and across the street) and the other cars in the modest lot.

Cold wind, bright sun. They walked quickly toward her car and were almost there when, just ahead of them, a backseat window exploded in a spray of safety glass pebbles. Rogers pulled Kevin down to the gravel and threw herself on top of him. She'd seen no muzzle flash, heard no report, but it sure as hell hadn't been a brick that took that window out. Rifle or handgun, she couldn't say—in either case a sound suppressor was in use—but she couldn't even be sure which way the shot had come.

"Stay down," she said.

"No problem!"

A second shot ricocheted off the concrete next to her, sending up sharp shards of cement, one of which nicked her cheek. She rolled off Kevin, said, "We're moving—stay low," and they crawled between two cars, getting behind one.

Both leaned against the rear of the parked vehicle. Neither was even breathing hard, it had gone down so fast, though Kevin wore an understandably startled expression.

"You hit?" she asked, her Glock out from her hip holster and in her right hand.

"No, I'm okay. Is it . . . the evil Beach Boy?"

"Not a clue, but we can't stay here."

The shooter—knowing he'd been seen, realizing the FBI agent would be armed—might have fled by now. But he could just as easily be waiting for them to present him a better target.

She said to Kevin, "Give me a shoe."

"What?"

"A shoe. Give."

He gave her his left loafer—a pity, as it was a nice Italian job—which she flung over to their right.

A bullet clanged off metal.

So the shooter hadn't fled.

"Why is he *doing* this?" Kevin shrieked.

"Because he thinks you know who killed Karma."

"I *don't*!"

"*I* know you don't. But somebody doesn't. Don't you go all Virginia on me now, Kevin. If there was ever a time for you to man up, this is it."

"Sorry."

"That shot came from the other side of the lot. I think behind that out-of-business gas station next door."

With her in the lead, they duckwalked back around toward the front of the car. When they were at the front bumper, she stopped.

"We have two choices," she said. "Stay here and hope he doesn't go looking for us in this lot. Or make it to my car before he does."

"How about none of the above?"

She pointed up and over the car they hid behind. "We're only two spaces over. I'll unlock it from here. It's the green Ford Fiesta. I'll go around on the driver's side, and if he's still here, that'll draw his fire. You get in on the left, and stay low, get down on the floor if you can."

"We can't just wait it out?"

"He could already be stalking us in this lot. We're doing this."

But before she could start, a couple came out of the diner, putting themselves in full view of the defunct gas station.

Without popping up, Rogers shouted, *"Get inside! Someone's shooting!"*

The couple did a deer-in-headlights freeze.

"Now! Federal agent! Call 911!"

That immediately thawed the couple, who scrambled back inside, a moment before the shooter fired another round that shattered the driver's side mirror of the car they were using as cover.

Kevin said, "Jesus!"

"Quiet. That was helpful."

"Helpful!"

"He hasn't changed positions. He's shooting from behind the gas station, all right. We're making our move."

She got the car-key remote from a peacoat pocket, clicked it, causing a honk, which unfortunately might've alerted the shooter. A risk but she had to take it.

Coming up in a crouch, on the move, Rogers fired off two rounds toward the rear of the gas station, a couple of cowboy shots that wouldn't do more than keep the shooter tucked behind his wall momentarily, but that was all she was after. Kevin's feet on the gravel told her he was just behind her.

As she got to her parked car and came around the front to the driver's door, the shooter popped out from behind his corner, but she was ready and sent him three more quick shots, whipcracks in the afternoon. He ducked back to safety and then she was inside the car, and Kevin was already in on the other side. She switched her Glock to her left hand as she got the car started. Kevin was tucked low, an oversize fetus jammed as close to the floor as possible.

The car was parked in a slot next to the sidewalk, but taking the exit, over to the left, would put the Fiesta in harm's way, so she gunned it and ran across the sidewalk and over the curb and into traffic, causing a symphony of screeching brakes, but nobody hit her.

Best of all, the shooter didn't hit them, either. He didn't even bother to shoot again.

She got her cell out and called it in, though she knew damn well the shooter was already making tracks.

Then she asked Kevin, "You all right?"

"I'm all right." No Virginia in his voice at all, though his face was whiter than his waitstaff shirt.

Sirens announced themselves, and she could have circled around and returned to what was now a crime scene, but she wasn't stopping till she got to the Hoover Building. She holstered her Glock.

Kevin asked, "Are *you* all right?"

"I'm fine. You did well."

"You're bleeding." He pointed in the rearview mirror for her to check it out.

From the cut in her cheek from the concrete shrapnel, red trickled like tears. She hadn't noticed, adrenaline rush pushing pain from her mind.

"It's okay," she said. "There's tissues in the glove compartment— get me a couple. If I use my coat sleeve, it might get stained."

"Can't have *that*," he said, just a little Virginia in there, and got her two tissues, and she dabbed the blood away. She used the rearview to guide her, but also to make sure nobody was following.

Then she got on her cell again, calling Reeder, filling him in. She didn't feel she should go hands-free with the witness in the car.

"I can't let you out of my sight," Reeder said.

"The other time somebody shot at me today," she reminded him, "you were right there."

"But my presence intimidated him and you were fine."

She laughed. It felt good. "Look, I'll be there in maybe twenty minutes. Traffic sucks less than usual. Anything to report?"

"Miggie's been struggling with all the financials—maybe having Elmore's name to plug in will get things moving. Might have something by the time you get here."

"Be nice to get somewhere. It's starting to feel like the OK Corral."

"You getting shot at," he said, "is a good thing."

"Really? Interesting perspective."

"You're not dead. You're not seriously wounded. But think about it—our blond assassin and whatever cronies he's working with are clearly rattled. After months of clean, professional hits, they're suddenly a bunch of sloppy amateurs."

"They're not the only ones rattled."

"See if you can get back here without getting shot at again."

He clicked off and so did she.

Kevin was looking at her with wide eyes. "This is the *second* time somebody shot at you today?"

"Yes," she said, "but this time I didn't get hit."

He got very quiet after that.

At the Hoover Building, Rogers turned Kevin Lockwood over to Anne Nichols and Luke Hardesy to interview, advising them to get whatever they could from him about Karma's suitor.

Before he entered the interview room, Kevin said to Rogers, "Thanks. You saved my life. That's not something I'll ever forget. Maybe when things settle down and this is all over, we can have a cup of coffee or a drink or something."

"I'd like that," Rogers said, wondering if she'd just made a date with a transvestite.

Nichols ushered Kevin inside to the table, but Hardesy lingered.

"Reeder says Kevin—or is it Virginia . . . ?"

"He's Kevin right now. Respect that."

"I will, I will. But Reeder says our witness here has IDed Elmore as DeShawn aka Karma's john."

"Tentatively, yes. You need to get everything you can out of Kevin about this gentleman friend. Maybe we can pinpoint some dates they were together."

Hardesy nodded. "Elmore works out of Ohio, like his boss Benjamin, but they both make plenty of DC trips. That's something to look at."

Back in the bullpen, Reeder was sitting next to Miggie, who looked up at her with a grin. "Having Elmore's name," he said, "made all the difference."

She pulled up a chair and joined them. "Good to hear. How so?"

"Remember Barmore Holdings? Company that owned the two buildings that blew up in Charlottesville?"

"Yeah, I vaguely remember the two buildings that blew up in our faces. Why?"

"Turns out, the company moniker derives from the surnames of the primary owners—Lynn Barr and Frank Elmore."

Rogers frowned. "We know Elmore. Who's Lynn Barr?"

"She's Adam Benjamin's VP of Special Projects," Reeder said. "I met her briefly at that Holiday Inn Express confab."

She shook her head. "Are we uncovering a palace coup here? Could the majordomo and this VP be behind the assassination attempt on their own boss?"

"Benjamin runs a pretty tight ship."

Miggie said, "The boss man's name isn't *anywhere* in *anything* Barmore is involved in."

Reeder said, "Jay Akers indicated Benjamin's security was lousy . . . and proved the point by getting himself killed."

Rogers mulled that, then said, "We have explosives possibly in the Capitol basement, and people being snuffed out like a room full of candles. Could this be a conspiracy of real size?"

"The Common Sense Movement itself?" Reeder asked. "That's a hell of a leap."

"How about a smaller group," Rogers said, "working clandestinely within Benjamin's movement? For their own purposes?"

Reeder's eyes narrowed. "Seems like we need to ask these questions to somebody besides each other."

"You mean, like Frank Elmore and Lynn Barr?"

"Yeah," Reeder said. "Like those two."

"Bravery is the capacity to perform properly
even when scared half to death."

General of the Army Omar N. Bradley

SEVENTEEN

Evan Carpenter had long since stopped believing in any notion of doing his duty. That, like many of his brothers in arms, died in a jungle hell.

But he still set stock in doing his job. When he signed on for one, he delivered, as he had when his boss was Uncle Whiskers, before Carpenter wised up and realized he had a marketable skill set. Today and yesterday, his employer got the full benefit of his abilities, just as Special Operations Command once had for far less money.

He didn't fear dying, but like any sane person, he would do his best to avoid it; and he feared no man, or at least not so far. Other than last week, and most of this week, the gig had been a snap—taking out clueless civilians, one at a time, months apart. Sometimes he felt he was damn near stealing his employer's money.

Tonight, though, the shit would be deep and he'd more than earn his paycheck. Not that he minded a challenge—that shiver up his spine was not fear, no fucking way fear, but excitement, anticipation, expectation.

The men he would face tonight were the real deal, even if they were getting soft guarding Adam Benjamin. Still, Benjamin delaying the announcement of his candidacy had been a godsend—wading through agents of the United States Secret Service might tax even Evan Carpenter's abilities. Taking out five mercenaries, a little off their game? That was not only possible, it sounded like fun.

Carpenter, in black duster-style coat, black fatigues, and Kevlar vest, sat in his car outside the Holiday Inn Express, weapons ready. Inside, people had no idea they were about to die. He sat back, scrolled mentally through his plan one last time, breathed deep, exhaled fully, did that again, and once more, then smiled slightly as he climbed from the car, wind whipping the duster skirt. But the cold meant nothing in the face of already pumping adrenaline.

Tonight he would impress his employer, always a plus, but his personal agenda would also be served—he'd have the opportunity to clear away the debris left by this recent bad-luck shitstorm.

Just outside the automatic glass doors of the hotel, he pulled on the black balaclava-style ski mask and withdrew the two sound-suppressed .45 automatics from the deep pockets of his duster. The pistols were in his hands as he went into the lobby, almost disappointed to see the four-man guard team in their usual places, as if they were lulled by the piped-in music (Dean Martin, "Winter Wonderland").

Lazy was just as bad as stupid in Carpenter's book—men hired to anticipate action, wholly unprepared for direct frontal assault. Unforgivable.

The two on the sofa midlobby were still seated when the head shots exploded through their skulls erupting blood/brains/bone and leaving halos of scarlet mist. They remained on the sofa with a ringside seat on a gunfight they didn't realize they'd been in.

The dipshit who just never got tired of flirting with that cute brunette desk clerk almost had his .38 out of the sideways hip holster when he gained a third eye in his forehead that would gain him no insight at all.

The blond merc hated, well anyway didn't love, having to shoot the cutie-pie clerk in her sweet head—these security bozos didn't deserve mercifully quick deaths, but he was glad she went out light-switch fast, anyway.

All this took enough time to give the guy who always lounged at a table in the breakfast area the chance to get to his feet, and even yank his gun partway out, but Carpenter's silenced shot caught him midface, opening his nose like a scarlet blossoming flower and spewing bloody matter out the back of his skull.

Nobody but Carpenter had gotten a shot off, and his silenced .45s only made sort of a *whuff* when he fired them. The only sound was that piped-in music—it always irritated Carpenter, having that old-timey crap continually foisted upon his generation.

As if he were delivering the mail, he went around to each fallen man and delivered a second head shot—overkill, he knew, but he'd seen head-shot men in combat go down and get back up again. Not everybody needed all their brains, it seemed.

Back around the check-in desk, he lingered a few seconds over the dead desk clerk. She really was a pretty young thing, or had been. Still, he'd hit her just perfect, the scarlet dot in her forehead almost like a bindi. The staring eyes and the little lake of red her hair swam in told him he needn't waste a round.

Five dead in under two minutes. Carpenter shook his head, smiling a half smile under the ski mask. Sometimes it was just too damn easy. He returned the left-hand pistol to its deep duster pocket, having used it only on the desk clerk, and reloaded the .45 in his right. He then headed down the corridor to where he knew Adam Benjamin waited, with only one guard in the room.

Carpenter eased past that door, however, saving it for last: he had other business first. He'd timed his assault to begin five minutes after the guards in the lobby would've done their usual every-thirty-minute walkie-talkie check-in with the especially well-trained man guarding their boss.

Four doors past Benjamin's room, Carpenter paused. His ear to the door reported a woman within, moaning loudly. Not in pain. Registered here was Lawrence Schafer, Benjamin's accountant. Finally he would get the chance to see the fetching Lynn Barr naked, a frequent daydream now about to come true, but not in the circumstances he might have wished.

The magnetic passkey wouldn't be silent, but the couple inside sounded suitably distracted. He slid the key down the slot, heard the lock click, then opened the door a few inches, just short of where the night latch would have stopped his action.

Bedsprings sang, a man grunted, a woman moaned. If they were aware that their door was now ajar, their performance gave no hint. Carpenter inserted a flat piece of flexible metal through the opening, then pulled the door almost completely shut as he slid the metal piece farther in, pushing the latch off the door.

His shoulder nudged the door open a few more inches. He slipped inside. Bedsprings sang, man grunted, female moaned, louder now, building. If they'd tipped to his presence, these were consummate actors. He very carefully shut the door, knowing it would make a click doing so and was ready to react.

But bedsprings sang on, grunts, moans.

Two silent steps took the blond down the short entry hall past the opposing bathroom and closet, and then there they were. Curtains drawn, room dark, but Carpenter could easily make out, on top of the covers, the beautiful naked woman riding the naked handsome man.

Grinding down on him as he thrust up into her, her brown hair down (usually in that uptight bun) and flouncing on her shoulders, she bounced and bounced on Schafer's dick. Carpenter could see the swell of her full breasts as they bobbed above a sex-drunk Schafer's gaping mouth.

Two high-class, powerful business types, going at it like the animals they really were at heart. Like everybody was.

They were climaxing and Carpenter let them. He wasn't devoid of mercy. When Barr, head back, moaned, "Give it to me, give it to me," he waited till Schafer had, then gave it to her, in the back of the head, much of the insides of which splattered abstractly on a realistic framed summer landscape screwed to the wall over the bed.

Her corpse fell, literal dead weight, onto her sexual partner, her flesh muffling his scream. Carpenter didn't even have to pull the female body off the man—he pushed her to one side, off the bed, and crawled out on the other, between screams.

And as the accountant widened his mouth to resume that screaming, Carpenter fired into the open hole, the bullet carving a groove in the victim's tongue on its way to severing his spinal cord.

A corpse on either side of the bed, sprawls of lifeless nothing. No need for second head shots here.

He exited without touching anything, went two doors back toward Benjamin's room, .45 up and ready, just in case the bodyguard had heard something and might stick his head out to check.

The passkey was enough this time. Frank Elmore never used the latch—it only slowed him down when his boss beckoned.

Carpenter went in, .45 leading the way down another mini hall past closet and can. But Elmore wasn't around the corner in bed, he was seated at a small desk against the wall, straight ahead.

The security chief looked up from his laptop and turned, expecting a staffer or possibly housekeeping, and instead saw the extended snout of the sound-suppressed .45.

No widened eyes or mouth yawning open to scream. No sign of alarm at all. It was as if this were a delivery he was expecting, and ready to sign for. His eyes were at droopy half-mast, red-rimmed, and the dried trails of tears were evident on a face smeared with five o'clock shadow. A whiskey bottle and an empty tumbler were at hand near the laptop.

"I don't give a shit," Elmore said.

Carpenter didn't either. He put one between the droopy eyes and Elmore went backward, taking the desk chair with him, like a doll somebody tipped over. His black-stockinged feet looked at the mercenary, who didn't bother with a redundant head shot here, either.

But when he checked Elmore's corpse, Carpenter glanced up and saw a photo that took up all of the laptop screen, a very, almost too pretty black woman who he immediately recognized. With a shudder of something that was almost fear, Carpenter slapped the laptop shut and took it by its edge in his gloved left hand, and slammed it into the lip of the desk with a metallic crunch. Then he tossed it.

He reloaded and stepped back into the corridor and headed for Benjamin's suite. The guard in there, Asher, a former Ranger, was the genuine shit. Elite. The others had been good—*had* being the operative word—and should have been better, but the easy gig had lulled them. But now they were history, with only Asher remaining.

The real threat among them.

He knocked, listening as Asher moved to the door. When the bodyguard was looking through the peephole, Carpenter fired a bullet through it. Then, in case he'd misjudged somehow, he quickly shifted alongside the wall next to the door, his back to it.

But the *whump* of the bodyguard falling to the floor spoke volumes. Some movement within the room indicated maybe Benjamin was trying to get out a window. He was just about to slide the key card down its slot when he heard coming from the lobby, "What the hell?"

A female voice.

Then from the mouth of the hall: "*FBI! Freeze!*"

That goddamned FBI bitch!

She was peeking around the corner. He pressed himself to Benjamin's door in its slight recess, giving her no real sight line to shoot at him, then fired three quick rounds in her direction. When she ducked back, as the quiet shots loudly chewed the edge of the wall she was tucked behind, he took off the other way.

The bullets had distracted her enough to give Carpenter time to start down the hall, but then she was coming, and he hit the deck as her shots went wide and over him. He rolled and had both .45s out now, pointed her way, forcing her to cram herself against a hotel room door. He sent her two rounds to keep her there, and then that fucking Reeder was in the mouth of the hall behind her, coming his way, an automatic in hand.

On his feet now, on the run, Carpenter emptied his magazine back up the corridor, not bothering to see if he hit anyone or anything. He hit the exit-door crash bar and let cold in and himself out, sprinting into the parking lot. The Nissan was around front, and he abandoned it, taking off on foot.

If Reeder and that bitch had brought backup, he would be running into a world of hurt. But it appeared they hadn't, and maybe he should lay back and wait and take them out.

But his larger mission remained, and that was the priority—that, and breathing.

He took off running.

"These are the times that try men's souls."

Thomas Paine

EIGHTEEN

Reeder helped Rogers up from the rough carpet—they'd hit the deck when their man emptied his weapon at them—just as the shooter went out the exit at the end of the corridor.

Arriving at the Holiday Inn Express, they'd spotted a Nissan Altima that, despite its different plates, seemed to be the vehicle the blond assassin had been using. Rogers called that in to the Falls Church police, and then they'd parked in the otherwise nearly empty lot and entered the lobby and its scene of unbelievable carnage.

"You okay?" Reeder asked her, still holding onto her arm.

She nodded.

"Go out the front," he said, "in case our shooter heads for his car. I'll go out the back."

"He may not be alone," she reminded him.

"Be careful," they said to each other in perfect sync.

Reeder trotted down to the end of the hall, pushed through the door in a crouch with his SIG Sauer gripped in both hands, fanning it around as he quickly scanned the empty parking lot on this side of the building.

Nothing out here but cold.

Rogers jogged around, her Glock in hand, barrel up. "He ditched the car."

Still scanning, Reeder said, "With the parking lots of these other motels and restaurants butted up against each other, he had plenty of escape-route options." He lowered the nine millimeter, which he'd only today started carrying again.

"I'll call it in," she said, "and say our perp's on foot."

Before she did, however, they compared notes on what she'd say: BOLO issued for male Caucasian, six feet, two hundred pounds, slender athletic build, black combat fatigues, duster-type coat, armed and very dangerous.

"And blond," Reeder said.

"All I saw was a ski mask."

"Blond hair on the back of his neck. The Nissan out front. It's our guy."

"Okay. But did he have help?"

"If so, they booked it even faster than he did. But I'd say no. He's good enough to pull this off himself, and the way he approached this meant other team members might just get in the way."

"Agreed."

"I don't think there were any survivors here, but you better check the fallen. Then wait for the cavalry to make their late appearance." No sirens yet. "I'll check on Benjamin."

They went inside, and Reeder stopped at Benjamin's door while Rogers returned to the bloodbath in the lobby.

Finding a bullet hole punched through the peephole, Reeder stood to one side, back to the wall next to the door, and called, "*Mr. Benjamin!*"

No answer.

"*Adam! It's Joe Reeder!* Are you all right, sir?"

Not anywhere near the door, voice muffled and distant, Benjamin called back: "My man Asher's been shot. He's right inside the door—dead. I've called the police."

"So have we, sir. But you best stay put till the building's been cleared."

Somewhat closer now: "What about my . . . man?"

Now came sirens.

"He's not going anywhere, and for right now, neither should you. I'll let you know when things are secure."

Reeder joined Rogers in the ghastly crime scene the lobby had become and then met the uniformed cops outside, three two-man units, and greeted them with displayed ID.

A passkey was quickly found in a drawer behind the desk, where a painfully pretty young clerk lay staring up at nothing. Rogers knew how to use the key card scanner and made three more passkeys, handing one to Reeder. One uniformed man stood watch in the lobby, the other five began to search and clear the building.

Returning to Benjamin's room, Reeder said, "Adam, it's Reeder. Open the door."

Behind it came: "I can't. Brian's body is . . . blocking the way."

"I'll handle it. Go back and sit down. You're inside a crime scene and it needs preserving."

Had the CSIs been there, they would likely have stopped Reeder from using the key card and carefully pushing the door open, moving the DB somewhat, so that he could edge in and step carefully over it. But they weren't and he did.

Reeder emerged from the short entry hallway to find the billionaire seated on the edge of a made bed. His silver hair slightly mussed, dark eyes glazed behind the black-framed glasses, Benjamin was suddenly just a senior citizen in off-white pajamas with brown trim and slippers—somebody's uncle or grandpa on a very bad night. A small automatic pistol was next to him. His face was blister pale and his expression blankly traumatized. After a moment, he looked up at Reeder, standing nearby.

"Joe. What the hell's going on here?" The words were strong but their delivery weak.

"Appears there was a second attempt on your life."

He looked up sharply, already coming out of it. "Have my men secured the building?"

"Your men are dead, Adam. A man in a black ski mask and fatigues came in and shot everybody. There's no sign that anyone had time to even defend themselves. The killer was outside your room when Agent Rogers and I got to the scene. We chased him away from your door, but lost him outside."

"I heard sirens. The police are here?"

"Yes. Clearing the building now." Reeder nodded to the little weapon next to Benjamin. "Is that your gun?"

"A .25 I've carried in my briefcase for years. I have a permit."

Reeder smiled. "I'm sure you do. I know it's not terribly pleasant here . . ."—the stench of cordite and the bodyguard's vacated bowels, laced with the coppery smell of blood, wafted nastily—". . . but until the crime lab unit allows us to clear this room, you'll need to sit tight. In the meantime, I'll open the windows."

"They don't open. They're sealed. Nobody trusts anybody any-more in this country. I'm . . . I'm afraid I tried to run."

Reeder sat next to him. "Adam, I would have tried to run, too. Don't apologize, and nobody doubts the necessity of someone like you carrying a gun for protection. You're the victim here."

The former professor gave Reeder a sideways look, the thin lips forming a rueful smile. "I'm supposed to be a leader. Not a victim."

"Leaders can be victims. Ask the Kennedys."

Benjamin sat slumped and silent for several long seconds, then he looked up abruptly. "Have you checked on my staff?"

"Where are they?"

"There's an empty room on either side of me, then Frank, Lynn, and Lawrence in the next three rooms, down the corridor."

Reeder called Rogers and told her what rooms to check. Several minutes passed, then his cell vibrated; he answered, and she gave him a report. He clicked off.

"Frank Elmore is dead," Reeder said.

"My God. My dear God." Benjamin's marble-eyed stare saw nothing. Like that poor desk clerk. "Frank's been with me for so many years. My right hand. My friend . . ."

He began to weep.

Reeder got him a tissue from a box in the bathroom, skirting the corpse again. Adding to the crap he'd get from the CSIs.

He brought several tissues to Benjamin, who dried his eyes and got control of himself. "What about Lynn and Lawrence?"

"Also dead. These are execution-style shootings."

He clenched a fist around a tissue. "It's a goddamn massacre. What in hell did any of us do to deserve this?"

"Adam . . . Darr and Schafer were on the floor, on either side of the bed, naked, where they fell after being shot, apparently. Were you aware they were in a relationship?"

He frowned. "I . . . I suppose I *suspected*, but I never gave it much thought. They were good at their jobs. Whatever their 'relationship' might be . . . it certainly didn't compromise their work."

Reeder's cell vibrated: Rogers.

"The CSIs and detectives are here," she said. "This is about to get very local and not our business, at least not yet. Just warning you that we're about to become temporary bystanders."

Reeder thanked her and told Benjamin to go ahead and get dressed. "Adam, you've got a long evening ahead. And prepare yourself for a circus."

Soon the Holiday Inn Express, despite its many empty rooms, was at capacity: more uniformed police, a quartet of plainclothes detectives, fire department personnel, paramedics, and, before long, media vans. The CSIs came in a now-unsealed window of Benjamin's room, took time only to scold Reeder and try to get him to turn over his shoes (he refused—the shooter had been outside the room, after all), and then America's favorite hero and its richest man had to crawl out the window, escorted around front by uniformed officers.

Walking through the lobby, Benjamin kept his head down and didn't take in the slaughter. He was led off to a vacant room for detectives to interview, while Reeder and Rogers cooled their heels in an employee break room. Rogers got hold of Miggie on her cell, which she set on the table between her and Reeder, putting Mig on speaker.

After filling him in, Rogers said to the computer guru, "Now, please tell us you've found something."

"I have—quite a bit, actually. The buildings in Charlottesville were in fact owned by Barmore Holdings, as we thought. Both Lynn Barr and Frank Elmore were on the board of Chemical Solutions, Inc.—another CSI, like Common Sense Investments."

"Please," Reeder said. "We've already got enough CSIs swarming over this hotel."

"None of this," Miggie said, ignoring that, "tracks back to Adam Benjamin. On its face, it appears to be a cabal of trusted employees doing their own thing on their boss's money. Embezzlement of a sort, on a crazy scale."

Rogers asked, "What about Lawrence Schafer?"

"Never heard of him."

"Benjamin's personal accountant," Reeder said. "One of the nine murder victims in this charnel house."

"Hasn't turned up in any of the records."

Rogers said, "Elmore and Barr were who Joe and I came here to talk to, now both conveniently deceased. This Schafer could be collateral damage—he was in bed with Barr. Literally, I mean."

Reeder asked, "Miggie, how is it the bad guys are always one step ahead of us? Could we have a mole on the task force?"

Rogers jumped in: "I trust my team."

Reeder held up a single surrender palm. "Okay, Miggie—let's say Patti's right, and we're all more honest than Eliot Ness. How about your computer system? Can you be hacked?"

"Joe, I'm good, and the government is careful. It's doubtful."

"But not impossible."

"I'll run diagnostics again. These guys have guys who have already done some pretty high-tech hacking."

"Do that please."

"So," Miggie said, shifting gears, "was this another assassination attempt on Adam Benjamin?"

Rogers said, "It appears so."

"'Appears,'" Reeder said, "may be the operative word."

Frowning, Rogers asked, "Why do you say that?"

"Something I've been mulling. If Benjamin's the target, why leave him for last?"

Miggie said, "To take out the bodyguards. First deal with the guys with guns, right?"

"Bodyguards, yes, and maybe the majordomo . . . but why a pretty VP and an accountant? What if we're supposed to *think* it was another assassination attempt? If your target is Benjamin, why kill anybody but watchdogs at all?"

Rogers, thinking out loud, said, "Our double-taps appear to be loose ends getting tied off, over a period of time. Now some sort of clock is running out, and maybe somebody is tying off *more* loose ends. Big ones now."

Reeder nodded. "Somebody like Benjamin himself, maybe. Elmore and Barr owned a company making unstable next-gen plastic explosives. Conceivably, their scientists figured out how to stabilize Senk. If they whipped up a batch, where is it? The two people who could most readily answer such questions are both freshly dead."

"Not a coincidence," Rogers said.

"Something else to stir in the pot," Miggie said. "Remnants of at least two 3-D printers were found in the debris of your exploded buildings in Charlottesville. Like it or not, Joe, you have the CSIs to thank for that."

Reeder and Rogers were exchanging glances.

Reeder said, "Sounds like somebody figured out how to stabilize Senk. And printed out something, apparently. *What?*"

"Neighbors at the industrial park," Miggie said, "reported seeing trucks come and go this past summer and fall. No one has any idea what those trucks were hauling. Closest thing we have are reports of seeing pipe being loaded up."

Rogers said, "And we have no idea where the trucks went?"

"None. But digging into the financials of Barmore Holdings, I see they have their fingers into all kinds of pots."

"Such as?"

"Such as the construction firm that built the new furnace in the Capitol."

Reeder frowned, but Rogers only shrugged.

"Then we may be fine," she said. "We've already determined that the new furnace is just so much sheet metal and typical parts. Ackley's people and our lab guys checked things out thoroughly. And, anyway, the Capitol maintenance crew installed it."

"A crew," Reeder reminded her, "led by the now murdered Lester Blake."

Miggie jumped back in. "Blake was theirs—Barr and Elmore's. His financials show substantial payments, over a period of a year, from *another* firm owned by Barr and Elmore."

Again Reeder and Rogers exchanged troubled glances.

Miggie was saying, "And when I checked GAO's Capitol records . . . don't ask . . . Lester Blake came up as the guy who reported a problem with the old furnace, paving the way for its replacement."

"Patti's right," Reeder said. "It's *not* the furnace."

Miggie said, "Doesn't have to be. The same Barmore firm that paid Blake off sold the Capitol all the PVC pipe for its recent ductwork."

"Call Ackley now, Miggie," Reeder said urgently. "Make sure they've checked any newly installed or replaced ductwork."

Rogers cut in: "And after you do that, call AD Fisk and tell her to speak to the President—the State of the Union address isn't that far off. We could still be in danger of its being compromised."

"Compromised" was a hell of a euphemism, Reeder thought, *in a world with Senk in it.*

Miggie asked, "What are you guys going to do now?"

Rogers looked at Reeder.

Reeder said, "We're going to go have a chat with billions of dollars."

When the Falls Church detective in charge had completed her interview with Adam Benjamin—in a room identical to the billionaire's previous one, minus such small details as a dead bodyguard inside the door—Reeder and Rogers were waiting.

The no-nonsense fortyish detective—who Reeder had never met but guessed had never caught a crime scene quite like this one before—reminded them to stick around for a full debriefing, then gave them a solemn nod and went off to check on the crime scene team.

Reeder and Rogers entered and found Benjamin in a wing chair in the corner, now in a gray suit and unbuttoned white shirt without a tie, looking exhausted. A straight-back chair left by the Falls Church detective was positioned in front of him.

Coming over with a smile, Reeder said, "I told you it'd be a long night," and sat. Rogers perched behind Reeder on the edge of the bed, not unlike the way Benjamin had earlier, in that other, bloody, unfragrant room.

"It has been that," the weary but composed Benjamin said. "I appreciate you stopping back to check on me."

"Not at all. This is Special Agent Rogers. I *know* that you know who she is, since she saved your life the other night, but you haven't actually met."

Benjamin rose, came over, and shook her hand. "I'm embarrassed that I haven't expressed my thanks before. I guess I owe you just about everything."

"Doing my job," Rogers said, nodding, smiling politely.

The folksy billionaire returned to his chair, eyes traveling from Reeder to Rogers and back. "You seem to have a somewhat . . . official demeanor, this trip. Is there something I can help you with, where this tragedy is concerned?"

"Nine people died," Reeder said. "So it's a tragedy, all right. But that could be just a drop in the bucket."

The crudeness of the cliché made Benjamin flinch. "What on earth do you mean?"

"Special Agent Rogers and I have uncovered a probable plot to blow up the Capitol Building."

He winced, frowning and smiling simultaneously. "You can't be serious."

"Does sound fantastic, I grant you, and I believe we've short-circuited the plan. These deaths, I should say murders, including this incident tonight, indicate a rather grandiose effort to tie off loose ends before shutting down a terrible, even mad plot."

A micro-expression tightened Benjamin's eyes. "You're actually serious?"

"It's not a night ripe for joking. Evidence strongly indicates that trusted employees of yours were in on this plot. I would like to think that you aren't part of it."

Benjamin's eyes and nostrils flared. He seemed about to lash out, but then he settled himself. Leaned forward.

"Joe, I quite honestly don't know what you're talking about. *What* employees? How could any of my people . . . blow up the *Capitol?* It's insanity. How would that even be possible in this day and age?"

"In this 'day and age,'" Reeder said, "many insane things have become all too possible. Technology can work miracles, and cause devastation. Take, for example, this crazy substance called Senkstone."

Benjamin tilted his head, a loyal dog who didn't quite get what he was supposed to do with that last command. "Never heard of it. What sort of substance?"

"A plastic explosive more powerful and dangerous than any before it. Your high-up employees Frank and Lynn had a company—well, several companies actually—but this one is called Barmore. Researchers in their employ figured out how to stabilize this explosive and what we've discovered suggests that they planned to use it—Senkstone, Senk for short—to replace the Capitol Building with a crater."

Some fury came into his frown. "And *that's* why they were murdered? Was this a . . . black op? The CIA, operating on our own soil, killing Americans without a trial? Or Homeland taking a page out of the Company's book? I don't care *what* they might have done, Joe, they deserved the usual procedures of arrest and trial. If you're soliciting my help in some sort of cover-up, you've come—"

"No. We believe the man who carried out these wholesale executions tonight—and a number of others, over several months—is the one tying up loose ends. For some group—terrorists either domestic or foreign. Or possibly an individual with an agenda."

Benjamin took off the black-framed glasses and stared at Reeder for a long time: he was trained in kinesics, too.

"Joe, you can't mean . . . you surely can't . . . suspect *me* in this? You think a man whose views are centrist, a concerned individual considering a run for the presidency, would want to destroy the *Capitol*? How much more insanity do you expect me to listen to, Joe?"

Reeder ignored the rhetorical question. "Elmore and Barr were neck-deep in this conspiracy. I thought they might be at the head of it, but then somebody had them killed. The killer himself is clearly a mercenary. Who hired him?"

"*. . . Me?*"

"Well, suppose . . . this is just a hypothetical now . . . you discovered this crazy plot by these true believers of yours. Maybe they'd drunk a little too much of the Kool-Aid and convinced themselves if they could reduce the government to rubble, the right man—Adam Benjamin—would step in and begin again."

He shook his head vigorously, put the glasses back on. "If that were true, I would never condone it. Never in a million damn years."

Reeder smiled, just a little. "No, but you might hire someone to remove the evidence—including human evidence. Because if any of this came out, even if you were wholly ignorant of a crazy plot launched by your followers? You couldn't get in the White House on a goddamn tour."

The former small-college professor gazed at Reeder with cold disappointment, as if his top student had handed in a grotesquely substandard paper.

"That's an interesting scenario, Joe. Ridiculous, preposterous . . . but imaginative, at least." The thin lips peeled back in a contemptuous smile. "Might I suggest a far more simple solution, even assuming this absurd Guy Fawkes plot has any reality? Have you considered that I was indeed the target tonight? Just as I was at Constitution Hall?"

"I've considered it," Reeder said.

"And have you considered that the logical people to want me, and my closest confidants, liquidated are not in the middle—where *I* am, and for that matter *you* are—but on the far left, and the far right. The fringes. If such a demented scheme exists as to destroy our beloved Capitol Building, God forbid, it was born on the lunatic fringe . . . one side or the other, or *both* . . . in a dark wedding of the damned."

"Wow," Reeder said. "I bet you write your own speeches."

Benjamin's expression turned hard and cold. "Please leave me, Mr. Reeder. I'm afraid I must ask you to go as well, Agent Rogers. It's indeed been a long and exhausting evening. And I hope, with a good night's sleep and this horrible evening put into context, the two of you will come to your senses. I may even be gracious enough to accept your apology. But not tonight. Not tonight."

They went.

"Few will have the greatness to bend history itself;
but each of us can work to change a small portion of
events, and in the total of all those acts will be
written the history of this generation."

Robert F. Kennedy

NINETEEN

On Monday morning, just a day away from the State of the Union address, Patti Rogers and Joe Reeder were again headed to the Capitol. What others might perceive as a mutual funk was more a sense of shared frustration merging on desperation. They had been unable to convince AD Fisk—or anyone else for that matter, including her task force team—that a threat to the Capitol was still out there.

Over the weekend, the "Holiday Inn Express Massacre" (the Fox News characterization, picked up by one and all) had dominated the news, with the cable outlets covering little else. As Reeder predicted, the victims were portrayed as martyrs, many of whom died trying to prevent Adam Benjamin's assassination, as opposed to helpless victims cut down in a mercenary's cold-blooded assault.

The Sunday morning opinion shows were devoted to trying to make sense of (as the *Meet the Press* host put it) "the targeting of America's greatest grass roots populist." This included much speculation by the right that an extreme leftist group might be responsible, and from the left assuming the same of the right. Both sides were careful to avoid directly mentioning either the Inhabit America group or the Spirit of '76 Movement.

For his part, the billionaire was avoiding the media storm by lying low back in Ohio. The media called it "mourning the loss of his friends and coworkers." Reeder referred to it as getting out when the getting was good.

Behind the wheel, Rogers said, "Catch any of the news shows this morning?"

"Do I look like a masochist?"

"Remember how Benjamin's popularity tripled after the Constitution Hall attempt? Well, now *that* figure's doubled. Everybody's favorite noncandidate is polling stronger than President Harrison himself."

Reeder said nothing.

"Better watch out, Joe," she said with a wry twist of a smile, "or Benjamin's going to be even more popular than you are."

"Finally," he said, "a good result."

Rogers, Reeder, and the task force team had spent the weekend searching for the blond assassin, scouring the District and its surroundings, calling in favors from contacts in the criminal life, and recruiting DC police and their own network of confidential informants . . . getting nowhere. The recovered Nissan was still going through forensics tests, but initially the results were nil—not even a fingerprint.

Rogers asked Reeder, "Have you had any luck with Amy?"

With the investigation still under way, the lid was on the apparent plot to blow up the Capitol, so Reeder was limited in what he could say to his daughter, to convince her not to attend the State of the Union address in the company of Senator Hackbarth.

"No," he said. "I asked her as a favor to her old man to take a pass, no questions asked."

"And?"

"She asked questions. And I couldn't answer them."

"We don't *know* that the State of the Union is the target. And we're alone in thinking there still *is* a target."

"If we have shut this thing down," he said, "great. But the State of the Union is optimum for the purposes of whoever is behind it. Taking out the President, the VP, Congress, cabinet members, Supreme Court justices, in one fell swoop? Broadcast live? The next American revolution could be won with just this one battle."

Rogers parked in a Government Only spot not far from the Capitol. As they walked, she was accompanied by thoughts of the one hundred sixty-nine dead and nearly seven hundred injured in the bombing of the Murrah Federal Building in Oklahoma City in 1995, the largest single domestic terrorist attack in US history.

Amy Reeder would be one of upwards of a thousand people in the Capitol tomorrow night.

Chief Ackley was waiting for them just inside the door and escorted them quickly through security. The trio immediately descended into the lower reaches of the building. Workers were putting new ductwork into place, adding percussive notes and the human voice to the oppressive *thrum* of machinery.

"PVC for the new furnace getting replaced," Ackley said, nodding that way.

FBI techs had determined that the innocent-looking pipe had been formed of Senkstone; removal had been after midnight, when the Capitol was at its closest to empty. The late Lester Blake had gotten it past security, as a longtime employee with clearance.

"When we were down here last time," Rogers said, "our blond friend must have been checking to see if everything was in place."

"That's my guess," Ackley said. "Happy coincidence that we showed up just then—otherwise, what they cooked up just might've worked."

Reeder said, "Do we know where the Senk is now?"

"Last of it was taken out Saturday. FBI bomb squad hauled it away. Where they carted it off to, I couldn't tell you."

Rogers asked, "How much of it was there?"

"Hundred feet or so."

Reeder grunted. "Our computer guy says a pound of this stuff could decimate a three-story building. A hundred feet, weighing maybe half a pound a foot? We're talking fifty pounds. The Capitol, and anybody in it, would just be . . . gone."

Ackley nodded. "Damn good thing we stopped it! Now and then we earn our paycheck, huh?"

The chief was feeling pretty damn good about himself. Rogers knew all too well that convincing this civil servant that a threat remained would be a tough sell.

Reeder asked, "How was it wired?"

"Remote device. Whoever planned this was no suicide bomber—he had zero plans on being in the building."

"Specifically."

"Cell phone hooked to the detonator, hidden in a pipe."

Reeder's eyes narrowed as he gazed out at the jungle of pipes and machines and a few workmen.

Rogers said, "A mobile phone call from anywhere in the world, to the cell in the pipe, would set it all off?"

"That's how I understand it," Ackley said.

His eyes still traveling, Reeder asked, "Can we be sure all the Senk is out of here?"

"According to the Bureau's bomb squad," Ackley said, "it's all gone. They did mass spec tests on the furnace, and any other work done down here in the last two years. The FBI's top hazardous devices guy says it's all clear, and that's good enough for me. Now I can get some good sleep tonight, and watch the speech from my upstairs office tomorrow."

"Can you," Reeder said.

Ackley put a hand on Reeder's shoulder and grinned. "Of course, Peep, I reserve the right to keep the sound down. *I* didn't vote for Harrison."

"If you're wrong, Chief," Reeder said pleasantly, "you won't need the sound turned up."

They left him to think about that.

On the way to the car, Rogers asked, "You figure we're wasting our time?"

"Trying to convince Ackley? Definitely. He's a good meat-and-potatoes cop, but this is way over his skill level."

She shook her head. "No, Joe, are *we* the ones who are wrong?"

They were at the car now.

Reeder said, "We might be, but a lot of lives hinge on 'might.' Something in that Capitol basement smells, and I don't mean dead rats . . . Let's get in and get the heater going."

They did, then she asked, "What does your delicate breathing apparatus tell you?"

He answered her with his own question. "Whoever is behind this conspiracy has been very careful, even methodical . . . right?"

"Right," she said. "Until the hotel shooting, at least. But otherwise, months, maybe years have gone into this. I was relieved, frankly, to hear they went back two years to check on any work done."

Reeder's face was typically blank but his eyes were moving. "The plot *has* accelerated. Tying off loose ends started at an almost leisurely pace. But even that frontal attack on that Holiday Inn—it was planned to the second. Doesn't it seem like we stumbled onto their Senkstone surprise package a little too easily?"

She goggled at him. "Are you kidding, Joe? Nothing's been easy about this investigation."

"That's because everywhere we go, the bad guys are a step ahead of us."

"No argument there."

His upper lip curled in a bitter smile. "So then is it just a 'happy coincidence' that our blond prick turns up in the basement of the Capitol, at the precise moment *you and I* are there?"

Her chin came up. "So that's what's got your smeller twitching. You don't think . . ."

"Don't I?"

"Did he *want* us to see him?"

"Oh yeah."

"But why?"

"So we'd think we caught him in the act. Setting the fuse, so to speak."

"Joe, I'm not sure I'm following . . ."

"Patti, a conspiracy this large, with this many moving parts? Whoever's behind it had to plan for the possibility that someone would begin putting the pieces together."

"Triggered by the double-taps, maybe."

"Yeah. So, if you anticipated that, why not have a dummy bomb set up?"

Her eyebrows climbed. "A bomb that we would find! . . . And then assume that the threat had been removed."

"Threat removed," he repeated. "Guard lowered."

"So it could still be *in* there."

He nodded gravely. "I think it is. And in this whole great big government . . . with its alphabet soup of law enforcement and anti-terrorist agencies . . . nobody but us is looking for it."

At the task force bullpen, the team pored over everything relating to Barmore Holdings, should anything have been overlooked. Again, all hands were on deck, Hardesy and Nichols pitching in, behaviorist Ivanek, too, everybody following Miggie's lead.

As the day dragged on, a long list of companies that Barmore had interests in had come to light: Clayton Pharmaceuticals, Davis Construction, Elgin Computer Services, even a one percent holding in ABC Security, Reeder's company.

"You're shitting me," he said.

"It's right here," Rogers said, showing him the updated list. "Maybe somebody was keeping an eye on you. Does your company send out e-newsletters and quarterly reports?"

"Of course."

"Well," she said, and shrugged.

"Damnit!" Miggie said.

Every head in the room turned the computer god's way, their expressions confirming that this was the first such outburst anyone here could remember from him. Rogers gave the room a look that said get back to what they were doing, and she and Reeder went over to Miggie's desk, pulling chairs up alongside him.

His voice down, his expression embarrassed, Mig said, "You were right, Joe. We were hacked. Sort of. Anyway, I figured out how they've been a step ahead all the time . . . They've been lying in the weeds, remotely monitoring everything I do."

Rogers frowned. "That's possible?"

"Absolutely . . . but they were buried so deep, it took me forever to even figure out they were there."

Reeder asked, "Can you track them?"

"I'm honestly not sure."

Rogers and Reeder exchanged surprised expressions—they'd never heard Miggie admit defeat so readily.

He was saying, "They're cloaking themselves well and have a revolving IP address that changes every thirty seconds. Tracking them will be next to impossible."

"Well," Rogers said, "how about shutting them down?"

"That I can probably do . . . but they're going to try to find another way in." He shook his head. "Most likely, we've been their best intelligence source about who's trying to stop them."

Rogers said, "Well, then, let's slam the door in their damn face, now!"

Reeder held up a hand. "Let's not be in too big a hurry . . . Do they know you're onto them?"

"Not necessarily. I spotted them when I was digging into the diagnostics, but backed out before letting them know I was there. Pretty sure of that, anyway."

"Perfect opportunity for some disinformation, don't you think?"

Rogers held out an open hand. "What about in the meantime? If things don't look like business as usual, we're blown."

Miggie shook his head. "No, Joe's right. We can do this. I go ahead and use my computer just like I have been, looking into aspects of the case. Every time I find something that might be helpful, I switch to a non-FBI device before pursuing it further. Rest of the time, they see me running into dead ends."

"Giving them more confidence in our incompetence," Reeder said. "I like it."

Rogers said, "Me, too. Pursue that approach."

By the end of the day, with everybody thoroughly beat, Rogers and Reeder gathered the team in the conference room to kick around theories, share discoveries, and exchange thoughts.

Ivanek, the deep-set eyes frowning under the shelf of brow, asked Reeder, "How did your friend Bryson get involved in this, anyway?"

"My guess? Chris was likely offered the same top security job I was, which Jay Akers had already taken—the kind of high-dollar position that discourages much due diligence before saying yes. But Chris Bryson started digging, and putting things together. Me, I turned 'em down flat, due diligence not an issue. Akers jumped in with both feet, but still noticed things that didn't seem kosher. That's why he wanted to talk to me . . . and maybe why he got killed."

Rogers said, "What Chris Bryson noticed, among other things, were the double-tap victims. Anne, you and Luke have been working on that. Anything?"

Nichols said, "Michael Balsin, the congressional aide, was looking into the sale of Senkian Chemicals. Must have been enough to get him killed."

Hardesy—his shaved head dark with five o'clock shadow—said, "Harvey Carroll did some accounting work for Senkian. Another loose end tied off."

"Presumably," Reeder said, "the factory foreman, William Robertson, was in some way moonlighting at Senkian, weekends maybe."

Hardesy said, "Now it gets really interesting. DeShawn Davis aka Karma Sabich was Frank Elmore's lover. Somebody in the conspiracy, not necessarily Elmore, considered the transvestite a poor security risk . . . or possibly an embarrassment . . . and she was next."

Reeder nodded. "Jay Akers may have been collateral damage in the first assassination attempt, although I tend to think he'd already learned too much. Like Chris Bryson. And like Chris, he tried to talk to me."

Ivanek said, "Lester Blake, Capitol maintenance man, did what he was paid to do . . . and his bonus was getting eliminated."

Reeder nodded. "People who will sell out for a buck forget that those they sell out to? Know that."

"Which brings us," Rogers said, "to the massacre at the hotel. Do we think Lawrence Schafer, Benjamin's personal accountant, is just more collateral damage?"

No one had an opinion on that one.

Going on, she said, "Then we have Lynn Barr and Frank Elmore, the putative coconspirators at the top . . . but if so, who ordered them killed?"

"The only person who can answer that one," Reeder said, "is their killer. Our ever-popular blond mercenary. It all comes down to him."

"We skipped one," Rogers reminded them. "Why was Carolina Uribe killed? Our reference librarian. No ties to anyone or anything else in the case that we know of."

Miggie said, "Actually, I think I know. Took a while, but I found something interesting, not fifteen minutes ago. Take a look at this, everybody."

On the big mounted monitor came grainy black-and-white footage of a library reference desk and an attractive Latina woman working behind it.

"This," Miggie said, "is the Burke Centre Library counter where Uribe worked. Security video."

A middle-aged, fairly average-looking guy, vaguely blue collar, came up to the counter and asked a couple questions that led to some brief, smiling conversation, then got her tapping away on a computer. After receiving his information, he walked away, frowning.

"Our factory supervisor," Rogers said. "William Robertson."

Miggie said, "This is the day before Carolina was murdered, and only a week or so before Robertson's death."

Hardesy was frowning at the screen, which Miggie had frozen on the frowning Robertson. "What the hell was he *doing* there?"

Reeder said, "Coming back from Charlottesville, most likely. Something about what was going on there bothered him. He stopped to ask someone who might have answers."

"A reference librarian," Rogers said.

"Exactly," Reeder said. "Answering Robertson's 'innocent' questions got her killed."

Hardesy asked, "Any way we can know what she told him?"

Miggie said, "We can try video enhancement and a professional lip reader, but that's a very long shot."

Nichols, generally a cool customer, seemed aghast. "Who would kill a stranger for answering a few questions? Information available to anybody?"

"Maybe," Reeder said, "somebody capable of blowing up the Capitol Building."

There had been some skepticism in these ranks about Rogers and Reeder's belief in that possibility. But no one was questioning it now.

"We're at the end of our workday," Rogers said. "We're less than twenty-four hours from the State of the Union. Joe feels that's when this conspiracy will come to fruition. And no one outside of this room thinks there's a problem. Who wants to go home?"

Nobody said anything.

"We'll break for supper," Reeder said, "and come back and hit it. Name your poison—I'm buying."

"We have it in our power
to begin the world over again."

Thomas Paine

TWENTY

Joe Reeder and Patti Rogers sat across from Margery Fisk's Omaha Beach of a desk. The perfectly coiffed, expensively dressed assistant director of the FBI was at her computer looking at the task force report they'd sent an hour before, explaining why the team believed a bomb still remained somewhere in the Capitol Building . . .

. . . and why tonight would likely see its detonation.

In two hours, the State of the Union speech would begin. Cutting it this close was nothing Reeder relished, but he had hoped the various cops and snitches out there, searching for the blond assassin, might come through for them.

They hadn't.

And nobody else in government, besides Reeder, Rogers, and their team, anticipated any problem tonight worse than some far-right Republicans heckling President Harrison at the big event.

Finally Fisk turned from the monitor toward them, her expression unreadable, even to Reeder.

"I'm not saying you haven't made a convincing case," she said.

It hit him like a blow. *Amy would already be in that building.*

Fisk continued: "But while you have solid facts here, the evidence for the continuing existence of a plot is highly circumstantial. And, if anything, you demonstrate that the threat has been found and removed. Dealt with."

Reeder said, "If we're right, Director Fisk, allowing the State of the Union to proceed isn't just a bad career move—it's a tragic mistake of epic proportions."

Her eyes flared, and *that* he could read.

But her voice remained cool: "If you think that President Harrison can be moved to cancel the biggest night of his political year, you are welcome to go over there, lean on your celebrity and prior dealings with the president, and see how far you get."

And that was that.

In the hallway, Rogers asked him, "Could you do that? Could we get in to see the President?"

"No. As a former Secret Service agent, I can assure you of that. No, no, and no. Fisk knows that. She blew us off."

In the task force conference room, Rogers informed the team of the fate met by the report they'd labored on for so many hours. Their response was a shroud of silence that draped over the room and everyone in it.

The image on the big wall-mounted monitor was divided into four panels of CNN, MSNBC, Fox News, and C-SPAN coverage. Wide shots on the exterior of the Capitol Building were interspersed with various angles inside the chamber itself, as it slowly filled up with dignitaries and guests.

Finally, their behaviorist, Ivanek, asked, "How many people will be in the Capitol tonight?"

Reeder, as if reading from a grocery list, said, "Five hundred thirty-five members of Congress, the President and Vice President, the Justices of the Supreme Court, a gallery full of visitors . . ."

including my daughter ". . . the Cabinet, save for the one member who won't attend to preserve the line of succession."

Luke Hardesy frowned. "Who is that?"

Miggie already knew. "Secretary of Agriculture Alexander Clarkson, the eighth man in line."

"Never heard of him," Hardesy said with a sour smirk. "I don't think *anybody* has."

"Unless we figure out a way to stop this," Reeder said, "that will change tomorrow."

Silence again. Able as they were, brilliant and brave though they might be, helplessness was pulling them down like quicksand.

Sighing glumly, Anne Nichols said, "All we have is the blond."

"But we *don't* have him," Hardesy said.

"I mean, in the sense that he holds the key. He can lead us to the man who hired him, and in all likelihood, he set the detonation device itself."

Rubbing a hand nervously over his shaved head, Hardesy said, "But we don't know that. And even if we *do* find him—and we've tapped every resource available to us, without success—who's to say he would talk in time?"

Nichols, with a hardness unusual from the woman, said, "Maybe we march him into the Capitol Building and see what happens as the clock ticks."

But Hardesy was shaking his head at his partner. "Annie, the guy may be a fanatic! He may relish being part of the big boom. All those famous people dead, and the next day, *he's* the one getting talked about."

"No," Reeder said firmly. "This isn't a suicide bomber. This isn't a muddled Muslim looking forward to virgins in the afterlife. He's a mercenary. In it for money. But, Luke, just the same—you still might be onto something."

"Yeah?"

"He's been handling everything himself."

Rogers said, "Not always, Joe. He was one of three or four who faked the Bryson suicide. And the timing is such that he probably *wasn't* the one who took those shots at me at the diner."

"You're right," Reeder said. "He's working with a small crew of other mercenaries—that's my thinking. But when it's something important . . . not to diminish somebody shooting at you, Patti . . . our blond has done the job himself. You can bet the double-taps are him. He came to Bryson's security office looking for what Chris had, then came back and torched it the next day. He was in the basement of the Capitol when we were. And he was alone at the Holiday Inn Express, wiping out nine people."

Rogers gazed at him with narrowed eyes. "He appears to be taking orders from the top. That seems to include not just loose ends, but high-up coconspirators. So maybe *he's* the man who'll detonate the Senkstone."

Hardesy was shaking his head. "We can't know that."

"For a certainty, no," Reeder said. "But it follows."

Ivanek was nodding. "I agree with Joe. Our mastermind, if you'll forgive the melodrama, has been delegating all his dirty work to this one mercenary. And the mercenary's mind-set—well, consider that the entire hotel massacre was carried out by him alone. He has an inflated ego. A self-image of considerable worth, with underlying doubts that only proving himself again and again can overcome."

"What he said," Reeder said.

Miggie's brow was knit. "But, Joe—if it's a cell phone detonator, like the one in the Capitol cellar, he can set it off from anywhere."

Reeder frowned. "No. I don't think he can."

"Of course he can," Miggie said. "He just has to dial the cell wired to the bomb and . . . you know the rest. He could be on the other side of the city, hell, by this time, the other side of the world."

"Not likely," Reeder said. "He takes pride in his work, and he's a micromanager. Trusts only himself with anything he deems important. Like detonating the bomb. Trevor, are we on the same page?"

Ivanek said, "We are. This individual will not only be compelled to push the button himself . . . he'll want to witness the result of his handiwork."

"Okay," Hardesy said, raising his palms in surrender. "I'll go along with all of this, since I don't have a better theory. But we *still* don't know where the bomb is, or what it looks like. Then there's the small detail of where the hell our blond *is*, and how do we keep him from making a mass-murder cell phone call?"

"Luke," Nichols said, calming her partner, "we all get that. But at least now we have a starting point." Her eyes went to Reeder. "How close a ringside seat do you think our man will want to have? I mean, you can see the Capitol from as far away as Arlington, if you find the right spot."

"He'd be closer than that," Reeder said. "He may figure we might expose his plan and send people streaming out of the Capitol before the speech starts. He'd have to be close enough to *see* that, so he could detonate earlier than planned."

"Joe's right," Ivanek said. "He won't be too far away."

Rogers—not participating in this discussion, since Reeder spoke for her on the subject—stood at his side with a thick printout of Barmore's financials folded back to a page she was staring at in frowning interest.

"What?" he asked.

Her response was a seeming non sequitur: "Did Frank Elmore love Karma Sabich?"

All eyes were on Rogers, as if she'd begun speaking Esperanto.

The best Reeder could manage was: "What?"

"Is it possible," she asked him, "that Frank Elmore was in *love* with his transvestite hooker?"

"Anything is possible, between two people. Why does it matter?"

"It matters," she said, "because looking at this data for the thousandth time? Something jumped at me. Something I should have noticed before—Davis Construction."

"DeShawn Davis," Reeder said slowly. "Karma's real name . . ."

"No excuse for missing it," she said, shaking her head, "but Davis is a top-five common surname, like Jones or Smith or Williams."

Reeder said, "Miggie—Davis Construction?"

"Already on it," the computer expert said as he typed the words into a search engine on his personal tablet.

Miggie quickly brought up the construction company's website and set the tablet on his desk, Reeder and Rogers gathering around to look over either shoulder, Nichols, Hardesy, and Ivanek crowding in, too.

Rogers asked Mig, "Can you put it on the big screen?"

He shook his head. "Not if we don't want the guys in the weeds knowing what we're up to."

The Davis Construction and Renovation home page had a line of tabs across the top: HOME, ABOUT US, FAQ, AWARDS, CONTACT, and so on. Prominent in the left lower corner was a smiling picture of their president, Cornelius Davis, a handsome middle-aged African American.

"Looks like DeShawn," Rogers said.

"Out of makeup," Hardesy added, getting a quick dirty look or two. "So, if DeShawn's daddy is the company president . . . where does Barmore fit in?"

"They own the company," Rogers said. "Cornelius probably owned it at one time, then sold out and stayed on as manager, retaining his old title. But the business is wholly owned by Barmore Holdings."

Reeder said, "Here's a quick scenario, just guesswork. DeShawn's father's business gets in trouble, and Frank has Barmore buy it, as a favor to DeShawn."

"All I got for Valentine's Day," Nichols said, "was flowers."

Checking the Barmore financials printout again, Rogers said, "They purchased the company less than two years ago. Was doing DeShawn a solid the *only* reason behind that?"

On the tablet's screen, the main photo in the center of the home page had been slowly scrolling, showing projects Davis Construction and Renovation had worked on. Several older buildings in the city revealed themselves, then came a shot of two bunker-like identical buildings separated by a parking lot—immediately recognizable to Reeder and Rogers, since the structures had blown up in their laps.

"Jesus," Reeder said.

The next pic rolled up and Rogers finished his thought: "Christ."

Davis Construction's current project, the company's biggest honor (according to the banner headline on the photo), was aiding in the restoration of the United States Capitol Building. The photo showed the dome encompassed in silver-pipe scaffolding courtesy of Davis Construction.

"It was right there in front of us," Reeder said through his teeth, "the whole goddamn time."

He looked up at the big wall monitor, where exterior views of the Capitol Building took up two of four panels.

"The scaffolding," Rogers said breathlessly. "It's Senkstone!"

Hardesy was almost glaring at them. "How could you *know* that?"

Reeder got up and went to the front of the conference room,

standing with hands on hips. "The only thing locals reported about the loading of trucks in Charlottesville was that they maybe saw pipe. We assumed that meant the PVC Senk we found in the Capitol basement. Bomb squad tests proved that no more Senk was *inside* the building, so . . ."

"My God," Hardesy said, finally onboard. "It's all *around* it!"

Nichols, trying to process this, said, "The repairs were due to an *earthquake*, Joe. You can't be saying a conspiracy caused *that?*"

"No," Reeder said. "I'm saying a conspiracy took advantage of it."

"The furnace's PVC, made out of Senk," Miggie said, with a sick smile, "was just meant to distract us from the real stuff."

"Or if the basement bomb wasn't found," Reeder said, "it could be part of a one-two punch."

"Either way," Miggie said, looking past everyone, "it worked." Everyone followed Mig's hollow-eyed gaze to the wall-mounted monitor and saw every network covering President Harrison and his Secret Service entourage entering the Capitol Building.

"We have to get this new information to Fisk," Rogers said, "right now. We have to get the chamber, the whole building, cleared, and send the Bureau bomb squad in."

"No," Reeder said.

"*No?*"

"We can inform Fisk, and should, but she won't have that building cleared. Or at least she shouldn't. It's too late."

Ivanek, his face bloodless, was nodding. "The blond assassin is out there somewhere, watching. Just like *we* are. And if he sees efforts being made to clear the Capitol, he'll detonate."

Rogers asked, "How the hell can we stop him then?"

Reeder was already heading toward the door. "Patti, inform Fisk of what we now know, and tell her we're taking steps. Don't ask her permission—*tell* her."

"All right," Rogers said. "But what steps?"

"We're each going to take a corner of the Capitol grounds and look for him. Old-fashioned shoe-leather police work. Hardesy, take the southwest . . . Nichols, the northwest . . . Patti, make your conversation with the AD brief, because you're taking the northeast and I'll cover the southeast. Trevor, you rove on foot. Miggie, call Bohannon and Wade, whether they're at home or Constitution Hall, and tell them to meet us at the Capitol and just drive around the area. They'll be our rovers on wheels."

"Got it," Miggie said.

"And tell them each to bring their personal cars and not a Bureau vehicle. We don't want to tip our hand. If he figures out we're there, he makes that phone call."

Hardesy said, "He could be in a building."

"No, they're all government buildings and it's after hours. Rooftops won't be accessible to him, which is good because we can't in this time frame bring in copters. We have to assume he's on foot."

Everyone was waiting, as if Reeder were the coach and he needed to blow a whistle.

"You all have to understand," Reeder said, "that if the explosion happens, we will likely be too close to it to survive. Patti, make sure Wade and Bohannon are informed of that. Miggie, you need to stay here and monitor what we're doing, and feed us anything we might need to know. Use your personal tablet only."

Miggie nodded.

Rogers said, "Any questions?"

No questions.

They were well armed, Kevlar-vested, earbud and wrist mic–equipped, and on their way in under ten minutes, riding in a single vehicle, no siren. Within another ten minutes, they had parked and dispersed to their stations.

Reeder wore a parka—the Burberry would have stood out—and the stocking cap was less for cold protection than to keep the assassin from recognizing that famous head of white hair. Breath visible, he walked between cars parked along the twisty drive on the edge of the Capitol grounds, checking his watch.

In ten minutes, the address would begin.

If the government lay in ruin—with Reeder and his colleagues and even Amy paying for a madman's vision—the irony would be how beautiful this winter night was, stars like holes punched in the sky letting in bright light from behind its dark-blue curtain, the moon a fat enough sliver for Huck Finn to sit on it and cast his line.

This kind of crisp cold evening did not scare off tourists, and plenty were strolling by, taking pictures, his own mental camera checking every face. Pedestrian traffic was a constant around the great building—people wanting to see it, feel the aura of the place—but tonight, despite the weather, more tourists were on tap than usual. Even if they couldn't be in there, visitors from around America liked to think that just inside that grand structure, the President of the United States would be delivering the State of the Union.

Telling them it was strong.

In Reeder's ear, Nichols said, "You'd think there wouldn't be so many people out in this cold."

Hardesy said, "Makes it harder."

"Keep looking," Rogers said, then the radios went silent.

These were good people. Rogers had done well; he was proud of her. Not one of them betrayed the pressure of knowing that if they failed on their desperate mission, none would get much closer to tomorrow.

In complete Secret Service mode now, Reeder studied each passerby, looking for the wrong gesture at the wrong moment, the hand that went into a pocket at the wrong second, the eyes in an otherwise expressionless face that revealed tension or occasionally cold hatred. Such threats he noted easily, almost unconsciously.

Striding north on First Street NE, Reeder kept his feet moving but also his eyes. Across the street, the Library of Congress's Jefferson Building looked particularly majestic to him, unaware of the looming threat to its seeming permanence. A few people passed in front, none fitting the blond's build, all in danger and Reeder dared not risk a warning. This part of the block was not the likeliest spot for the bomber to be, but their little group must cover all the bases.

Seconds ticked by.

Minutes.

A small ball of anxiety in his belly represented the full-blown fear he had learned so long ago to keep back. He managed his breathing, forced time to slow down. He saw a man with light-colored hair wearing a plaid jacket and earflap hat, moving on the other side of the street in Rogers's direction. Reeder, resisting the urge to run after the guy, was about to key his mic to warn her when the guy hailed a passing taxi, got in, rode off into the night. Plaid-jacket, at least, would see tomorrow. Maybe the cabbie, too.

Or had it been the blond?

Had the merc made Reeder? Impossible. No, the man's back had been to him. Let it go.

Heading back south, Reeder strode toward Independence Avenue, the ball of anxiety burning. Down this way was a prime spot for the bomber, the kind of place Reeder himself would pick in the blond's shoes: good vantage point and just a block's walk to a metro station where, after making that fateful phone call, a bad guy could stroll away in easy view of flaming rubble, the smell of what he'd done scorching his nostrils, and disappear forever.

With how much money? Reeder wondered.

However big the fortune, the per-death payoff would be meager.

Reeder had assigned this station to himself, knowing it was prime, hoping he'd guessed right. This was the most likely quadrant for the bomber to be in, and it gave him the best chance of saving all those lives.

Of saving Amy's life.

The cold helped him keep the tears from his eyes and retain his focus. Wade's car passed him, slow but not conspicuously so; but Reeder gave no sign of notice. Everyone looking, no one finding, radios painfully silent.

At the corner, he turned east, crossing First Street SE. He considered walking a block to Second, on the off chance the blond might be up that way. Glancing over his shoulder, he saw a puff of breath from the recessed doorway of the Cannon House Office Building to the south, as if someone had tucked in there for a smoke.

Or *was* that smoke? Could be a tiny cloud of condensation, almost immediately disappearing.

That could be him.

Or a janitor who really was smoking, and was just between puffs.

Reeder walked farther east, out of sight of the Cannon House doorway. *It had to be him. The clock insisted.* Using the Madison Building as cover, Reeder trotted back west toward the corner of First Street SE and Independence Avenue. No tourists at the moment, not here.

At the corner, he peeked around the building and saw, halfway down the block, another puff of breath from the recessed doorway. Reeder checked his watch, the speech under way, not much time left . . .

No telling how long the bomber would let the President talk before ending so many lives and making—and destroying—so much history with the tap of a fingertip on SEND.

No leeway for fancy plans now.

Reeder, SIG Sauer in hand at his side, stepped out around the corner and walked diagonally across the street, stopping on the sidewalk in front of the Cannon House door where he had seen the puff of breath. Someone was tucked in there, all right.

The blond, bareheaded, cheeks red, face flecked with tiny scars, hands in the pockets of his thermal jacket, stepped out of the shadows. The bastard did something terrible: he grinned.

"I was beginning to think you weren't coming," he said.

Reeder said nothing.

The blond, looking at the pistol trained on him, withdrew his hand from his jacket pocket. So that Reeder could see the cell phone detonator.

"Let's not get overly excited, Joe. Okay I call you Joe? I feel like we know each other now. We've been through a lot together, haven't we?" He gestured casually with the phone-in-hand.

"You want to talk?"

"Why not? We understand each other, don't we? Who knows, maybe you can reason with me."

Reeder shot him in the head.

"Not interested," he said, but the blond didn't hear him.

Reeder plucked the cell phone from dead fingers as the assassin crumpled empty-eyed toward the cement, scarlet trickling from the black hole in his forehead to drip down over his nose. A crimson mist sparkled in the air like dying fireworks.

Rogers's voice came on the comms system, distant in his ringing ears. "*That was a shot!* Everyone report."

Reeder said, "Clear. Blond is down and dead. I have the cell phone. Tell Fisk to get the bomb squad over to the Capitol."

"You're okay?" Rogers asked, out of breath, on the run.

"Sure," he said.

Rogers found him sitting on the sidewalk, back to the wall, ten or so feet from the fallen assassin. He was crying. She went down and checked on the dead man, came back quickly.

Kneeling before him, she said, "You *are* okay?"

"Amy's okay," he said, and swallowed, smiling, still crying. "That's what matters. She's okay."

"To argue with a person
who has renounced the use of reason
is like administering medicine to the dead."

Thomas Paine

TWENTY-ONE

Patti Rogers sat in first class next to Joe Reeder, who had paid for both their airfares. She was taking a personal day to fly with Joe to Toledo, Ohio, for reasons that remained somewhat obscure. They were on their way to talk to Adam Benjamin. That was all she knew.

She had asked only one question: "What is this about?"

"When we get there," he said, "just follow my lead."

She knew Reeder well enough to know that was the end of that discussion.

The immediate aftermath of Reeder taking down the blond assassin had been a media blackout as the federal government—by way of the Bureau, Homeland, NSA, and even the CIA—undertook a massive cover-up in the name of national security. Reeder appeared mildly outraged, but Rogers understood—public panic might ensue should it become known how close the nation had come to having every leader of its two parties killed, and the great symbol of the democracy—the Capitol Building itself—destroyed.

Beyond that was the issue of Senkstone, a weapon of such frightening proportions that the ramifications of any wide knowledge of its existence could hardly be calculated. Reeder said that the Pentagon was no doubt trying to get its "grubby hands" on the stuff: "They must be giddy finding a new way to kill people, with no consideration of how any enemy might use it against us."

One thing could not be covered up: at the same time the blond was supposed to be blowing up the Capitol, three men thought to be the dead man's comrades-in-arms assassinated Secretary of Agriculture Alexander Clarkson at a supposed safe house in Arlington, taking out a team of four Secret Service agents, including two Reeder had worked with.

As the pundits speculated on the reason for such an obscure assassination—absent the context of the greater plot—Reeder said, "Makes perfect sense. The idea was to remove the government, and that meant taking out the remaining man in presidential succession, too."

Over the past two weeks, the task force had remained in place, putting the pieces together but very glad those pieces weren't of a destroyed Capitol Building. Through the efforts of every team member—but of course especially Miggie—it had all come together.

First, pictures of DeShawn Davis, aka Karma Sabich, had been found on Frank Elmore's laptop.

Next, a subsidiary of Barmore Holdings proved to have paid off the Constitution Hall shooter, Thomas Stanton, by way of the Cayman Island trust funds for Stanton's children.

Meanwhile, the hacker monitoring Miggie's computer turned out to be a tech support woman just two floors down who'd been a Common Sense Movement true believer—in custody now.

And finally came the dropped shoe everybody had been waiting for—the identification of the blond assassin.

Fingerprints led to Evan Carpenter, a Michigan boy who'd done poorly in school but excelled in the military—US Army Special Forces, as the arm tattoo in the hotel video indicated.

"We might have IDed him sooner," Miggie said to Reeder, "if he hadn't already been dead when you killed him."

She and Joe were pulled up at Miggie's temporary workstation in the task force bullpen.

"Explain," Reeder said.

"Remember that dustup with the Muslim extremists in the Philippines back in 2019? According to service records, Carpenter and his whole squad went missing in action, presumed dead—declared legally dead three years ago."

"How many men?"

"Including Carpenter, eight."

"And none has ever turned up?"

"Other than Carpenter, no."

Reeder's eyes narrowed. "I'm not so sure. Three of them may have helped him remove Chris Bryson. And the same three may be behind the killings of Secretary Clarkson and his Secret Service team."

"They don't have a leader now," Rogers pointed out. "We'll find them. Bohannon and Wade are working with the Secret Service on the investigation of Clarkson's assassination. Anyway, I have a vested interest."

Miggie said, "You do?"

But Reeder answered the question: "One of them took a few shots at Patti coming out of that diner—remember?"

The next day Miggie had more for them: he'd managed to track down a string of the mercenary's aliases, one of which led to a Swiss bank account where a money trail ended at another Barmore subsidiary.

"That was the missing piece," Reeder said. "Now we know."

"We do?" Rogers asked.

"Unless, of course, Frank Elmore and Lynn Barr were suicidal."

"Why suicidal?"

Reeder's eyebrows went up. "Well, do you think they hired Carpenter to assassinate themselves?"

Later that day, Reeder had announced he was heading back to ABC Security the first of next week.

"Understood," Rogers said. "You have a business to run."

"And media to duck. But there's one thing left for us to do, if you're up for it."

"What would that be?"

"Call on Adam Benjamin."

Rogers drove the rental Chevy from Toledo to Defiance, where they had a two o'clock appointment with the small town's favorite son. She had made the arrangements herself, getting through to Benjamin surprisingly fast, almost as if he expected her call. Maybe he had.

At any rate, she'd merely said the FBI wanted to speak to him, off the record; essentially this would be an unofficial visit, and she'd appreciate it if he paid her that courtesy. He had readily agreed.

Now she was driving along a quiet, snowy street in Defiance, Ohio, where Adam Benjamin lived in a two-story Prairie School–style house built around the turn of the twentieth century, the kind of home that had a lofty bearing without losing its middle-class flavor. The homes on either side, neither as imposing, were also owned by Benjamin—the 1920s bungalow to the right had been Frank Elmore's, the 1950s crackerbox to the left was a bodyguard station.

But just driving by, the notion that America's richest man lived here was the last thing that would occur to you.

They parked on the street in front of the house, the sloped lawn snowy but the sidewalks clear. Rogers had gone the dark suit/sensible shoes route, under her peacoat, no gun, and Reeder wore a Brooks Brothers number beneath his Burberry. No one was in sight, but by the time they were up the short flight of stairs to the covered porch, a bodyguard in a black suit emerged, flat-nosed, dead-eyed, with military-short hair as dark as his suit.

She displayed her credentials. "Patti Rogers, FBI. This is my consultant, Joe Reeder. We're expected."

The bodyguard frowned. The voice came thick, like he was tasting molasses. "You're expected. He isn't."

"Check with Mr. Benjamin, please."

The door closed on them, but reopened only thirty seconds or so later. The bodyguard gestured them in.

Dark wood stairs rose before them, a living room to the right, decorated with vintage mission furnishings—they could be Frank Lloyd Wright originals for all she knew—and the floor was a gleaming parquet. Somebody well-off lived here. You might not guess billionaire, but no other home on this street would likely rival it.

Adam Benjamin emerged from sliding double doors at left, smiling warmly. The silver hair, the dark-rimmed glasses, the kind, professorial manner, all of it was in full force, set off perfectly by a light-blue sweater over a yellow shirt and baggy tan trousers. Your favorite uncle.

"Joe," Benjamin said, offering his hand. "I was hoping you might come along. Pleasure to see you. Special Agent Rogers, a pleasure seeing you again, as well. Please, join me in my study. Anything to drink? Coffee, tea, something stronger?"

"We're fine," Reeder said.

Then they were seated before a big old pine desk that had seen a lot of years and plenty of use, probably dating back to Benjamin's teaching days, and indeed the whole study had a warm folksiness suited to their host. The only sign of money was the wall of books whose famous titles, both fiction and nonfiction, went back not just decades, but in some cases centuries. One shelf was devoted to multiple copies of Benjamin's own *Common Sense for the Uncommon Man*.

The only clue that this wasn't 1952 was the sixty-inch wall-mounted monitor to his left on the far wall, above a tufted leather couch on which his briefcase sat. But his desk lacked any sign of a computer setup, just some framed photos and the usual suspects, pen holder, stapler, IN and OUT box and so on.

"Thank you for seeing us," Rogers said. "And again, this is an informal, off-the-record chat."

Benjamin nodded, smiled. "Certainly . . . though I believe I know why you're here."

"Probably you do. We'd like your thoughts on Frank Elmore, in particular, and possibly touch on Lynn Barr."

A sorrowful expression washed away the smile and he rocked back in his swivel chair. "Let's start with a question. Why has there been nothing in the media about their actions? Other than the assumption that they were . . . what is the unfortunate phrase? 'Collateral damage' in the second attempt on my life?"

Reeder said, "Well, that will come. The Bureau has been investigating, and a full in-depth report to the public is imminent."

Rogers kept her face blank—Reeder had taught her well—but of course what Joe had just told Benjamin was an outright lie.

Their host rocked. "I'd be interested to know what's in that report . . . if I'm not stepping into some kind of classified area."

Rogers said, "We'll be glad to share at least some of what we've discovered, only . . . what's your take on Frank Elmore and Lynn Barr?"

But Reeder jumped in. "First, Adam, we should update you, specifically on those two. Seems Thomas Stanton, the would-be Constitution Hall assassin, was hired through a subsidiary of Barmore Holdings."

"Good heavens. How can you be sure of that, Joe?"

"Stanton was dying of cancer. You're a student of history—remember Zangara, who was hired to pretend to go after FDR, when

Chicago Mayor Cermak was the intended target all along? Barmore set up one-hundred-grand trust funds for both of the dying man's kids."

Benjamin's expression was grave; he shook his head slowly. "That confirms my worst suspicions."

Rogers asked, "Which are?"

"That you were right in advising me that Frank and Lynn betrayed my trust and feathered their own nests, in a scheme of widespread corporate embezzling. Starting companies I knew nothing of, and stuffing their own pockets with the results. Do their bank accounts indicate payments beyond their salaries?"

"They do," Rogers confirmed. "For the last three years. They were both millionaires several times over."

"But if I'd discovered their actions," Benjamin said firmly, frowning, raising a fist, "they'd have had those funds seized, and gone to prison. I have no compassion for traitors."

Reeder said, "Their scheme was much more than monetary, Adam. What I'm about to tell you won't come out until tomorrow. We need your word that you won't share this with even your closest and most trusted inner circle . . . if any have survived."

"You have my word," Benjamin said.

Reeder told him that the plot to blow up the Capitol had been confirmed, indeed using the next-gen explosive perfected and stabilized in Barmore laboratories. He did not get into how the plot was foiled.

"It's fantastic," Benjamin said, seemingly stunned. "But why is this being kept from the public?"

"That's just for now. Until the report is made public."

He was shaking his head, staring into nothing. "Then it may be possible that Frank and Lynn were well-meaning but misguided souls, who thought they were helping me. Who misunderstood and perverted my goals."

Reeder asked, "What do you think they were trying to accomplish?"

He sighed, shook his head again, apparently overwhelmed. "Frank, like many of us, thought that our great country might be . . . beyond repair. Certainly America has been paralyzed by the extreme right and their equally feckless counterpart on the left. My guess is . . . Frank must have thought the only way to return this country to the people, the majority in the sane middle who have been so badly served by major-party loyalty to special interests . . . was to . . . start over. Tabula rasa, clean slate."

Reeder said, "Sounds more like scorched earth."

Another grand sigh was followed by a grander shrug. "I only mean to say, I understand his motivation. I abhor and condemn his methods . . . if indeed my theory about the 'why' of his actions is correct."

"Let's explore your theory further," Reeder said.

"All right. If that's really necessary."

"Necessary or not, it might be . . . illuminating. Would you agree that Elmore and Barr hired Stanton in order to boost your popularity as a presidential candidate? By having you survive an assassination attempt?"

"That seems a bizarre reading of the facts. If they wanted me to become president, would they expose me to so terrible a risk?"

"Was it a risk?" Reeder asked. "Jay Akers was right there on stage, and for that matter, so was I, and Agent Rogers. Seems to me the person at risk was the man coming up out of the audience with a gun in his hand."

Benjamin was shaking his head. "Improbable. I might say preposterous."

"Well, maybe Elmore and Barr were fanatics. Assassinated, you become a martyr, and someone else from the Common Sense Movement steps forward."

Benjamin frowned. "I . . . I suppose that's possible. But there's not really anyone else in the movement who could step in and effectively mount a campaign . . ."

"No, I guess there really isn't," Reeder said. "But of course, it wasn't Elmore or even Barr who saw to it that I was on stage that night. That was your doing."

"Was it? That's kind of a blur at this point. I know I offered you a position on my staff."

"It's possible," Reeder said, "that Elmore and Barr wanted you out of the way. If they were, as you say, embezzlers on a grand scale. Maybe they wanted to get rid of you before you got onto them."

He nodded. "A possibility."

"But there's a problem with both interpretations of Elmore and Barr's actions. Whether these failed assassinations were for monetary reasons, or were intended to boost your candidacy . . . *you don't hire an assassin to kill yourself.* And for either theory to work, that's exactly what Elmore and Barr would've had to do."

He shifted in the swivel chair. "Not sure I follow."

"Have you ever heard the name Evan Carpenter?"

"No."

Rogers wondered if the people reader had picked up anything in the suddenly blank expression Benjamin presented them.

"Carpenter's a mercenary," Reeder said. "Hired to tie off loose ends. The one-man army who committed all that mayhem at the Holiday Inn Express. And the man I captured before he could use a cell phone to trigger the explosives in the scaffolding around the Capitol Building."

Everybody wore a blank expression, including Rogers, who hoped she had in no way betrayed Reeder's lie.

"Mr. Carpenter is an interesting man," Reeder said, "with a strong sense of survival instinct. He appears to be waiting for just the right deal before giving up his employer."

And Rogers saw it: the slight relief around Benjamin's eyes.

"My only explanation for all of this," Reeder said, "is that Frank Elmore really was a true, pass-the-Kool-Aid believer in the Common Sense Movement. So extreme that he *did* add himself to the list of the loose ends Carpenter was hired to tie off, and added Lynn Barr, too."

"It's incredible," Benjamin said softly. "But Frank truly was dedicated to the movement . . . and to me . . . what a tragic outcome."

Shaking his head, Reeder asked, "But whatever would possess Elmore to think blowing up the Capitol was in any way a good idea?"

Benjamin thought about that, staring into nothing again. "I suppose . . . he must have thought that, had the Capitol been destroyed, the people who stand in the way of progress would be gone. The country would be . . . would *have* to be . . . reborn."

"With you as the new father of the country."

He waved that off. "I would give of myself in whatever way my country needed."

"Think you'll still run?"

"Too early to say. Not an appropriate time to even consider it. But—whatever my country needs."

Reeder smiled. "Well, we'll see what your country needs from you, when that report comes out tomorrow."

Benjamin frowned. "You really believe that will have an impact on their decision, and mine?"

"Yeah, I do. One thing I forgot to mention. Carpenter hasn't talked yet, but before you reach out and find some way to silence him, don't bother. Seems he recorded all the cell phone calls between you two. I'm guessing he doesn't know who hired him, and you didn't contact him directly until after Elmore was dead. See, killing off your insulation was not smart. The techs have already done voice comparisons between the man on Carpenter's cell phone and you. Perfect match."

Benjamin didn't say anything, although in a way he did, since all the blood was draining from his face.

Rogers, rather stunned by the enormity of Reeder's bluff, did her best not to show it.

Reeder was saying, "We're only here, Adam . . . *I'm* only here . . . because I was once a fan. And I think you started out meaning well. But you've pushed this ends-justify-the-means thing over the line. Your middle-of-the-road followers are not going to take to your brand of megalomaniacal extremism."

The voice that emanated deep from Benjamin's chest was one neither Rogers nor Reeder had heard before, as if it came up from dark depths within the man.

"Why *did* you come, Mr. Reeder?"

"Out of respect for who you were. Of how you started. On the assumption you once were who you've come to pretend you still are. And if you're thinking that your money will bail you out? Well, keep watching the financial news, and the little scrolling down below, and see just how far and fast your stock drops after the report comes out. Think of this as a courtesy call."

Behind the black-framed glasses, the dark eyes were cold and unblinking. "Courtesy?"

"Yes. Advance warning. For you to get your affairs in order. Ducks in a row kind of thing. Your next visit from the FBI will *not* be unofficial. They will bring warrants and disgrace. You may still have enough money to fight this for a while, Adam. But it's over. I hope you have the common sense to know it."

They were almost to the car when they heard the gunshot.

"The work goes on,
the cause endures,
the hope still lives
and the dream shall never die."

Edward "Ted" Kennedy

TWENTY-TWO

Joe Reeder sat at the head of a table in the Verdict Chophouse dining room, his daughter Amy to his left, her boyfriend Bobby next to her—the kid wearing a suit for the first time in Reeder's memory.

But then everybody was dressed up tonight, including Patti Rogers, looking very feminine in a silky-looking dark-blue dress with some neckline and pearls, in the seat to Reeder's right. An empty chair was between her and Melanie at the far end—they were waiting for Patti's date.

Melanie's husband, Donald Graham, couldn't make it because he'd been called out of town on business. Reeder had tried to sound sincere telling Mel he was disappointed, but she clearly didn't buy it. If he could have read people half as easily as she did him, he'd have deserved his reputation.

Mel looked fashion-model lovely, as usual, in an emerald designer dress, all of that long brown hair up in a currently fashionable tower. Kind of silly looking, but he wouldn't tell her that under torture.

His ex sipped her martini, then said, "You just never know about people."

Reeder said, "You don't, huh?"

"That Adam Benjamin. You really admired him, didn't you, Joe? He seemed so strong. So warm. Always made such good sense."

"Agree to disagree," Bobby mumbled, and gulped his own beer.

Mel was saying, "Here he was at the head of an entire grassroots movement, richest man in America, and yet . . . What could make him take his own life?"

Looking like a younger version of her mother, minus the towering hairdo and in a white silk blouse and black skirt, Amy said, "I don't think that's so hard to figure out. So many of his friends and associates, wiped out in a crazy shooting spree. At a Holiday Inn Express? What's *that* about?"

Eyes narrowing, Bobby—who could really use a haircut, in Reeder's opinion—said, "I'm telling you, there was something going on there. I bet Benjamin was *murdered*. I mean, do you survive two assassination attempts and then *kill* yourself?"

Amy, sipping her sparkling water, shook her head. "Honey, you see conspiracies everywhere."

"He was a real threat to the left and right both. There's a very interesting website that suggests elements of both parties came together to get rid of him."

Reeder said, "It would be one thing they agreed on, anyway."

Bobby said, "Ms. Rogers, you're in the FBI, right?"

Rogers smiled a little. "Right."

"Do *you* buy what happened to that guy?"

"What guy? Benjamin?"

"No, that Carpenter character. Goes all Manson Family at the Holiday Inn, then days later shows up suddenly a suicide himself. Doesn't it seem like an awful lot of convenient suicides to you?"

She sipped Chablis. "Not my case, Bob. Sorry."

He smirked. "And if it was, you *still* wouldn't tell me."

Amy said, "Bobby . . . be good."

Holding up a surrender palm, Melanie said, "My fault. I brought up a topic not suitable for friendly discourse at an evening out of fine dining . . . at my ex-husband's expense."

"Hear hear," they all said, and Rogers lifted her glass to him and everybody followed suit.

Reeder tasted his beer and shrugged. "I'm with Bobby."

Bobby blinked. "You are?"

"Yeah. I'm a big believer in conspiracies. I mean, hell, it's only been, what? Five years since they finally cleared Oswald?"

Melanie, brightening, said to Reeder, "Say, I heard from Beth Bryson! She and Christopher just got back from Florida. Said they had a lovely vacation down there." She shook her head, turned to Reeder. "Too bad you weren't able to help her out, Joe, where, uh, her husband . . . you know."

Reeder nodded, flashed her a sad smile, had more beer.

Unfortunately the real reason behind Chris Bryson's "suicide" was buried in the general cover-up of the Capitol bombing plot. Nonetheless, Reeder had privately assured Beth and her son that Chris had not taken his life, and that Reeder had personally settled the score.

Not entirely true, because Carpenter's cronies were still out there. Some day.

Mel said to Rogers, "So, Patti—where's this guy of yours?"

"He's just a friend."

"Sure he is," Amy said with a wicked little smile.

"Anyway, he marches to his own drummer."

Reeder said, "Even when a free meal is in the offing?"

Rogers, looking behind her, said, "*Here* he is . . ."

A slender, dark-haired, very handsome guy in his early thirties—his suit a sharp gray number over a blue dress shirt, open at the neck—stood poised at the door between the bar area and the dining room.

Rogers waved him their way. He came over and stood shyly behind the empty chair beside her and she smiled up at him, squeezing his elbow.

"Everybody, this is Kevin Lockwood. Kevin . . ."

And she made the rest of the introductions.

Frowning in confusion as he shook hands with Kevin, Reeder asked, "Haven't we met?"

Rogers glanced at Reeder with an impish smile. "Joe," she said, "it'll come to you."

STATE OF THANKS

The following books were of help in the creation of this novel: *The Definitive Book of Body Language* (2006), Allan and Barbara Pease; *Images of America: Arlington National Cemetery* (2006), George W. Dodge; *Reading People: How to Understand People and Predict Their Behavior—Anytime, Anyplace* (1998), Jo-Ellen Dimitrius and Mark Mazzarella.

Thank you to Eleanor Cawood Jones and Aimee and Eric Hix for helping make Matt's research trip to Washington, DC, so productive.

As usual, thanks to Chris Kauffman, Van Buren County Sheriff's Office (ret.), and Paul Van Steenhuyse for their expertise with weapons and computers, respectively.

We wish to thank our in-house editors, Barbara Collins and Pam Clemens, for improving our work with patience and skill.

Thanks also to our agent, Dominick Abel, and everyone at Thomas & Mercer, with special nods to Jacque Ben-Zekry, Kjersti Egerdahl, and Alan Turkus.

ABOUT THE AUTHORS

MAX ALLAN COLLINS has earned an unprecedented twenty-one Private Eye Writers of America "Shamus" nominations, winning twice for best novel and once for best short story. In 2007 he received the "Eye," the PWA life achievement award, and in 2012 his Nathan Heller saga was honored with their "Hammer" award for its major contribution to the private eye genre.

His graphic novel *Road to Perdition* (1998) is the basis of the Academy Award–winning Tom Hanks film, and his innovative "Quarry" novels are now a Cinemax TV series. He has completed a number of "Mike Hammer" novels begun by the late Mickey Spillane, his full-cast Hammer audio novel, *The Little Death* (with Stacy Keach), winning a 2011 Audie.

Collins has written and directed four feature films, including the Lifetime movie *Mommy* (1996), and two documentaries, including *Mike Hammer's Mickey Spillane* (1998), which appears on the Criterion Collection's *Kiss Me Deadly* video. His many comics credits include the syndicated strip *Dick Tracy*; his own *Ms. Tree*; and *Batman*. His movie novels include *Saving Private Ryan, Air Force One,* and *American Gangster* (IAMTW Best Novel "Scribe" Award, 2008).

Collins lives in Muscatine, Iowa, with his wife, writer Barbara Collins; as "Barbara Allan," they have collaborated on twelve novels, including the successful "Trash 'n' Treasures" mysteries, including *Antiques Flee Market* (2008), winner of the *Romantic Times* Best Humorous Mystery Novel award in 2009. Their son, Nathan, is a Japanese-to-English translator, working on video games, manga, and novels.

MATTHEW V. CLEMENS is a longtime coconspirator with Max Allan Collins, the pair having collaborated on over twenty novels, fifteen short stories, several comic books, four graphic novels, a computer game, and a dozen mystery jigsaw puzzles, for such famous TV properties as *CSI, Bones, Dark Angel, NCIS, Buffy the Vampire Slayer,* and *Criminal Minds*. Matt also worked with Max on the bestselling "Reeder and Rogers" debut thriller, *Supreme Justice*, published by Thomas & Mercer in 2014. He has published a number of solo short stories and worked on numerous book projects with other authors, both nonfiction and fiction, collaborating a number of times with Karl Largent on the late author's bestselling techno-thrillers.

Matt lives in Davenport, Iowa, with his wife, Pam, a retired teacher.